Bloody Beginnings

Bloody Beginnings

Laura Hysell

This is a work of fiction. Names, characters, businesses, places, events and incidents are either the products of the author's imagination or used in a fictitious manner. Any resemblance to actual persons, living or dead, or actual events is purely coincidental.

Copyright © 2015 Laura Hysell

All rights reserved. No part of this publication may be reproduced, distributed, or transmitted in any form or by any means, including photocopying, recording, or other electronic or mechanical methods, without the prior written permission of the publisher, except in the case of brief quotations embodied in critical reviews and certain other noncommercial uses permitted by copyright law.

Dedication

To my husband for pushing me

To my daughters for believing in me

To my friends for just being there

Prologue

The phone was ringing. I roused myself from a deep sleep and pulled the phone to my ear. "Hello," I mumbled into the receiver, struggling to wake up.

"Izzy? Oh, thank heavens! I was afraid this call wouldn't go through."

"Justin!" I sat bolt upright in my bed, brushing a strand of blonde hair out of my eyes. Adrenaline was pumping through my body and I was immediately alert. "Where are you? Are you okay? I haven't heard from you in months and now there are all these strange reports about your expedition all over the news! What's happening?"

"Shh, it's okay. I'm okay. We...we were attacked, Iz. I can't say over the phone, but I'll explain everything when I get home. Just know that I'm okay."

"What about everyone else? Sarah? Kirk?" My heart thudded at the thought of my ex-fiancé, Kirk. We may have broken up, but he still held a place in my heart, and he was one of my brother's closest friends.

"Kirk's been hurt but he's going to live and Jared's all right, but everyone else is dead."

Everyone was dead? "Sarah?" I asked timidly.

There was a short pause before he spoke. "Sarah's gone,"

Justin said softly. His voice was strained, as though he was holding back tears. "Listen, I don't have much time to talk. I just called to warn you. Whatever you do, Iz, don't get the vaccine."

"Vaccine? What are you talking about? What vaccine?" The line went dead. "Justin? Justin?"

I stared at the receiver in my hands for several minutes, listening to the incessant beeping indicating an empty line. I set it down and picked it back up, but there was still nothing there. I finally set the phone down and glanced at my clock, thinking five in the morning was too early to get up, but knowing I wouldn't be able to sleep any more after that phone call.

Slowly I pulled myself out of bed and wandered into the kitchen to start coffee. I felt numb all over. Justin was alive, but most of the expedition was dead. Sarah, Justin's on-again off-again girlfriend was among the dead. I tried to wrap my brain around that. I had never been a big fan of Sarah, but I knew her death would crush my brother. He hadn't sounded sad though, he'd sounded scared on the phone, or maybe he was just hurried. And what was this vaccine he was talking about?

I grabbed my favorite mug and filled it with hot, bitter coffee. Then I lovingly dosed it with my favorite caramel flavored creamer. I held the mug to my face, breathing in the intoxicating aroma before taking a tentative sip. The coffee helped my brain to come awake, and my mind began wandering over all the strange things Justin had said in that short conversation. As I sipped and turned the conversation over in my head I realized I just kept coming back to the same thing. What vaccine was he talking about?

It must be some vaccine his research company was making. Maybe it had something to do with the trip to Romania he and his team had gone on. Justin had been close-mouthed about the trip when they left eight months ago, but he had kept in touch through e-mails weekly. Then, about two months ago, the e-mails had stopped. About the same time news reporters had pounced on the story of the

American research team missing from the Carpathian Mountains, near Brasov, Romania.

I gulped down my coffee, wincing as it burned my throat before I headed toward the bathroom. I had just opened the door when the phone rang again. I rushed to it and picked it up before the second ring. "Hello!" I yelled into the receiver, hoping it was Justin again.

"Hello, I'm looking for a Miss Isabella Howerton," said the official-sounding male voice on the line. I glanced at the clock, seeing it was only 5:18. Who calls this early in the morning?

I took a deep, steadying breath before I replied. "This is Isabella."

"Hello, my name is Agent Rodcliffe, and I need to speak to you regarding your brother, Justin Howerton. Have you heard from him?"

My heart began pounding and my fingers tingled. I had learned long ago to trust my intuition, and my intuition was telling me not to trust this stranger on the phone. "Sorry, no I haven't," I replied. "May I ask what this is all about?"

"I happen to know Justin called you about fifteen minutes ago. Now, let's not play games, Miss Howerton," Agent Rodcliffe replied, his voice dropping to a frightening deep bass.

I shivered and stared at the phone in my hands. My heart was beating quickly and my palms were sweating. I pulled the phone away from my face and looked it over briefly. Was my phone bugged? The more I thought about it the angrier I became. "Well, since you started playing games in the first place, I'm going to end it. You either tell me what you want or leave me alone."

"Is your brother planning on meeting you anywhere? Is he back in the States?" the voice on the other line asked, ignoring me.

"I think you know more about what's going on than I do! He didn't tell me anything. Now, what do you want?"

"Miss Howerton, your brother is in extreme danger. I need to find him right away. I also need to find Sarah Ellister, Kirk Daughtry,

Jared Bushing, Ronald Dawson, Jin Hao and George Brisby. Has he mentioned anything about them? Has he mentioned anything about his team or the events that took place in Romania?" Rodcliffe asked, his voice dripping with sincerity. I didn't buy it for a minute.

"Well, if you have my phone bugged you should know exactly what he told me," I retorted.

"You are Justin's only family, Miss Howerton. I am sure he has communicated with you in other forms than just this phone call. Has he e-mailed you perhaps?"

I powered on my laptop and waited for my e-mail to come up as I spoke to the man on the phone. "Look, all I know is what he told me on the phone. His team is dead, except him, Kirk, and Jared," I added, dropping to sit on my couch. I felt drained already from this short conversation.

"Oh, they're not dead, Miss Howerton. Apparently your brother doesn't tell you everything after all. Thank you for your time." The line went dead.

I slammed the phone down and stared at my e-mail. I had no new messages from my brother. I grabbed my cell phone as well, but there were no new texts there either. My whole body was shaking now. I hadn't felt this type of panic since the night of our parent's death. Something big was happening. I just didn't know what yet.

Chapter 1

"Hey, Isabella, what's with the rush?" Mark asked as he hurried to catch up with me.

I glanced at him, noting his usual attire of basketball shorts and a t-shirt, but continued as fast as my short legs would go without actually running. "I'm late for the staff meeting, Mark. Obviously you are too," I added.

"Oh, yeah, staff meeting... um, I'm not going."

I stopped suddenly and he had to skid to a halt to keep from running into me. His hands braced against my waist briefly before he immediately let go. I turned and flipped my hair over my shoulder and narrowed my pale blue eyes at him. "What do you mean? They made it seem serious. If you don't go it's an automatic suspension. That's more than enough incentive for me to go. What makes you so special?" I placed my hands on my hips as I waited for a response.

Mark shrugged and glanced in each direction down the hallway nervously. It was after school and there were no students in sight. He grabbed my hand and pulled me into a vacant classroom. I stumbled in my heels, bracing myself against a table. He shut the door quietly and leaned back against it. I noticed for the first time that he seemed to be perspiring even more excessively than usual. He ran a hand through his thick brown hair, a nervous gesture I was secretly very fond of.

I sighed and adjusted my beige skirt. "What's going on Mark? Are aliens attacking?"

Mark frowned at me, crossing his arms across his very muscular chest. "That's not funny," he said dryly. Mark was quite the conspiracy theory buff. He fancied everything from aliens to ghosts and was convinced the government was behind all sorts of strange plots. He was lucky administration didn't know about all his theories, or he would be sitting in a padded room instead of teaching P.E.

"Look, Mark, I'm already late for the meeting and I don't particularly want to be suspended. What's so important?" I sighed, pulling my eyes away from his muscles. Oh, but the man was good to look at!

"Have you been listening to the news?" he whispered, leaning toward me.

I shook my head, my blonde hair falling across my eyes. When my brother had disappeared I watched the news every night, hoping for some clue as to what had happened. Then after he called I watched the news even more. A month after his mysterious phone call the news reported that the expedition team had all perished while hiking in the mountains. A bear attack, so they claimed. There had been a big memorial service, but no funeral. No bodies were recovered. I didn't believe it, not after Justin's weird phone call, but I still hadn't heard from him. I stopped watching the news after that. That was five months ago.

"Look, you said your brother warned you about some vaccine, right?" I nodded, and he seemed to gain strength, rushing on. "They want us to get some sort of vaccine here at work. They have doctors lined up at this meeting just for that reason. It's the vaccine that's been all over the news. Geez, Iz, you can't shut out the world because your brother's gone."

"I didn't shut out the world!" I snapped. It was just too hard to listen to tragedies on the news anymore. "Just because I don't watch the news doesn't mean I don't hear things. I heard about some vaccine that Petri Co. created that's supposed to suppress every form of the flu permanently. That sounds like a good thing to me."

"Aren't you worried that maybe this vaccine is the one your brother was talking about?" he pushed, moving his body closer to mine as he spoke.

Mark was so close I had to take a step back to look up at his face. I shook my head in response. "My brother didn't work for Petri. He worked for NuvaDrug, which I seem to recall went bankrupt just after Justin's team disappeared. So I don't think there's any vaccine to worry about from them."

"Oh, Izzy, you're ridiculously naïve for someone so smart. Petri bought NuvaDrug! They own all their work."

"No, Mark, Cascade bought NuvaDrug and shut down most of their facilities. See, not naïve at all!" I retorted angrily.

"You really need to dig deeper, Iz. Petri owns all of it!" Mark's voice rose in volume, but he quickly quieted, glancing through the small window in the door to check the hallway. He turned back toward me, his brown eyes soft. "Petri has a new owner, who bought out Cascade, NuvaDrug and Pharm Tech. Sure, Cascade and Pharm Tech still work under their original names, but Petri Co. bought all of it. They've done it secretly, but if you know how to look you can find the information."

I shook my head, growing tired of Mark's incessant theories. I didn't want to hear it, especially if this one concerned my brother's company. Mark wouldn't relent until I had heard him out. He was like a dog with a bone. "Look, Mark, I have to keep this job. If you have a point, please get to it!"

Mark leaned up against the door and ran a hand through his hair again. He took a deep breath before speaking. "They are going to force us to get a vaccine, Iz! I overheard these men in suits talking to Principal Tourney about it. That should be illegal, but the government's making it mandatory for everyone. They're starting with anyone who is in contact with young children or elderly, who could be susceptible to transmit the flu to them. That means all hospital staff and all teachers, along with all government workers as well. I heard the military's on board too! Parents are lining up to get their kids this vaccine, not even stopping to think about the repercussions. First there was the swine flu, then the Equine flu, and now this vaccine!"

"People died because of those flus, Mark! People were killing their own horses in a panic that they would catch the Equine flu. Then what happened? One of the drug companies came up with a vaccine, and they saved people's lives! Nothing bad happened!" I practically yelled, my irritation getting the better of me.

Mark was speaking in a loud whisper as he leaned toward me. "Nothing happened you say! Nothing but people panicking and thinking they had to rush out to get the cure! People lined up for hours like a bunch of mindless sheep to get a vaccine that might work, or might not. Now they're doing the same thing, only this vaccine has serious side-effects."

"What side-effects? Diarrhea, vomiting? I think most people will live with a temporary side-effect if it keeps them from getting the flu *forever*." I was done. I tried to push past Mark to hurry to the meeting but it was like trying to move a brick wall. He shook his head and pulled a piece of paper from his pocket, thrusting it into my face.

I glanced at the top, noting it was just a copy of an e-mail. "Wow, Mark, you do know how to e-mail. Amazing," I added sarcastically, as I continued trying to push past him. He moved the paper in my face and I swatted his hand out of the way.

"It's from Justin," he whispered softly.

I think my heart stopped. I looked up at Mark quickly, trying to see if he was joking or not. His eyes were soft and warm and completely devoid of deceit, not that Mark knew how to lie anyway. I swallowed hard and took the paper from him, unfolding it carefully. It was dated five weeks ago! My hands were shaking as I stared at the paper. Five weeks! Mark had received an e-mail from my brother five weeks ago and hadn't told me. Why Mark? Why not me? I shook my head and smoothed out the paper, my hands shaking.

Mark,

I know you have a lot of conspiracy theories, so I knew this would be right up your alley. I can't contact Iz. They'll find out, or intercept it. They might intercept this, but I had to take a chance. Whatever you do you can't get the vaccine. Make sure Iz doesn't. She's my only family, and I have to keep her safe. I don't know if I'll be able to get to a computer again. I'm being tracked, but I'm trying to get home to her.

This vaccine does do what they're saying, but it has serious side-effects they won't mention. It's corrupt. It's not natural. It's evil. I can't explain any more, you'll just have to trust me.

Delete this email right away, and don't tell Izzy I've contacted you. She needs to go on acting like she knows nothing, like she thinks I'm dead. It's safer that way. Please! Take care of my sister. I'm counting on you.

-J.

Tears were leaking from my eyes as I finished reading the e-mail. My brother was alive, and he was trying to get to me. Why was it taking so long? What was stopping him? Who's tracking him? And what is so damned important about this vaccine? He could have been a little clearer, or maybe he couldn't. I swallowed hard and wiped the tears from my eyes. "So, you think this is the vaccine he's talking about?" I asked Mark.

He nodded slowly, taking the e-mail from my hands. He carefully folded the paper in half, and then proceeded to rip it carefully. My eyes widened in shock, but he shook his head and continued ripping. "It's for the best, Iz. We need to get out of here. This meeting is mandatory so we can get the vaccine. Your brother said this thing is evil, and I certainly don't want anything like that inside of me. Do you?"

I shook my head and dried my tears. "Maybe we should talk to

Principal Tourney first."

"What's that old saying? It's better to ask forgiveness than permission? I say we leave now and find out the whole story from the other teachers later."

I nodded my head in agreement and sniffled. "Okay, I suppose that would work. We could say I got sick or something. Let's just go," I said, turning towards the door. Mark nodded and followed behind me as I opened the door.

I glanced out into the hallway, making sure no one was around, before striding purposefully towards the doors. Mark shadowed me as we walked hurriedly towards the exit. I pushed the door open and walked into the storm. There was no rain yet, but thick black clouds obscured the sun, making it ominously dark for only four o'clock. I shivered in my thin sweater and skirt, realizing I had left my jacket in my classroom. Too late now.

We hurried down the front steps and began crossing the parking lot, my heels clicking on the pavement. "Isabella? Mark? You're late for the meeting!" I heard the voice of the Superintendent behind us.

I stopped and Mark ran into the back of me. My breath expelled with a whoosh. The man was built like a tank. "No, Isabella," he whispered, but I jabbed him in the stomach. I'm pretty sure this hurt me more than him, since my funny bone immediately began tingling and he didn't even flinch.

"Oh, we were just getting some things out of Mark's truck," I said sweetly, rubbing my elbow all the while. "He needed a hand carrying things so I volunteered. We'll be right there." I turned and rushed over to Mark's Jeep Cherokee, pointing for him to unlock the door.

"Do you need another hand? I can help as well," Superintendent Blanks said as he started walking towards us.

"No, no, it's just a few things. Don't miss the meeting on our account. I promise we'll be right there. I know this must be an important meeting," I smiled sweetly back, waving the superintendent away as I pretended to reach inside Mark's Jeep for something. What was the superintendent doing at a high school staff meeting? The man rarely left the district office across town.

"He's leaving," Mark said softly.

I stood up and watched with Mark as the door closed behind the superintendent. Mark's hand brushed across my back, sending a shiver down my spine. "He'll be back if we don't hurry. Get in the truck now!" Mark said as his hands encircled my waist, guiding me into the jeep.

I climbed in the driver's side and scooted across to the passenger seat, smoothing my skirt out beneath me. Mark climbed up behind me and immediately started the truck. I looked back toward the high school and saw Superintendent Blanks running back towards us, waving his arms and yelling. Beside him were two men in dark suits running towards us. Mark glanced at me, and then quickly backed the jeep up and we were out of the parking lot in seconds. I glanced behind us and my breath caught. The two men in suits had jumped into a black car and were peeling out behind us.

"They're following us?" I whispered, more to myself than to Mark. I watched the car back out of the parking lot and swerve onto the road behind us. "They're following us!" I screamed. Mark glanced in the rearview mirror as the black car sped to catch up with us.

"Damn, why do I have to be right about this shit now?" Mark swore as he sped around a corner and shifted gears. The jeep groaned and bucked as he missed a gear in his panic. "Shit!" he swore as he corrected the truck.

My hands were shaking uncontrollably as I watched the car behind us. "Seriously, Mark? Fuck!" I exclaimed. Mark shot me a surprised look. Being a high school English teacher, I usually refrained from using profane language. I found it degrading. Shit, damn, fuck!

I gripped the dash as we sped around another corner. Were

we on two wheels? It certainly felt like it as we careened around corner after corner. Mark turned suddenly onto the main street through town, zipping in between cars. If this was a big city we might have been able to pull off a great escape, but this was a small town. The sleek black car behind us had no problems keeping up with Mark's rugged Jeep.

Why were they following us? What was the big deal if we didn't go to this meeting or get this vaccine? I glanced behind me again, seeing the car right on our bumper. "We need to do something different, Mark. We're not going to lose them this way," I screeched, my voice raising an octave.

"I know!" Mark jerked the wheel again, sending me flying towards him. My leg hit the shifter hard and I had to grab the passenger door to move myself back into my seat. I'd forgotten to buckle my seatbelt in the rush. I grabbed the seatbelt now in a panic, buckling myself in just as we veered around another corner, the tires squealing in protest. We were going to die! I glanced at Mark, noticing he wasn't wearing his seatbelt either. My hands were shaking as I reached across his chest and began buckling him into his seat.

"What on earth are you doing, Iz?" he growled as he reached around me to shift.

"I'm buckling your seatbelt! What did you think I'm doing?" I screamed back at him as I heard the buckle click.

He shook his head but said no more as he continued driving like a maniac. I was surprised no cops were following us. We were on the outskirts of town on a long expanse of road. We weren't going to lose them on this stretch of highway. Mark slammed on the breaks and turned us off the highway suddenly. We slowed down as we turned onto a gravel road. I glanced around, recognizing our location. We were on an old logging road that led up to a small natural lake that kids usually frequented in the summertime for skinny-dipping and make-out sessions. A quick glance behind us showed that the car was still following us, but our distance had increased.

"What are you planning to do, Mark? Take them swimming." I quipped.

"Oh, you're just so funny," he said dryly. "This truck is 4-wheel drive with nice big tires, unlike the little car behind us. We can go places they can't, sweetheart. I know what I'm doing. They can't follow us now!" he added as he turned off the road and began following a muddy track that could barely be called a path. I smiled at Mark's logic. This was it! We weren't going fast, but Mark's jeep had no problems navigating through the terrain. We were getting out of here!

Bang! Bang! I ducked my head in terror as gunshots ripped through the air. I felt the truck lean towards its left side as the back driver's side tire was shot. The path we were on climbed upward through thick mud.

"Mark! They're shooting at us! What the fuck?" I screamed.

"Hang on," Mark said as our momentum slowed in the thick mud. Mark stopped and quickly put the jeep into 4-wheel drive. The jeep groaned and bucked before continuing slowly up the steep, muddy path. The jeep was struggling in 4-wheel drive and I knew the car behind us wouldn't even get this far. If we could just get some distance between us we'd be safe.

Bang! Bang! The whole back of the truck seemed to sink into the mud. Putting the truck in 4-wheel drive wouldn't do any good if we had no tires. My face was wet and I realized I was crying. I could hear yelling and realized the men in suits had gotten out of their car and were climbing up the path after us. I looked up at Mark as the truck stopped moving forward, utter defeat on his face. "I'm so sorry, Iz," he said as another gunshot rang through the air. Blood splattered across my face and I stared in horror as the light left Mark's eyes.

Chapter 2

My head was pounding and I was hearing voices. Hmm, isn't it usually a bad thing to hear voices? Wait, there were people talking about me. Okay, good, not hearing voices in my head, but actual voices. My eyes wouldn't open though. I tried with all my might but it seemed as though my whole body was numb. My brain seemed slow, sluggish. What had happened? Where was I? Mark!

Memory returned to me with increasing speed. We were in the truck, driving away through the woods. Mark knew a way. He would get us away from the bad men. Oh, and they were definitely bad men. Hmm, why did I think that? My mind was growing fuzzy again as I tried to access my memories. I knew they were bad but couldn't recall why I thought that. Where am I?

The voices were growing louder. They must be walking towards me. I strained my ears to hear. My breathing sounded hollow and I could hear a steady beeping noise. Was I in a hospital? Footsteps were coming closer now, along with two voices.

"I'm not sure why she's still unconscious," a male voice was saying. "The tranquilizer should have worn off hours ago. We think it's most likely stress-related."

"You're sure she's not having a reaction to the vaccine?" a second male voice said. This voice was deep and rich, with a strange accent I couldn't place. "It doesn't seem to be working right."

"No, no reaction, sir, I'm quite sure. She'll receive the second dose tomorrow and you'll see she's just like all the rest." The first voice sounded nervous now. "Her body is just working quite a bit slower because of the tranquilizer. We don't normally administer this if there are other medicines in the person's body, but since you insisted…" the voice trailed off.

"There'd better not be any negative effects, *doctor*," the man with the accent was speaking slowly now, enunciating his words. "I will hold you personally responsible if we have to dispose of this one. Give her the second dose right away."

I strained my ears, but heard nothing for several moments. Then there was a shuffling noise and I felt something on my ear, then I heard a beep. Thermometer? "105 degrees," the doctor's voice murmured. Yes, a thermometer, but was my temperature really that high? I didn't feel like I had a fever.

I struggled to open my eyes again but they wouldn't open. I told my fingers to move, but they didn't feel like they moved at all. The doctor who hovered over me certainly didn't indicate he noticed my feeble attempts at moving. I could hear papers flipping and the sound of someone scribbling on paper. The distinct sound of heels clicking on the floor indicated another person had just walked in. I heard a swish of clothing and caught the scent of a sweet perfume.

"Doctor Douglas?" a woman's voice said.

"Ah, Patricia, what is it?" the doctor asked. His voice was softer sounding now than when he'd spoken to the man. I sensed he liked this woman. Or perhaps he just really didn't like the other man.

"Is she all right?" the woman, Patricia, asked. I didn't know anyone named Patricia and I certainly didn't recognize her voice.

"She's burning up and I'm pretty sure she's blind. I don't know what this vaccine did to her, but I honestly think a second dose will kill her," he sighed. I swallowed hard, or tried to. My body didn't seem to respond with any of the usual movements it should. I was blind? No, I just couldn't open my eyes. How could he know if I was blind?

Wait, maybe he's talking about someone else. Yes, that's it. He's talking about someone else.

"Geez, Max, she's been through enough!" Patricia exclaimed. Oh, yes, I definitely had the sense there was something more going on between the doctor and this woman. Yes, Max, listen to her! I have definitely been through enough.

"I can't go against his orders, Patricia. He'll kill me! I'm sorry. I have to go prepare the second dose now." I heard footsteps as someone walked away. It must have been the doctor leaving because the smell of perfume suddenly grew stronger and I sensed this woman leaning over me.

"I know you can hear me, Isabella Howerton. I slipped something into your IV to give the impression you are in a coma. I was hoping it would stop Max from giving you the second dose, but he doesn't dare go against orders. He'll die if he disobeys. I couldn't stop him from giving you the first dose, but I switched the batches. I hope it helps. I'll explain later if I can." She paused but I still felt her breath warm on my cheek. She kissed my neck then and I felt wetness roll down my neck and across my collar bone. I felt her tongue move across the wetness, licking it up. What the hell? Did she slobber on me when she kissed me and now she's licking it up? Gross!

Her voice was velvety sweetness now and I felt my heart beat faster with her words. "When you see your brother tell him our debt is repaid," she laughed softly then and I sensed her leave. I would have been shaking if I could have made my body function properly. What the hell was going on?

***

I dreamed. Heck, I was hooked up to machines and unable to move. What else was I going to do? But the dreams were strange and very disturbing. I kept dreaming about a woman with deep brown hair that cascaded in waves across her shoulders and black eyes. And I do mean black, not a dark brown that looks black. Her eyes were like twin coals waiting to be lit on fire. Her eyes sought to capture mine, but I refused to look at her. Every time I evaded her eyes she laughed. She spoke to me, though I have no idea what she said, and her voice was the velvety sweet voice of Patricia. Her skin was milky white and she was covered in a dress that appeared to be made of smoke. It shifted back and forth, revealing portions of her body I'd rather not see.

A man entered the dream then, vying for my attention. Patricia seemed aware of his presence, but acted as though he wasn't there. The man was god-like! I could barely keep my eyes off him, but some part of me told me not to look. I found myself shifting glances between these two irresistible beings, unable not to look, but knowing that to look would be a very bad thing to do.

His hair was pale gold but his eyes were black too. I avoided looking at those eyes and he too laughed when I did, though he was definitely not amused. Where the woman was made up of darkness and smoke, this man was gold and fire. He was completely nude and my breath caught at his perfection. I examined him from the neck down, not daring to look at his handsome face in case his eyes bewitched me somehow. His shoulders were broad and well-muscled. Every inch of him was muscled perfection. My eyes trailed hungrily down his ripped abdomen, lower, lower... WOW!

I quickly averted my eyes as he laughed. My face must be on fire! Oh, but he was quite a man! Hmm, I'd seen Mark without a shirt on and I wondered how he'd compare to this man. Mark! No! Memories of blood splattering my face shattered the image of these two beautiful beings. I woke suddenly, my heart pounding in my chest.

My eyes were open and I squinted, looking around at my surroundings. The room was dark, but I could make out shapes. I held my hand up to my face. Yup, that's my hand and I can see it. It's just dark in the room. Whew, I was worried when the doctor had mentioned blindness. It must have been a temporary side-effect of whatever that woman had given me, along with the 105 degree fever. I felt my forehead, but it felt completely normal to me.

I looked around the dark room, waiting for my eyes to adjust to the dim light coming through the curtains Looking down at myself, I noted there were no IV's or wires attached to me, although I did appear to be in a hospital gown. I pulled the blankets off and careful stepped onto the cold floor. Slowly, I moved toward the window and pulled back the curtain. I had expected to see outside, but instead my window looked out into a dimly lit hallway. The hallway seemed to be gray concrete and I gave an involuntary shutter. Where was I?

I pushed the curtain back in place and felt my way around the room until I came to a small closet, hoping my clothes were inside. Nope, there was nothing in the closet except a hospital robe and slippers. I pulled the robe on and slipped my feet into the slippers, then began feeling my way around the room until I reached a door. I quietly turned the handle and peeked out into a brightly lit hallway that appeared very similar to the one I viewed outside my window. The floor was tiled slate, but the walls were cold gray concrete.

The hallway was quiet and seemed the same looking both directions. I quietly tiptoed down the hallway to my right, looking for anything to indicate which way to go. Doors were spaced out along both sides of the hallway, but there were no signs anywhere indicating what was behind the doors. I took a deep breath and turned the knob on the first door I found. The light from the hallway illuminated the empty room, which looked precisely like the room I had just come from. I closed the door and moved on to the next room, which was another empty carbon copy. The hallway continued on the same until I reached a dead end. I turned around and scurried back the way I had come, unsure which room was the one I had started out in.

After checking over 20 rooms I finally came to a secondary hallway that seemed exactly the same as the one I was in. Sighing in frustration, I decided to just continue the way I had been going instead of taking the new hallway. I was beginning to think I was completely alone when I opened a door to peer in and noticed a person lying in the bed. I tiptoed toward the person, squinting in the darkened room. I saw a slender arm hooked up to IVs and long, blonde hair. A woman, I figured as I inched closer. Her head was turned away and she seemed to be dreaming, tossing in her sleep. She rolled toward me and I gasped, stumbling backwards several steps. She looked just like me!

I jerked awake, sitting straight up in bed. Was that a dream? I looked around the room, then down at my arm and the IVs running to the machine beside the hospital bed. I carefully removed the tape holding the needles in my arm and pulled the IVs out. There weren't any more wires hooked up to me so I hopped out of bed and went immediately to the window. It was just as I had seen it in the dream. Next I went to the closet, pulling out the robe and slippers that were right where I expected them. I walked to the door and stopped before pulling it open. What if I'm still dreaming? I thought I was awake last time. I pinched my arm for good measure, wincing at the slight pain. I seemed to be awake this time. I ran the back of my hand across my forehead. I didn't feel clammy or feverish.

Slowly I opened the door and immediately noticed the difference. The walls and floor were the same materials as before, but the hallway ended to my right. I opened the door further and stepped out into the hallway, listening for sounds. Everything seemed quiet, so I ventured down the hallway until I reached the next room. I opened the door and was immediately disappointed. The room was completely empty of people as well as furnishings. I quickly closed the door and moved down to the intersecting corridor. Three ways to go, but all directions seemed the same. I was about to turn left when I heard the faint sound of voices coming from the right. I scurried down the hallway toward the voices and stopped outside the second door on the left. It sounded like people were arguing, but I couldn't make out any words through the thick wooden door. Then one voice grew louder, sounding as though he had moved toward the door.

"... permanent damage! I'm going to go check on her now." I recognized the voice of Doctor Douglas, but had no time to listen further as I watched the door handle turn. I ran to the next room and quickly shut the door behind me, hoping I had made it in time. Several minutes passed and my breathing returned to normal. I glanced around the room I was in, noticing for the first time it appeared to be a hospital room like mine, complete with a patient on the bed.

I pinched my arm again, just to make sure I was awake before I moved toward the bed. The arms peeking out of the blanket were large, muscular and covered with hair. Okay, that's definitely male. The IV liquid was silver in color and the man was hooked up to the liquid on both arms. I moved closer, squinting in the darkness at his face, sure I was mistaken about whom was lying on the bed.

My heart was pounding in my chest as I leaned over his face, taking in the unruly brown hair, the strong jaw with a day's growth of facial hair, and the large white bandage wrapped around his head. I gingerly reached out and touched his cheek, then let out a sob. Mark was alive! I wasn't sure how, but here he was.

Chapter 3

Mark's skin was covered with a fine sheet of sweat. I touched his forehead, and it felt clammy and slightly colder than usual, but he was alive! "Mark!" I whispered in his ear, shaking him gently. I wasn't sure what to do, but I knew I didn't want to stay here and I certainly couldn't leave him behind now that I'd found him. I pinched my arm again, just for good measure. This wasn't a dream! "Mark, wake up!"

There were no heart monitors or any other machines hooked up to him other than the IVs, so maybe that was a good sign. The bullet must have only grazed him, I thought, remembering the blood splattering across my face. Then I remembered the look in his eyes and how they had gone blank as his body had slumped down in his seat, held up only by his seatbelt. Then I'd felt pain in my shoulder and everything had gone dark.

I touched my shoulder, pulling back the gown to look for any marks. There didn't seem to be any wounds, so my guess was I'd been hit by some sort of tranquilizer. I frowned back down at Mark, pursing my lips together in thought. What was I going to do? Should I unhook the IVs? I had unhooked my own IV, but it hadn't contained the weird silvery-colored substance that Mark's did. *What is this stuff?*

I stepped closer to the bags hanging on metal poles next to his bed, looking for something written on the bags that might indicate what was in them, but had no luck. There was nothing written on the bag, but maybe he had a chart. I moved around the bed, looking for a medical chart that might give me a clue as to what I should do next. No luck. The room was sterile and empty, devoid of anything that would lend me a clue as to what I should do next.

I moved around to the far side of Mark's bed and gently moved the bandage on his head, peeking underneath to get an idea about the wound. There was dried blood on the bandage, but as I pulled it back further I couldn't find a wound on his skin. Wouldn't there be a wound beneath all this blood? Getting bold now, I grabbed the wrappings and pulled them off his head. Dried blood was matted to his hair where the largest part of the bandage had been, but as I moved his hair I found no sign of a wound at all. After a few minutes I gave up trying to find a bullet hole and moved back to the strange IVs. Was the weird fluid in the IVs what was healing him? Was it keeping him asleep? Do I dare take them out? But he's healed now, so I should be able to take the IVs out, if they are in fact some sort of healing medicine.

I'm not sure how long I stood there debating, but eventually I figured I may as well take one of the IVs out to start with. I'm sure I could get it back in if I really needed to. Maybe if I can wake him up I can just take the IV bags with us. Sighing, I decided to just take the leap and quickly removed the tape from his left arm and pulled the needle out. Nothing happened immediately. Mark was still lying on the bed, breathing shallowly. For several moments I stood there watching him, praying I had made the right decision. I felt his head and I swear he felt warmer. Yes, he was warmer. His skin was already taking on a more normal color, instead of the sickly pallor he had moments ago.

Taking it as a good sign, I ran around the bed and quickly removed the other IV as well. Fingers crossed, I scrutinized Mark's appearance with each passing moment, watching the color return fully to his face. He began moving around slightly, and I scooted close to the bed, grasping his hand. "Mark!" I whispered once again. "Wake up!"

His eyes shot open and I stumbled back as he rolled off the bed, groaning. "Mark, are you okay?" I asked, leaning down beside him as he curled his naked body into a ball on the floor, the sheets tangled around his ankles. "Are you in pain?"

"Get back!" he growled, his voice threatening. His whole body began shaking, hands flat on the floor, head tucked in. It was almost as though he was having a seizure, except he was on all fours and seemed to be aware and talking. Maybe I shouldn't have taken the IVs out after all?

After a few minutes he stopped shaking and his sweat-covered body relaxed onto the floor. I stepped forward gingerly and knelt down beside him. "Mark?" I asked tentatively, reaching a hand out toward him.

"Don't touch me yet," he said, and I pulled my hand back quickly. His voice sounded almost normal, but he was breathing hard like he'd just run a marathon. "Just... give me... a minute."

I nodded my head, even though he couldn't see me. After a few more minutes he took a deep breath and sat back, running his hands through his hair. My eyes were involuntarily drawn to his chest as the muscles rippled with his every movement. He wore absolutely nothing and I found my eyes transfixed on his body. His head turned toward me and I blushed, looking away quickly and standing up. Hopefully it was too dark for him to see how red my face was. "There's probably a robe or something in here," I said, rushing to the closet. My heart was beating quickly and my hands shook as I opened the closet doors.

Just like in my closet there was a pair of slippers, but no robe. Instead there was a pair of long striped pajama style pants that I grabbed out and tossed behind me toward Mark. He barked a low laugh behind me, and I felt my face flush again. I am such a dork! I grabbed the slippers out as well and waited a few minutes before turning around and handing them to him.

The pajama bottoms hung low on Mark's waist, emphasizing his defined abs. He took the slippers from my hand, but didn't put them on. "So," he started, "where are we? And why are we in the dark?"

"Um, I actually have no idea," I began in a whisper, moving closer to Mark so he could hear me better. I looked up at his face, my eyes scrutinizing him for any signs that he might drop to the ground, or go into seizures, or something. He seemed perfectly normal. "As far as I can tell we're in the weirdest version of a hospital ever. The walls are concrete, the floors are tile, and I think we might be underground." I shivered, pulling my robe tighter around my body and pointing toward the window. "Take a look."

Mark turned and walked to the window, where a small amount of light was filtering into the room, just like in the room I had woken up in. He cautiously pulled back an edge of the curtain and peered through. He dropped the curtain quickly and walked back to me. "We need to get out of here now!" he whispered urgently, grabbing my arm and steering me toward the door.

"Mark, wait," I stopped, pulling against his hand on my arm.

He let go of my arm and moved his body in close to mine. He lifted my chin, turning my head from side to side. He stopped, holding my head off to one side as he ran a hand along my neck. "Mother fucker!" he exclaimed. I jumped back, shushing him to be quiet while he continued to rant a trail of obscenities. "Damn, damn, fucking pieces of shit mother fuckers!"

"Mark, shh, they'll hear you!"

"Let the mother fuckers hear me!" he roared, then continued another litany of colorful cussing.

I ran to the door and held my ear up to it, hoping the doors were all as sound proof as they had appeared. I didn't hear any running footsteps, so I hoped we were safe for a few more minutes. I turned back to Mark, who seemed to have run out of swear words although he was now standing with his head in his hands, breathing hard. "Mark, are you all right?" I asked timidly.

"No, I am not all right," he said tensely. He lowered his arms and stalked towards me, pulling me into his body and wrapping his arms tight around me. I breathed in his scent and listened to his pounding heart while he held me tight. After a few moments he finally loosened his grip and I stepped out of his embrace.

"So, you want to explain what that was all about?" I asked, crossing my arms.

He smiled but it didn't reach his eyes. "Let's worry about getting out of here first," he said, turning for the door. "I think I have an idea where we are."

He opened the door and peered out both directions before grabbing my hand and pulling me along behind him. "Where are we?" I whispered as he rushed down the hallway past the door I had heard the doctor in.

Mark shook his head and put a finger to his lips as he stopped before another hallway branching to our left. He peered cautiously around the corner and took a deep breath. He looked back at me then pointed at me feet. "Off," he whispered quietly. I nodded as I pulled the slippers off my feet and shoved them into one of the large pockets of my robe. The slippers had been making a slapping sound as we had scurried down the hall.

Mark began jogging down the main hallway once more, pulling me along behind him. His bare feet made virtually no sound as he ran, but I felt as though I was stomping with every step. By the time we stopped at another hallway intersection I was breathing heavily, and loudly it seemed. Mark peered around the corner and pulled me behind him to the left, where the hallway ended at elevator doors. Beside the elevator was another door for the stairwell, which Mark pulled me into quietly.

We stopped there for a moment, listening for any sounds before Mark began slowly climbing the concrete stairs. He paused at the next landing and put his ear up to the door, listening intently for several moments before taking my hand once again and pulling me up the stairs behind him. At the next landing he stopped once again and put his ear to the door. The sound of a door opening on the stairwell below us urged Mark into action and he quickly opened the door and pulled me behind him. He cautiously closed the door behind us and it clicked softly shut.

The hallway we were in looked like a hotel, a fancy hotel. The walls were painted a pale golden color and the floor was a beautiful matching marbled tile that was shiny enough to view your reflection in. Beautiful landscape paintings dotted the walls, but I had no time to admire them as Mark pulled me quickly behind him as he rushed down the hallway. Doors lined the hallway with keycard locks on them as well as numbers on gold plaques stating 1045, 1044, 1043. We stopped at an intersecting hallway, then turned and followed the signs that pointed toward the lobby, walking at a casual pace.

Mark reached over and grabbed my hand once again as the murmur of people talking grew louder. An elderly couple in rich clothes exited a room and stopped, frowning at us. The woman clutched her small purse to her chest as the man pushed her ahead of us into the lobby. We followed behind them, leaving a space between us and the couple as we entered a large lobby area.

The high vaulted ceiling had a large, beautiful chandelier hanging down, casting a warm light on the room. Plush furniture in red and gold decorated the room, adding to the expensive feel of the hotel. The elderly couple turned toward a dining room, where the rich smells of bacon and coffee were coming from. Several people mingled near the dining room doors, casting glances our way. I looked at Mark, with no shirt on, and wondered what people must be thinking. It looked like the two of us had just rolled out of bed and come down to the lobby for breakfast. My stomach rumbled as we continued past the dining room and toward the massive front doors, where two large security guards were standing on either side.

Before we reached the door the two security guards moved to block it, their hands reaching toward the guns strapped to their hips.

"Mr. Andrews, Miss Howerton, please come with us," the security guard on the left said, his hand resting on his gun.

My heart was pounding in my chest, but Mark appeared suddenly very calm. He pushed me back behind him and stepped toward the security guards casually. Both men pulled their guns out, and guard number one leveled his directly at Mark. Mark stopped moving and held his hands out to his sides. Security guard number two replaced his gun and grabbed a set of handcuffs off his waist, moving cautiously toward Mark as guard number one kept his gun held steady.

The security guard reached out and grasped Mark's right arm, and as soon as he did Mark grabbed him and pulled him in front of his body. Several gun shots rang out, peppering the security guard and covering the ground with blood. People were screaming and running around as I watched transfixed as Mark threw the dead security guard at the other guard, knocking the man back into the wall. Faster than I could see, Mark had knocked the gun away from the man and kicked him in the face, breaking his nose with a loud crunch. Blood gushed from the man's face as he tried to wrestle Mark, but Mark was a high school PE teacher and wrestling coach and he knew what he was doing. Within seconds Mark had twisted the man onto his stomach, pulling his arm back until it popped out of socket. The man screamed and Mark pulled back his arm and punched the man out cold.

Footsteps sounded behind me and I turned to see five more security guards in uniform running towards us, guns drawn. Mark wasted no time grabbing my arm and pulling me out the front doors. We squinted in the bright early morning sunlight as we quickly ran across the parking lot, dodging through cars. A valet was parking a car and gasped when Mark ran up to the car, yanked the door open and pulled him out. Gunshots rang out and I ducked as I ran for the passenger door. Mark pushed the door open before I got there, and I jumped in and slammed it behind me. Mark quickly back the car up and zipped through the parking lot.

I ducked down again as several more gun shots rang out, but nothing seemed to hit us as we sped out of the parking lot and onto the street. I was shaking and kept glancing behind us for pursuit as Mark raced us through city streets. After a few minutes I recognized the city we were in, just under two hours from our home town. Mark changed lanes and quickly took a side road, randomly zigzagging through the city, until we found ourselves downtown amidst a bustling Saturday Market.

Chapter 4

Mark slowed the car down as we turned into the downtown area, where street vendors lined the waterfront. We slowed down and parked the car illegally near the base of a bridge. Mark took a deep breath and turned off the car, leaning his head back with his eyes closed. "You're not going to sleep, are you?" I asked after watching him like that for a minute.

He smiled and opened his eyes, sighing deeply. "No, I'm not going to sleep. I just needed to stop and regroup." He turned to face me, then reached out and caressed my cheek. I felt my heart flutter at his tentative touch and my cheeks warmed. I looked away as he dropped his hand. "We should probably dump this car, and get some clothes. Check the glove box and under the seats. Maybe we can scrounge some money."

After several minutes of us searching the leather interior of the car, we came up empty handed. The car was immaculate and obviously well taken care of. A quick look in the trunk only showed a spare tire. We got out of the car, wiping down the seats and anything we might have touched, and locked the keys in the car before walking toward the Saturday Market.

Mark looked like he had just gotten out of bed, and I looked like I had just escaped from a mental institution. I kept brushing my hair down and looking behind us, while Mark casually strolled through the streets as though he knew exactly where he was going and what he was doing. A few vendors eyed us warily, but Mark had an easy way about him that seemed to put people at ease. We wound our way past the food vendors, my stomach growling the whole way, and down a side alley I would never have ventured on my own. Debris and glass littered the ground and I walked gingerly, even with the slippers placed back on my feet. Mark walked barefoot and seemed to avoid all the glass and debris, even though he was watching ahead of us and not watching the ground at all.

We followed the alley to another small street that wasn't quite as debris covered, but the walls of the buildings on either side were painted with gang graffiti. I felt a shiver up my spine and peeked behind us to see three young men following behind us. One of the men held a baseball bat in his hand, and they definitely appeared to be gang members to my mind. "Mark," I whispered, moving close beside him. He nodded his head and stopped walking, turning quickly to the men behind us. Why were we stopping? All I wanted to do was turn and run very quickly away.

"Well, well, well, what have we here?" the young man in the middle said. He looked to be in his early twenties and had dreadlocks hanging to his shoulders. He spoke slowly, his hands reaching casually into the pockets of his big puffy green jacket. "Looks like you twos escaped from a hospital."

The man with the baseball bat laughed, lifting the club onto his shoulder casually. He was bigger than the other two and had dark, greasy hair. I looked at the third one, thinking he looked more like a kid than a man. Pimples covered his face and he seemed nervous, his eyes shifting back and forth. His long hair was stringy and greasy and his clothes were about three sizes too big.

Mark stepped toward the men, pushing me back behind him as he did so. "I could use some money," Mark said as he moved slowly toward the three of them. "Why don't you empty your pockets for me?"

"Ha, that's funny man, real funny," the leader said, pulling a gun out of his pocket. "Why don't I put a bullet in your head and take your woman?" My heart thudded in my chest. I did not like the sound of that.

Mark put a hand to his head, where the bandage had been. "I've already had a bullet in my head, and it wasn't pleasant, so I think I'll pass. Let's go with option B," he said, moving so fast he was a blur. Mark simultaneously grabbed the gun with one hand, while slamming his fist into the man's face, sending the man sprawling across the pavement while the gun spun across the ground the opposite direction. The baseball bat swung out, glancing off Mark's shoulder as he rolled to the ground. He kicked out, sending the thug with the bat flying onto his back. Mark grabbed the bat out of the thug's hand and slammed it into the ground beside his face. The bat splintered on impact, sending pieces flying. I covered my head with my arm; feeling pieces of splintered wood hit me.

I lowered my arms, watching Mark lean over the man until his face was inches away. The man moved slowly, pulling his wallet out of his pocket and handing it to Mark. Mark opened it and took the cash out before dropping the wallet back onto the man's chest. Mark stood up and walked back to me, snagging the gun on his way. He moved up beside me and dropped the gun into one of the pockets of my robe. I yanked on the robe as the weight of the gun pulled it crooked. Mark placed an arm around my shoulders and led me out of the alley, steering me back around to the edge of the Saturday Market.

"Wait here," Mark said, as we stopped before a bench. "You look a little conspicuous. I'll go get us some clothes. Don't move!"

I watched Mark jog over to a clothing vendor, crossing my arms in irritation. I immediately winced in pain and uncrossed my arms. Splinters had embedded in my skin from the bat breaking, and I gingerly pulled the largest one out. Blood oozed out of the open wound and I wiped it off, turning my arm so I could see how bad the injury was. I watched in fascination as the wound closed before my eyes, leaving only a smear of drying blood behind. I frowned, running my finger across the skin. I quickly pulled the other smaller splinters out, but they didn't even bleed.

I was still staring at my arms when Mark came jogging back over to me, holding a tote bag with clothes. He didn't say a word, just grabbed my hand and pulled me along behind him. I think I was in shock. My brain certainly seemed to be working slower than usual, and I couldn't seem to form words. I followed Mark numbly as he led us down the street until we reached a fast food restaurant. We walked in and made our way towards the bathrooms. Mark retrieved a couple things out of the bag, and then left me to go change in the bathroom.

I entered the small women's restroom and immediately caught sight of myself in the mirror. Wow, I looked terrible! My pale blue eyes were wild and dilated, and my usually sleek blonde hair was sticking up all over. I turned the faucet on and splashed water on my face and arms, eventually sticking my whole head under the sink until I was shivering. I moved toward one of the stalls and looked inside the tote bag. Mark had bought me a long spaghetti-strap dress in a horrific blue cheetah print. No bra, no underwear, no shoes. I plopped the gun into the bottom of the bag and threw my robe in on top of it. I untied the hospital gown and used it to dry my hair off a little before pulling the dress on. The dress was simple, shapeless and thin! Wow, you could practically see everything I *wasn't* wearing.

I threw the hospital gown into the top of the bag and pulled the slippers back onto my feet before leaving the bathroom. Mark was leaning against the wall outside the bathroom, waiting for me with a bag of food in one hand, a soda in the other. He was wearing a pair of board shorts, a plain green t-shirt and a pair of flip flops. His eyes took me in, lingering on my chest for just a touch too long before he handed me the bag of food. He slipped his empty arm around my shoulders and led me back outside.

I shivered as the wind gusted, and Mark tucked his arm tighter around me. We walked quickly down the street, turning toward the business center of town. Mark stopped at the edge of a parking garage and handed me the soda. "Be right back. I'm going to grab us a car," he said before jogging off into the parking garage.

I opened the bag of food and munched on some fries, trying not to think about how he was going to grab us a car. Minutes later a silver four-door car pulled up to the curb beside me, and the passenger door opened. "Get in," Mark said. I peeked in at him before jumping in the car.

The car was a little old, but seemed to be in good shape and smelled of citrus thanks to the car freshener hanging from the mirror. I buckled my seatbelt in and pulled a cheeseburger out of the bag. I handed it to Mark before grabbing another burger out of the bag for myself.

After Mark and I had finished six burgers and two large fries together, I felt immensely better. Mark was eyeing the bag, looking sad that his four burgers were already gone as he drove us onto the freeway headed north. It was barely noon and already it felt as though a lifetime had passed. A million questions were running through my mind, but I didn't know where to start.

"So," I began, and Mark looked at me warily. "How are you alive?" I asked. I sounded casual, as though I was asking about the weather. This was the question that had been in the back of my mind since I'd seen him in the hospital.

Mark barked a laugh and shook his head, but his hands tightened on the steering wheel. I waited patiently for several minutes, until it became obvious Mark wasn't going to answer me. Guess it's time to try a new question. "What was that place we were in? You said you knew where we were."

"I didn't *exactly* know where we were," he muttered, his eyes never leaving the road. I waited for him to explain more, but as before he said nothing. I shifted in my seat and bit my lower lip. This wasn't getting me anywhere. "Where are we going?" Home was in the opposite direction we were traveling.

He glanced at me, then back to the road. "I have some...

friends near here. They'll be able to help, I hope."

Hmm, that got me a little bit of an answer. "So, you have some sort of plan?"

"I have a temporary plan, yes," he said, glancing at me again. "I'm sorry; I just can't really say anything right now. First thing is to get us safe."

"And these friends of yours will keep us safe?" I asked, trying not to let my frustration show.

He didn't answer, but I could tell he was thinking hard about something. Frown lines creased his face and he suddenly crossed several lanes of traffic and pulled into a rest area. He drove to the far end of the rest area, backing the car into a spot and shutting the car off. "I don't know if taking you to these people will keep you safe or not. Fuck! This is turning into a fucking catastrophe!" he yelled, slamming his hands on the steering wheel repeatedly.

"Well, maybe if you communicated with me as to what's going on I could help!" I yelled back, my anger finally getting the best of me. "You've been acting strange since I unhooked you from those weird IVs."

"IVs?" he asked, looking at me. "What do you mean?"

I crossed my arms under my breasts, and noticed his eyes being drawn there. "I'll answer your questions when you start answering mine."

"Damn it, Isabella," he shook his head, but his eyes travelled to my breasts once more and stayed there. I cleared my throat and his eyes shifted up to my face, but there was a hunger in them that made my face flush. He leaned across the seat, reaching his hand out toward me. "You are a very infuriating woman, did you know that?"

"You won't answer my questions," I replied, my heart pounding in my chest as he drew a fingertip across my lips and down my chin. His hand gently brushed back my hair as he leaned forward. I closed my eyes, waiting for the kiss, but it didn't come. His hand stopped on my neck and a low growl emanated from his throat.

My eyes shot open, wondering what that growl was all about. He was looking at my throat and growling, and I felt a sudden fear in the pit of my stomach. I tried to push him back, but he held me tight as he leaned in and sniffed my neck. "Who bit you?" he asked, biting off each word.

"What?" I asked, my hand coming up to my neck. Mark moved back from me as I pulled the visor down, examining my neck. Two small dots I hadn't noticed before were on the side of my neck. I ran my finger along them, but could barely feel them.

"I noticed them before, at the hospital," he added. I remembered how he'd moved my chin around earlier, examining my neck. Is this what he'd been looking at? "So, who bit you?"

"I don't know what you're talking about? All I see is a couple small dots, Mark. Where do you get the idea that someone bit me?" I asked, turning to face him once again.

"Those dots are bite marks, Izzy. Vampire bite marks. So, who bit you? Who are you protecting?"

Was he insane? Mark was always full of theories, but this was a new one even for him. Vampires? He had to be joking. I touched my neck again, remembering the woman from the hospital. "A woman licked my neck," I said softly, looking Mark in the eyes. "I was in my room under some sort of medication. I couldn't see anything and I couldn't move, but I could hear. A woman named Patricia was talking to the doctor, and after he left she kissed me on the neck, and I thought she slobbered on me because then she licked me. I think I would have remembered if she'd bit me," I added.

He shook his head, "Not necessarily." He touched my neck again, his fingers sending a shiver down my spine. "Is this where she licked you?"

I nodded and he leaned in close to me again, pressing his face against my neck. My heart began pounding in my chest as I felt his warm breath across my neck. He leaned back and took my face in his hands, staring intently into my eyes. "I think we'd better take this from the top. What happened after we got caught?" Mark leaned back in his seat and I shivered as his warmth moved away from me.

"You mean after you died?" I asked, the words coming out in a choked sob. "I saw them shoot you, Mark. Your blood splattered on my face and you were gone! And then I felt something hit me, and the next thing I know there's nothing. Then I wake up and I can't see, can't move, but I can hear them talking about me. They gave me the vaccine, Mark, but the woman whispered that she switched the batches. She did it in repayment to my brother, or something like that. I don't know. Everything's all a blur. I was dreaming again, and again, and everything was confusing. I was wandering around that place, or I thought I was. Then I woke up and I didn't know what was real and what wasn't. Then I found you with these IVs full of some weird silvery stuff in them." I stopped talking as the tears began pouring down my cheeks as the emotions I'd been holding in came flooding out. Was this even real?

I heard Mark move closer and felt his arms wrap around me, pulling me across the seat to him as I cried. He stroked my still damp hair as tears continued to come until I couldn't cry any more. Mark turned the heater on, and I realized I'd been shivering. "I'm not dead, Iz," he whispered, again and again. "I'm right here."

I pulled away, searching through the fast food bags for napkins to wipe my face with. "You want to explain?" I asked, blowing my nose very unladylike into a napkin.

He sighed and leaned back, running his hand through his hair in one of his usual nervous gestures. "Vampires are real," he said bluntly.

I looked at him blankly, waiting for him to expand on that. When he didn't add any more, I asked, "Are you a vampire?"

He laughed then, shaking his head and pointing at the sun. "Nope, I am not a vampire. I'm not actually supposed to say anything unless... well, I guess that doesn't matter now." He shook his head, as though he was arguing with himself.

I waited while he battled whatever internal struggle he was going through. After several muttered curses under his breath he finally seemed to come to a decision. "I didn't die, Izzy, I was just badly wounded. But, the thing is, I heal really fast. I'm not sure who those men were who took us, but they definitely took us to a vampire den."

"Okay," I said slowly, taking in his words. "So, the woman who licked me...?"

"Bit you," he corrected, nodding. "Yes, she's a vampire. Do you remember her name or anything about her?"

"I couldn't see anything," I replied, trying to remember the conversation she'd had with the doctor. "Patricia. Her name was Patricia." I closed my eyes, remembering the strange dream I'd had of a woman I suspected was Patricia. And then there was the man, all gold and fire. No, I mustn't tell Mark about him, or the dream.

"And she said she switched batches for your brother?"

I nodded my head, "She said something about her debt to him being repaid." Thoughts of the man from my dreams invaded my thoughts, his pale muscled body walking through fire. He tossed his blond hair back, smiling at me, summoning me to him. I found my eyes growing heavy as I slipped toward sleep, and the man of fire.

"Izzy! Izzy! Iz!" Mark was screaming distantly and I felt myself wondering why. The man gestured for me to come to him, and suddenly he was lying in a bed of silken red sheets. I found myself walking towards him, admiring the muscles in his chest and the sheer perfection of his body. But I was nothing compared to this man, this god. I am just a simple school teacher. I suddenly felt ashamed, looking down at the plain dress I wore.

Where was my dress? I was standing mere feet before this resplendent man and I was completely naked. I started to cover myself with my hands, but the man shook his head and beckoned me forward. He sat up on the bed and the sheet that had been covering him slid to the floor, revealing the rest of his perfection. My mouth was dry as I stared at him, but he only smiled and held out a hand for me.

Timidly, I stepped forward until I was standing naked before this beautiful man. His eyes were large dark pools and I felt myself falling forward as I looked into them. I reached out a steadying hand, feeling suddenly lightheaded. He grasped my arms and pulled me down onto the bed, his mouth finding mine in an exploratory kiss. His strong hands trailed down my body, caressing intimate places. His mouth moved down my neck and across my breasts, kissing and licking as he moved lower and lower. My eyes fluttered as I gave in to the pure pleasure, angling my body to give him better reach. Just when I thought I'd climax he stopped and removed his hand. I opened my eyes in time to see him climb on top of me, spreading my legs to either side to give him easy access. Wait, what was I doing? I didn't do this. I'd only been with one man in all my life! I most certainly didn't sleep with men I didn't know. Hell, I didn't even kiss a guy unless I'd been on several dates. I tried to scurry away and he shook his head, prowling after me on all fours. Oh but he was amazing to look at.

No, no, I wasn't looking at him. I was leaving. I turned on the bed and tried to crawl away, but the bed went on and on. I looked around, but there was nothing but the bed and him. This must be a dream, I thought, but why can't I wake up. "Izzy, come back to me," I heard Mark's voice.

Mark? Where was he? I could hear him, but I couldn't see him. "Mark!" I screamed, falling off the bed and jolting awake.

Chapter 5

My heart was pounding in my chest and I was panting like I'd just run ten miles. I opened my eyes and looked around, quickly realizing I was not in the car anymore. I was lying on a black leather couch with several thick blankets on top of me, and a man's arm around me. "Izzy?" Mark asked tentatively. I sat up, pulling the blankets around me.

"Yeah," I croaked, swallowing hard. Mark handed me a glass of water, which I greedily gulped down. I set the glass down on the coffee table in front of me and looked around. The room we were in seemed to be a small but modernly decorated sitting room, with shiny dark wood floors and several black leather couches and chairs circling around the coffee table. A roaring fire blazed in a hearth along the wall by our heads.

"Are you all right, Iz?" Mark asked, reaching out to feel my forehead.

I leaned away from him, nodding as I pulled the blankets tighter around my body. "Where are we?" I asked. "And how long have I been out?"

Mark dropped his hand and sat up beside me. "We're at my friend's house, and you've been out for almost two days."

"Two days!" I screeched, standing up and immediately regretting it as the world tilted beneath me. Mark's arm was suddenly around me as he pulled me down onto the couch beside him. He tucked the blankets back around my shoulders and pulled me into his arms. I folded my legs underneath me, curling into a ball beside him.

I sighed, letting myself relax into his warm embrace. His hand brushed across my forehead and cheeks, and then curled possessively around me. "You wouldn't wake up," he muttered, his voice hoarse.

I tried to turn and look at his face, but he pulled me in tighter so I could hardly move. I lay there for several minutes, letting him hold me. "Did I have a fever?" I asked, thinking about the cold chills I kept getting and the way he kept trying to touch my forehead.

"No, not a fever," he murmured. "You've been freezing cold, and you still feel like ice. I think the last temperature we took you were at 84 degrees. I'm guessing you're up in the 90s now, but you still feel colder than you should. According to the doctor, your body was basically shutting down. The longer you were out, the more likely..." he stopped talking and cleared his throat, letting the words go unsaid.

A tall dark-haired woman walked into the room and knelt in front of me. She was wearing black slacks and a crisp button-up white shirt. "Hello, Isabella, I'm Dr. Humphry. It's nice to see you awake," she said, smiling as she held up a digital thermometer. "I'm just going to take your temperature now."

"Okay," I replied as she inserted the thermometer into my ear.

After a moment there was a quiet beep and she removed the thermometer. "Well, you're up to 91 degrees. I'd say that's a vast improvement, but you're not out of the woods yet. I'm going to bring you some nice hot tea to try and warm you up from the inside. How do you take it?"

"Sweet," I replied, shivering as another cold chill shook my body. I closed my eyes after the doctor left, suddenly feeling very tired.

"Hey, don't fall asleep," Mark whispered in my ear, shaking me gently.

I opened my eyes and turned my head, looking back into Mark's face. His eyes were red with dark circles around them. Another shiver shook me and Mark pulled himself underneath the blankets, so I was lying right next to his warm body. I could feel his chest against my back and his legs intertwined with mine. I peeked under the blanket, seeing I was wearing a thin spaghetti strap nightgown. I reached down and attempted to pull the gown down so it was actually covering my butt and my hand brushed up against Mark's skin. I was pretty sure he wasn't wearing clothes, and I felt the blood rush to my cheeks at the thought.

The doctor walked over to me, setting a hot cup of tea on the table. "Well, it's good to see some color in your cheeks," she commented, and I knew my face must be bright red. I felt Mark's chest move in what I presumed was laughter, even though he was quiet about it.

The doctor took my temperature again, and I think we were all happy to see it was up to 94 already. As soon as she left the room I sat up and grabbed the mug, carefully taking a sip of tea. Mark moved behind me, wrapping me in a cocoon of blankets before he stood up. Mark's back was to me as I peered over the rim of my cup, taking in the pair of black silk boxers he was wearing. Well, at least he had *some* clothes on. He stretched his arms, the muscles of his back rippling with the movement, before he looked over his shoulder at me.

"I was on strict orders to keep you warm," he said, turning and looking at me, his face looking very serious. "You scared the crap out of me, Izzy. I didn't know what happened. One minute, you were talking to me. The next thing I knew you were passed out and your body was seizing or something. You were moaning and thrashing around for the longest time. I couldn't wake you so I just drove here as fast as I could, but you started getting so cold. I was sweating with the heater on full blast, and you just got colder and colder."

I was *moaning*? Oh, the dream, I thought. I felt my face flush once again and I hurriedly looked down, hiding my face behind my hair. I took a sip of tea, and ended up gulping down the rest of it. I set the mug down and stood up, pulling the blankets with me. Mark followed me like a large shadow, hovering behind me. I moved toward the fireplace, warming myself in front of it. "So, where are we?" I finally asked.

"We're at Jed's house," he said as though that was explanation enough.

Mark moved up beside me, his hands nervously running through his hair. "You need a shave," I said casually, observing the thick growth on his face. He barked a laugh, but he seemed nervous. "So, who's Jed? The friend you mentioned?"

"I don't know if friend is the word I would use," he said softly, suddenly stiffening and turning around. I peeked over my shoulder and turned as well as a tall, dark-haired man wearing a navy flannel shirt, jeans and cowboy boots walked in.

The man smiled and walked towards us. He was tall and obviously muscular, and I have to admit a little intimidating. He held his hand out to me, "I'm Jed Harris."

I shook his hand while tightly holding the blankets with my other hand. "I'm Isabella, but most people call me Izzy," I replied.

He nodded and rocked back on his heels, his brown eyes darting from Mark to me. "So, Mark tells me you've had quite the interesting last few days. Run-ins with vampires usually don't end well for humans."

Another person who says vampires exist. Great, just what I need. "Well, it has been an interesting few days. I must be having a weird reaction to the vaccine," I muttered.

Jed laughed, shaking his head. "I get it," he said softly, still chuckling. "You don't want to admit in a thing such as vampires. Normally I'd say it'd be better for you that way, but since you're already under vampire control, I think it's a moot point. Vampires do exist, as do other things."

I'm under vampire control? What was that supposed to mean? I shivered, and Mark immediately placed his arm around me. He wasn't normally this protective of me, but I guess my almost dying may have something to do with that. Or maybe he just didn't trust this Jed guy.

The doctor walked in with the thermometer in hand once again and I waited patiently while she took my temperature. "Well, well, well, looks like you're back to normal," Dr. Humphry said, smiling as she looked at the thermometer. "I think Isabella has had a rough day, so why don't I get her some food and clothes." The doctor looked pointedly at Jed, then at Mark.

Mark dropped his arm from around my shoulder and I let Dr. Humphry lead me out of the room and down a hallway that branched off toward another large living room and a staircase. I could hear people talking beyond the living room towards what I assumed was a kitchen by the delicious aromas wafting my way. The doctor continued to lead me up the staircase at the end of the hallway. The second floor opened up in a hallway that appeared to be made up of bedrooms and a single bathroom.

We stopped before the bathroom, where a set of towels and several clothes were lying on the counter. "Hopefully the clothes fit," the doctor said, pointing at the pile. "Why don't you take a shower and get cleaned up, then come downstairs to the kitchen. Talk can wait until after you've been fed."

The doctor left and I immediately stripped and turned the shower onto its hottest setting. I winced at the heat until my body adjusted. The shower felt wonderful and I would have lingered if it weren't for my stomach rumbling a protest. My skin was red from the heat by the time I turned off the shower. I dried off with a luxuriously soft towel and pulled on a pair of jeans and a blue buttoned shirt. Once again there was no underwear, but I couldn't complain too much since the clothes fit perfectly. I looked at myself in the mirror and wondered at how great I looked, despite the fact I wore no makeup. I didn't think after all the ordeals I'd been through that I'd look good, but I think I actually looked better than ever.

I toweled off my hair and ran my fingers through the damp

strands before heading down the stairs toward the smells of food. The large living room I had passed opened up on a massive dining room, complete with a thick mahogany table laden with food. Several people bustled from the dining room to the kitchen beyond, carrying food and drinks to the table. I counted eight place settings and there was still room at the table for more. I stood back, watching the people bustle back and forth, laughing and joking as they went.

Dr. Humphry walked into the dining room on the arm of a giant of a man. The man had shaggy auburn hair and a massive beard and was carrying a large platter of ham in one hand. He dropped the tray on the table and looked over at me, the smile that had been on his face vanishing. A smaller brunette woman walked in carrying a tray of biscuits, followed by two other men who were identical in looks but were dressed very differently.

"Isabella," Jed said from behind me, making me jump. "You've met Mirabelle Humphry, our good doctor. This is her husband, Hugo."

I held my hand out to the red-haired man, but he just looked at me and sat down at the table. The doctor, Mirabelle, smiled apologetically at me before sitting down beside her husband. "This is Beth," Jed continued, indicating the pretty brunette woman who nodded to me before sitting down across from Mirabelle. She had a pixie-like face and large brown eyes. Jed pointed at the two twins. Both had sandy brown hair and rugged good looks. One wore a suit and tie, his face clean-shaven and his hair cut short. The second was dressed casually in jeans and a t-shirt, with slightly longer hair and a 5 o'clock shadow. "These two are Logan and Lucas."

The twin in the suit and tie walked over and shook my hand, smiling at me with perfect white teeth. "Logan Hill, investments," he said by way of introduction.

The second twin shoved Logan aside, laughing. "And I'm the better, more handsome brother, Lucas," he said, taking my hand in both of his. "You have such soft skin," he commented before he kissed the back of my hand, his blue eyes twinkling mischievously.

"Come, sit down," Jed said, pulling out a chair for me beside Beth.

I sat down and looked across the table at Hugo, who glared at me menacingly. I shivered, looking around for Mark. Lucas sat down beside me, pulling his chair close to mine. "So, are you single?" Lucas whispered in my ear.

"Lucas," Jed said warningly, and Lucas laughed before grabbing a fork and piling several slabs of ham on his plate.

No one seemed to stand on ceremony, everyone simply filling their plates with whatever food they wished. I looked around the table, noticing the empty plate where Mark should be. Lucas leaned across me, his hand brushing across my breasts as reached for the bowl of mashed potatoes. "You'd better get some food before it's all gone," he said as he piled potatoes and ham on my plate.

"Thanks," I muttered, taking the gravy boat from him. He smiled again, his eyes darting toward my chest. I poured gravy on my potatoes and began piling food on my plate. There was enough food to feed an army and everyone had their plates overloaded, except for the doctor and me.

The food was delicious and I savored every bite, helping myself to extra crescent rolls smothered in cranberry jelly. To me it seemed like an early Thanksgiving, although I couldn't help but notice Mark's absence more and more as the food vanished. At first it was quiet at the table, an almost uncomfortable silence, until Lucas started throwing peas across the table at his brother. For several minutes Logan ignored it, until he finally scooped a spoonful of peas up and chucked it back at Lucas.

Lucas laughed as the peas splattered across his face and suddenly people were laughing and talking, the atmosphere in the room changing. I turned toward Jed, who was speaking quietly to Mirabelle. I opened my mouth to ask Jed about Mark, when I noticed Beth out of the corner of my eye shaking her head. "Don't," she said softly.

"Do you know where Mark is?" I asked her quietly. She shook her head again, darting nervous glances at Jed.

"Mark went for a run," Jed said, and the room went silent. I looked up to see Jed staring at me and I felt my heart pounding in my chest. Polite as he was, there was still something very dangerous about him. "He'll be back shortly. Eat."

Everyone returned to their food and conversation slowly resumed as though nothing had happened. I don't know why, but I was scared. My palms were sweating, my heart was pounding, and I was looking around the room for a quick escape. Just then I heard a door bang closed from the kitchen and Mark sauntered in, wearing a pair of ripped jeans and an unbuttoned flannel shirt. He certainly didn't look like he'd been running, especially since he wasn't wearing any shoes, but his skin was drenched in sweat.

Mark didn't look at anyone, just grabbed a plate and began piling food on it before sitting down on the other side of Lucas. I looked over at him, noticing the bruise developing on his cheek and the drying blood on his chest. Mark glanced up at me briefly before buttoning his shirt and continuing to shovel food in his mouth. Lucas leaned toward me, placing a hand on the back of my chair and blocking my view of Mark with his body.

"So, sweetheart, you never answered my question," Lucas said softly as he leaned closer to me, his eyes blatantly trailing down my body. "Do you have a boyfriend, or maybe a husband? Is there a man in your life? I could be that man," he added, placing a hand on my thigh.

Mark's chair dumped on the floor as he stood up. In one swift move he had grabbed Lucas by the back of the neck and threw him into the wall behind me. I jumped up in surprise, but Mark simply righted his chair and sat back down. Everyone else resumed eating as Lucas picked himself up off the floor, laughing the whole time. I was still standing in shock, wondering what had just happened while everyone resumed eating. I slowly sat down, before turning to Beth.

"What was that?" I asked. She shook her head and stood up, gathering plates and taking them into the kitchen.

As people finished eating, they gathered their own plates and started clearing off the table. Appetite gone, I stood and picked up my plate, but Beth quickly took it out of my hand and told me to sit back down. I watched Mark shovel a large quantity of food into his mouth, seemingly without stopping to breathe as everyone else cleared the table of food and moved into the kitchen.

"Mark?" I asked tentatively when we were alone. He glanced at me, shook his head, and finished cleaning his plate. As soon as he was done he stood up and took his plate into the kitchen, leaving me alone.

This place was strange to say the least, but at least the doctor seemed nice. I smelled coffee and got up, making my way into the kitchen. The kitchen was huge, but barely large enough to hold everyone. The twins and Hugo were at the sink doing dishes, while Mirabelle and Beth were getting trays of coffee and pie together. Jed and Mark were nowhere to be seen. There was only one other way they could have gone, so I moved through the kitchen toward the back door, but was stopped by a menacing Hugo.

"They'll be back. Go into the living room," Hugo said, moving his massive body to block my way outside.

The kitchen got quiet, until Lucas moved up beside me, placing an arm around my shoulder. "I'll escort the pretty lady into the living room. No need to get your frilly, lace panties in a twist, Hugo." Lucas smiled up at Hugo, but Hugo just moved back to the sink and helped with the dishes.

I let Lucas lead me into the large living room that was attached to the dining room. This room was packed with furniture, all leather and all expensive looking. I sat down on a couch and Lucas sat uncomfortably close to me, his arm still draped around my shoulder. "Do you need to help your brother?" I asked, scooting away from Lucas until I was pressed up against the end of the couch.

Lucas scooted closer, his leg touching mine. He leaned

forward, sniffing the air. "You smell good," he reached out and touched my neck and I jumped up, moving away.

The doctor and Beth walked in carrying a couple trays of pies and cookies, followed by everyone else carrying trays of mugs, coffee carafes, cream, and sugar. Jed and Mark were the last to enter, both taking seats in chairs. I stood stupidly as everyone sat down and helped themselves to cookies and coffee, chatting amicably the whole time.

"Come, join us," Jed said to me, indicating the vacant chair beside his own.

I eyed the chair warily before grabbing a mug of coffee, dosing it with sugar and sitting down. I felt exposed, sitting alone in the chair beside Jed, while the others lounged comfortably on couches chatting amongst themselves. Mark moved from across the room and sat down on the floor in front of my chair, wrapping his arm around my legs. It was an odd thing to do, but it made me feel better, safer.

"So," Jed began, and the room grew quiet, all eyes turned toward him. "Mark has come back to us with some disturbing news regarding the vampires. You've all been briefed on the facts so far, but this situation with Isabella is interesting." I shot a look at Jed, then down at Mark. What situation with me? "Considering the circumstances, I have determined that no rules have been broken regarding Mark and Isabella. The vampires are the ones at fault, and as such they will be the ones punished."

Huh? What was he talking about? What rules? And here we were talking about vampires again.

"He told her," Hugo said, standing up. "She's not his mate! The rules are clear on this."

"I decide here, Hugo, not you!" Jed said, standing up. "Mark has been punished as I see fit. This is not up for debate. You will sit down, and you will abide by *my* rules."

"Maybe I don't want to abide by your rules!" Hugo roared back, his facing growing red with anger.

"Is that a challenge?" Jed asked softly, crossing his arms. There was a great deal of menace in his quiet voice. "Is that what you want, Hugo? You want to be in charge here?"

Hugo stood still, his whole body vibrating with anger. His eyes darted from Jed to me, until his eyes finally rested on his wife. His eyes softened and he dropped to his knees, head bowed before Jed. "Forgive me, Alpha. I forget my place," he murmured.

Alpha?

Chapter 6

Jed relaxed back in his seat while Hugo remained on his knees in the center of the room. What was going on? Mark was rubbing his hand up and down my calf, but I wasn't sure if the gesture was for my comfort or his own. All eyes in the room were focused on Jed, waiting. Finally Jed spoke, his voice soft and calm. "Isabella, what do you think about vampires?"

All eyes turned to me, waiting and watching. "I, uh, I'm not sure. If you asked me that question two days ago I would have said they were fiction, make-believe, and a complete myth. Now, I'm not so sure," I added, touching the spot on my neck where I had supposedly been bitten. I looked around the room, trying to read the people around me. They all stared at me, but their expressions gave nothing away. I looked back to Jed and shrugged.

Jed smiled as he leaned back in his chair, his hands relaxing on the arm rests of his chair. "You don't believe in vampires." It was a statement, not a question.

I shrugged, glancing around the room. "Mark seems to think I was bitten by one, and there have definitely been some strange things the last few days. None of that says vampire to me though." It wasn't that I didn't necessarily believe Mark. It was more that it was hard to believe someone who constantly talked about aliens and government cover-ups.

"What about your dreams?" Jed asked, and I heard a sharp intake of breath from someone in the room. I glanced around, but I wasn't sure who had made the noise.

"What dreams?" I asked, but I couldn't keep the quaver out of my voice. My thoughts turned to the man of gold and fire, who had been seducing me in my dreams. How would they know anything about that dream? My heart sped up as I pictured the man who had stalked me across an endless bed. I felt my face flush as I thought of his muscular body. Ouch! Mark squeezed the back of my calf, making me wince.

"It's best not to think overly long of the vampires, Isabella. To do so can allow them access to your thoughts and your dreams. Tell us, who is this vampire who has been invading your dreams?" Jed asked.

"I don't know what you mean," I replied, my heart pounding quickly. "I told Mark about the woman who he thinks bit me. Patricia was her name. I did have a dream with a woman in it and I think it was her, but I really have no way of knowing for sure. I've never actually met her, just heard her voice, and she didn't speak in the dream."

"What about the dream you just woke from?" Dr. Humphry asked from across the room.

I shifted uncomfortably and Mark began rubbing my leg again. I didn't like being put on the spot, and I certainly didn't like these questions. Everyone was watching me, with the exception of Hugo who was still on his knees in the middle of the room with his head bowed. "Who are you people?" I asked, and Mark's hand immediately tensed on my leg.

"I'll let Mark answer that for you," Jed replied softly. "I have given him permission to let you know certain information we wouldn't normally share with an outsider. So, please just have some trust that your questions will be answered soon enough. For now, would you answer ours? Tell us about the dream you were having when Mark brought you here?"

"Why do you think I was dreaming?" I retorted. I was most definitely not going to tell a room full of strangers that I was having some weird sex dream about some guy I've never seen before.

"Tsk, tsk, tsk, now let's not play games, Isabella," Jed leaned toward me and I felt my heart beat faster with fear. What was it about these people that had me so scared? Jed, in particular, was disturbingly intimidating. "You were thrashing, moaning and talking in your sleep, plus the smell of vampire was so thick in the air you could practically taste it. Does this vampire have such a hold on you already that you won't dare speak of him?"

What? This was getting nuts. Now he's saying he could smell a vampire that was supposedly in my dream. Why was I even listening to this nonsense? "No one has a hold on me," I snapped angrily. "I dreamt of a man, yes. He didn't speak though, so I couldn't tell you anything about him except he has blond hair. He was in the dream I had about Patricia, too. He was just a man though. There was absolutely nothing in my dreams to indicate vampire." There, I told them. They didn't need to know any details.

"Did he bite you in this dream? Did you have sex with him?"

"No!" I yelled, standing up and spilling my full cup of coffee all over the floor. "No, no, no, no, no! I've had enough!"

I slammed my half-full mug of coffee on a side table and stormed out of the room. I reached the hallway, and there I was lost. Where should I go now? Mark was suddenly behind me, wrapping his arms around my waist. I grabbed his arms and pushed him away, turning on him. He held his hands up in surrender, a small smile playing at his mouth. Damn him and his adorable little quirks. I turned away and stalked off toward the front door, Mark following closely behind me.

It was dark outside and there was a chill in the air, but it felt good. I walked gingerly, since I still wasn't wearing shoes, wandering around the side of the house. A large garage and some sort of shop were set around the back of the house. In the distance there was a barn with a light on, which I started walking toward. The moon was almost full, so I could easily pick my way across the soft grass.

The barn was enormous, and must have once held dozens of animals, but not anymore. What once were probably horse stalls were now massive cages, with thick bars completely surrounding them. They all appeared freshly cleaned, with thick piles of hay lining the bottoms. Several sets of fluorescent lights illuminated the interior of the empty barn.

I walked to the end of the barn where the tack room was and stopped. Inside the room was a single cot, mounds of blankets, and several totes stacked against one wall. I leaned up against the wall, breathing in the animal smells that came with all barns. I was disappointed there weren't any animals in the barn though.

I closed my eyes and took a deep breath, sensing Mark close beside me. What kind of people was he mixed up with? "So, you want to tell me what the hell is going on? Who are these people? What is this place?" I asked, opening my eyes to look directly at Mark.

Mark looked away and ran his hands through his hair. As he did so his shirt lifted, and I noticed more dried blood on his stomach. I reached a hand out and Mark grasped it before I could touch his shirt, his facing turning toward me. "Don't," he said.

"Mark, he *beat* you! I can see the blood. Look, I don't know what the deal is with these people, but let's just leave."

"You don't understand," Mark muttered. He dropped my hand and stepped into the tack room, unbuttoning his shirt as he walked. I watched as he peeled the flannel off, tossing it on the ground before turning back to face me. Blood was dried to Mark's chest and smeared across his stomach and arms, but I didn't see any marks. I stepped forward and ran my hand across his chest and stomach, feeling the taut muscles, but no wounds. I looked at the side of his face where I'd seen a bruise developing earlier, but there was nothing there now. "I told you before; I heal fast."

My heart was racing as I ran my hands across Mark's muscular body, the events of the evening replaying in my head. "He said he punished you," I murmured, looking up into Mark's soft brown eyes. "You have dried blood all over you."

Mark took my hands in his and led me over to the cot, sitting down and pulling me beside him. "I was rightfully punished for a number of reasons, like telling you about the vampires. The rest of the punishment concerns things that you really don't need to worry about. There's no permanent damage, as you can see," he took a deep breath before continuing. "Jed has given me permission to tell you about me, about us. You must understand that if I had told you before it would have been like signing our own death warrants. Some members of the pack don't necessarily agree with Jed's *leniency*, but the rules were technically violated by the vampires first, so we get to live."

"What rules? Mark, I have absolutely no idea what you're talking about."

He laughed, shaking his head. "Yeah, I guess this doesn't make a lot of sense. Okay, here it goes. I'm a werewolf," he said bluntly, looking me squarely in the eyes.

I mulled that over for a few seconds, wondering when the rest of the joke would kick in. Mark stared at me, his brown eyes soft and almost puppy-like, not wolf-like. "So, you're a werewolf," I said. "I guess if there are vampires running around biting people, it'd make sense there are werewolves also running around biting people. I'm sure there are dragons and unicorns too, we just never see them, right? Ooh, what about leprechauns? Is there really a pot of gold at the end of the rainbow?"

"You don't believe me."

I continued on, ignoring the look on Mark's face. "Maybe there are little fairies flying around us right now, but we just can't see them because they're invisible. And trolls live under bridges, demanding a toll for passage unless you can answer a riddle. What about gnomes and goblins? Are those running around too? They're probably with the elves and dwarves, right?" I asked acerbically.

"Do you have a lot of sex dreams about random men?" Mark asked bluntly, stopping my tirade.

"It wasn't a sex dream," I retorted.

"Really? It certainly seemed that way to me with how you were moaning and clawing at your own body." Mark leaned in close to me, his face right next to mine. "I could smell the sex on you. Do you know what it was like being in a car with you while you moaned and smelled of desire? All I wanted to do was stop the car and rip your clothes off! Then I'd cover your body with *my* scent, obliterating the putrid, rotting scent of the vampire who was *in your head!*" Mark yelled and his eyes began turning from a soft brown, to a golden yellow.

He held his hand out to me and I watched in fascinated horror as his hand elongated, his nails turning to claws before my eyes. Thick hair was rapidly spreading across his arms and bare chest. "I must warn you that I'm not such a gentleman when my wolf takes over. Do you believe me now, or shall I continue to change for you?"

I looked up into Mark's yellow eyes and felt an overwhelming fear. He looked roughly the same, but his face was more angular, rougher, and changing by the minute. I was fascinated and terrified at the same time, not sure if I wanted him to stop or not. Then he let out a howl heard only in the wilds and I found myself backing up against the wall, my feet curled under me. "Stop, please, stop," I cried, feeling the tears coursing down my cheeks.

Mark sniffed the air above me and spoke, his voice deep and husky, "Do you believe me now?"

I nodded my head furiously, "Yes, yes, I believe you. Please, Mark, just stop."

He grunted and leaned away from me, closing his eyes. I stared at him as the fur that had been forming across his body slowly faded away and his hands returned to normal. When he opened his eyes they were still a golden yellow color, but other than that he seemed mostly normal. "Vampires and werewolves are real," Mark stated gruffly before he leaned back away from me.

I untangled my feet and stood up, rubbing my arms to take away the chill. I found myself backing up until I reached the wall, my eyes still on Mark sitting on the small cot. I tried to wrap my mind around what had just happened as I scrubbed the tears from my face.

Mark was a werewolf, with claws and everything. Part of me really wanted to see the full thing, but from a safe distance, maybe with binoculars. I looked over at him and he looked just like the old Mark, the funny, quirky gym teacher I'd worked with for over three years. Was *this* the real Mark? Was the Mark I'd known just a cover for this version? How could I have been so blind? Now I knew the truth that behind the conspiracy theory-obsessed teacher was this new Mark, who had yellow eyes, claws and was very, very scary.

Chapter 7

I was speechless, yet I had a thousand questions running through my mind. Mark was definitely something else, something not human. But if I was going to admit to werewolves being real, I'd have to admit to the vampires as well. Everything over the last few days began clicking into place. Mark had known the truth since I'd woken him up in that weird hospital room, maybe sooner. Had he known what was happening back at the school? I looked over at Mark, who sat still on the cot watching me with his eerie yellow eyes. I took a couple slow, deep breaths, trying to calm my racing heart before walking back to the cot.

I slowly sat down next to Mark, trying to appear nonchalant despite my heart pounding in my chest. "I'm not going to hurt you," he said softly and I glanced up into those yellow eyes. "You don't need to be afraid of me."

"I'm not afraid," I lied immediately.

He laughed gruffly, but there was no humor in it. "You can't lie to a werewolf, Izzy. I can smell the fear on you, and hear your pounding heart. You're most definitely afraid of me." He looked away from me, staring down at his hands.

"Okay, you're right; I'm absolutely terrified." Mark nodded his head at my words, still not looking at me. I reached out and grasped his hand, which was thankfully just a normal hand again. "But I also know that you'd never hurt me. If you can tell whether I'm lying or not, then you know I'm telling you the truth. I do trust you."

I must have passed the werewolf lie detector test, because he looked up at me and smiled, simultaneously squeezing my hand. "I wish you would have just believed me. I didn't like scaring you like that, but you need to know the truth. And you also need to be honest with me. I know a lot more about the supernatural than you do, so you're just going to have to trust me."

"Telling you is one thing, Mark. Telling a room full of... werewolves," I looked up and he nodded, "is a lot different. I don't know these people, and I don't trust them. And Jed scares the bejeezus out of me!"

Mark barked a laugh, shaking his head. "Jed scares everyone. That's why he's Alpha."

A sat for a couple of beats, taking that in. "So, I have to know some key details," I started, and Mark's face turned serious as I began. I could sense the tension in his body as he stiffened, waiting for my questions. I didn't like this serious side of Mark. It was unnerving and so not like him. "So, do you turn into a wolf or is it more like Michael J. Fox?"

"Michael J. Fox?" he asked, a frown creasing his forehead.

"Yeah, you know, from that movie Teen Wolf back in the 80's. He was a little furry, but really good at basketball."

Mark tipped back his head and laughed at that, his whole body shaking with mirth. I smiled watching him, glad to ease the tension a little. When he finally stopped laughing he looked directly at me and I was surprised to see his eyes were back to their usual warm brown. "Being a werewolf does not make you good at basketball," Mark replied, smiling. "It does give you added strength, speed and coordination though, so it definitely helps with sports. Most of us just turn into wolves on the full moon, but those of us who have been around a while longer can change at will, or partial change into a sort of wolf-man hybrid. Like most things, the more experience you have, the better and easier it gets. I can completely resist turning on a full moon if I wish to, where a newly turned werewolf is helpless to the power of the full moon. That's why there are so many cages in the barn."

"It's almost a full moon. Does that mean everyone's going to be in cages in a couple days?"

Mark shook his head, "No, only the newer wolves go into cages. It takes a while, but with each full moon you retain more and more humanity, until eventually you run as a wolf with a human mind. We only cage the newest because they can be violent, and it's never good to wake up naked with no idea of where you are after you've been running around as a wolf. Plus, we don't want anyone getting shot by accident."

"You said you can resist changing on the full moon. Can any of the others? Jed? Dr. Humphry?" I asked, wondering who would be running around as a wolf. Would I be safe?

"Jed and the twins can resist, but they usually don't. It's freeing to run as a wolf. And Dr. Humphry isn't a werewolf; she's just married to one."

I thought about that. There were so many questions running through my head. I had always thought of Mark as a friend, but I was finding I really knew very little about him. "So, how did you become a werewolf?" Mark's face looked sad at my question, and I immediately regretted asking. "You don't have to tell me if it's too difficult. I'm sorry."

"No, it's all right. I know this is all new for you," he sighed and grasped my hand tightly. I could feel the tension in his body and his eyes began turning golden yellow once more. I felt my heart speed up as he turned those golden eyes on me. "This close to the full moon it's harder to control the wolf, especially with everything that's been going on. I'm normally a lot calmer."

"It's okay," I said, patting Mark's hand. "I don't mean to make things more difficult for you."

He smiled at me and brushed a hand across my cheek. My heart sped up again at his touch and he grinned, looking very smug. "I don't really want to talk about my wolf," he said softly.

I was disappointed, but I nodded anyway sensing this was a difficult subject for him. "We can talk about that some other time," I replied and he nodded, his hand still caressing my cheek.

Mark was definitely acting differently, and I wasn't sure if it was the full moon, his wolf, or just the fact that we weren't at the school in a work setting. Three years I'd worked with this man, secretly staring at his hardened body when I thought no one could see me. The Mark I'd known just weeks before had always been great to look at, but he had been quirky and goofy. This new Mark was darker and more dangerous, but he had a sadness to him I'd never seen before. His hand continued to caress my cheek and trail down my neck and I felt my face blush. This new Mark was also much sexier, and considerably more direct.

Mark leaned his body toward me, his yellow eyes watching his hand travel down my neck and shoulders. I looked down and noticed for the first time that the flannel shirt I was wearing was unbuttoned to show a considerable amount of cleavage. When did that happen? Mark's hand trailed across the top of my shirt, his fingers brushing across the mound of my breasts. He leaned in closer and I closed my eyes as his mouth brushed across mine in a soft kiss.

The kiss grew slowly as he explored my mouth with his tongue. His hand held my face in place as he continued to kiss me. I returned his kisses eagerly. I had wanted him to kiss me for almost three years. One of his hands moved across my neck and traced along the line of my shirt again. I felt his hand pulling at my shirt, unbuttoning the top two buttons with deft fingers.

He lowered me down onto the cot, and I opened my eyes to look at him. Yellow eyes stared back at me as he ran his fingers through my hair. He leaned forward and kissed me again, his kisses trailing across my chin. Mark moved and angled his body over mine on the small cot as one of his hands trailed down the center of my shirt, skillfully unbuttoning the remaining buttons. His kisses moved down my neck, light and soft as his hand ran along the edge of my shirt, peeling it back slowly to reveal more skin.

I closed my eyes as his mouth moved back across my chin and to my mouth once more. He ran his hand lightly across my breasts, pushing my shirt off further. He growled quietly and my heart sped up significantly. His hand that had been softly caressing my skin now moved down my side and across my butt, grabbing me fiercely. Mark's kisses moved down toward my breasts, punctuated with growls low in his throat. His hand suddenly moved to the button on my jeans and I felt a flutter of panic as he swiftly unbuttoned my jeans and began sliding them down.

"Mark," I said softly, grabbing his hand before he could pull my jeans down further. He growled loudly and I think my heart stopped for a second. "Mark?"

Mark lowered his face to my stomach and nipped my skin lightly before looking up at me, his yellow eyes glowing eerily. "Stop?" he asked, his voice husky. I nodded, not trusting my voice. He jumped up and was across the room in the blink of an eye, his back to me as he stared out the doorway, breathing heavily.

I quickly stood and pulled my pants back up, buttoning them as I watched Mark. His back was to me and he appeared to be arguing with himself. I waited until my heart rate calmed down before I walked over to him, buttoning my shirt as I did. I reached out and ran a hand gently across his shoulders. He turned his head and looked at me with his strange wolf eyes. "I'll take you back to the house now," he muttered, turning and walking away.

"Wait a minute," I said, catching up to him and grabbing his hand. "I don't want to go back to the house."

Mark pulled my hand to his face and kissed it gently before looking at me. "I got carried away, Izzy. I never should have let things go this far, especially this close to the full moon. I... I'm sorry," he murmured. "It won't happen again."

"Wait a minute! What do you mean by that? Maybe I want it to happen again," I said angrily. Mark looked up at me in surprise and I felt myself blush at my brazen words. Where had that come from? I hadn't meant to say that. I swallowed, wondering what I really wanted and what I should say. "I just... I liked kissing you. It was just... too much," I said softly.

Mark smiled at that, running his free hand through his hair. He may have been smiling, but his face took on a serious look. "I truly did get carried away, Iz. You've been driving me crazy for three years and this close to the full moon my wolf decided to take the reins a little more than I usually allow him. And to think, I've been trying to get up the guts to ask you on a date for three years, and all I had to do was put you in mortal danger with vampires and werewolves."

"You didn't put me in mortal danger, Mark. You're not responsible for the vampires. And... wait, three years?"

He grinned nervously, looking around the barn as though for an escape. He finally sighed, "Yeah, three years. Of course, when we first met you already had a boyfriend, and then I guess I just talked myself out of asking you, even though your brother kept pushing me to. You can be kind of intimidating."

I frowned at that, thinking I was probably one of the least intimidating people I knew. "That makes no sense, you know that right? I'm this tiny 27-year-old schoolteacher and you're, well, look at you! How on earth can I be intimidating?" I said, pointing at his well-defined abs.

He laughed, shaking his head. "You're brilliant, sweet and completely out of my league. Besides, I'm a werewolf, Izzy. I'm not exactly safe. You should be with a nice, normal human."

I thought about that, remembering how intense he'd become. "How do you keep the wolf hidden from regular humans? I've known you for three years and never had a clue."

"People don't see things they don't want to see. Plus, I'm

usually much better at this. I wouldn't be on my own away from the pack if I wasn't good at hiding my beast." He ran his hand through his hair again, and I knew he was nervous talking about this. "It's too close to the full moon," he said simply, and I knew he wouldn't talk about his wolf any more. I watched him shut down and I figured I'd let it go and not push him about it any further.

I still had a lot more questions I needed answered, and not all about werewolves. "So, tell me about the vampires. What's true about the myths?"

"A lot of it, actually," he replied, smiling. "Vampires can't abide sunlight, or they burn to a crisp. Holy water also burns them, but they can heal from that eventually. A stake through the heart works on newer vamps, but the best way to kill them is to cut off the head and burn the body. They are immortal and drink blood from the living to stay looking young. If a human drinks their blood, they form a weird bond with the vampire and the vampire gains control of the human's mind, for a time anyway. We're not sure on all the logistics around that, but it seems that vampires need to maintain the bond with their humans or it slowly fades away. That's where I think this vaccine thing comes into play. One dose initiates the connection. The second dose solidifies it. I heard on the news they're requiring a third injection now."

"I was given the vaccine," I muttered, "and possibly a second dose, but I don't really have any way of knowing. So, wait, does that mean this vaccine has vampire blood in it?"

Mark nodded, "That's exactly what we think. You said this vampire, Patricia, claimed to have switched the batch?" I nodded my head. "And you had a dream with this Patricia vamp in it?"

I nodded again. "Well, I think it was her. I never saw her, but I have a feeling that's who it was. I can't really describe it as anything but that; a feeling."

"And what about the other dream?" he asked slowly, his yellow eyes staring directly at me.

Oh, man, here we were again. It always came back to that dream. I felt my cheeks grow warm at the thought and I quickly looked away. "Okay, so I keep dreaming of the same man. The first dream I had with Patricia, he was in it. Then he was in the other dream, the one in the car."

Mark's voice was low and deep, coming out in a raspy growl. "Did he bite you in the dream?"

I shook my head, looking at Mark's face out of the corner of my eye. "No, he didn't bite me."

Mark nodded his head and began pacing back and forth nervously. I had a feeling I knew what he was going to ask me, and I wasn't looking forward to it. He finally stopped pacing and stood in front of me, his hands behind his back. "Tell me about the dream."

Oh, I did not want to tell him about that. It was embarrassing! I shook my head, and looked down at my feet. Mark stepped in close to me and put a hand under my chin, lifting my face slowly. "It's okay, Izzy. Please, just tell me."

I sighed and looked up into his very bright yellow eyes. He outwardly appeared calm, but his whole body was thrumming slightly. I wasn't so sure that telling him would be a good idea. "Mark, maybe we should talk about this some other time."

"I've got my wolf under control, Izzy. So either you tell me, or we go inside and you tell the whole pack."

Damn him and his pack of wolves, I cursed. I didn't like ultimatums. I crossed my arms angrily and took a step back. Fine, if he wanted to hear it, then I'd tell him. "He doesn't speak in the dreams, but he is completely and utterly naked. And, oh, what a sight it is," I added bitterly, taking grim satisfaction in seeing Mark's face harden. Well, that's what he gets for trying to order me around. "He is strong and muscular and wow, what a package!"

Mark growled and his fist slammed into the wall beside me, making me jump. I looked up into his face and felt a shiver of fear. "Get on with it," he muttered.

"He's hard to resist. During the last dream, I remember standing there thinking how inadequate I was compared to this god of a man, and the next thing, I'm naked and he's beckoning me to come to him on a bed of silken sheets. And I did go to him. I was drawn to him, like a moth to a flame. He kissed me and touched me." I stopped talking, swallowing as Mark began growling again. "He started to climb on me and that's when I kind of panicked and came to. I turned and tried crawling away, but he was always there behind me. I realized it was a dream then, and I swear I heard your voice. Then I was falling off the bed and waking up in a house full of werewolves."

"You didn't have sex with him and he didn't bite you?" he asked in a deep, husky voice. I shook my head, and he seemed to relax slightly. "What about the woman? How many times have you dreamed of her?"

"Just the once."

"Is there anything else I should know?"

I shrugged. That was a loaded question. "Is there anything else I should know about you?"

He chuckled and leaned away from me. "No, I think you know enough for now. Come on; let's go back to the others."

I followed Mark back to the house, not at all anxious to face a room full of werewolves. There was a big black truck parked in front of the house that I hadn't seen before, and I wondered if more werewolves were joining us. Mark sniffed the air as we drew close to the truck, but didn't say anything. I fidgeted with my clothes, making sure the buttons on my shirt were properly buttoned, and sufficiently covering me.

Everyone was in the large living room when we came in, with three new additions to the group. A teenage boy who couldn't be more than 17 sat on the floor by Jed's feet, nervously clutching at his hands. He sniffed the air when we walked in, turning yellow wolf eyes toward me. Another man sat on the floor facing Jed, his head bowed. He had long, scraggly hair and his clothes were tattered and dirty. A large man with long black hair pulled back in a ponytail stood behind him wearing all black, with his hand resting on a gun. I could sense the tension in the room, and the focus seemed to be on the man on the floor.

Jed seemed focused on the man on the floor, but he spoke to Dr. Humphry. "Mirabelle, would you please escort Isabella upstairs?"

Dr. Humphry was standing at the far edge of the room and jumped when Jed said her name. Hugo was standing protectively in front of her, and she gave him a quick kiss before moving around the edge of the room to me. Mark nodded to me before moving to stand beside Jed's chair. I backed out of the room and followed the doctor down the hallway to the stairs.

At the top of the stairs, Mirabelle led me down a short hallway to a bedroom at the far end of the house. The bedroom was plain and clean, consisting of a queen size bed, a dresser and a small nightstand. "Are you tired?" she asked. "You can rest here."

The moment she said it, I realized that I was exhausted. It seemed strange, since I'd been asleep for so long, but a lot had been going on. "I am tired, but I don't know if I can sleep."

"Because of the dreams?"

I nodded, "Yes, those too. Also, what's going on downstairs?"

"Mark explained to you about where you are and who you're with?"

"You mean the fact that I'm in a house full of werewolves? Yeah, he might have mentioned that."

Doctor Humphry smiled kindly and glanced toward the hallway, as though she could see what was transpiring downstairs. "That man down there, on the floor, isn't from around here. He claims he has no pack. John, the big guy in black leather, was bringing Michael here for the full moon when he stumbled upon this guy."

"Michael? Is that the kid?"

"Yes, we found him last full moon. He had no idea he was a

werewolf. We're still trying to find out who turned him. It wasn't one of our own," she added defensively.

"So, what are they doing with this new guy?"

She shrugged, glancing back toward the hallway once more. "Jed won't let a stray wolf run around his territory. I guess it depends on why this guy is here. From the sounds of it, he was waiting for John, as though he wanted to be found. I don't like it, but I don't get a vote." She moved to the doorway of the bedroom, then stopped and turned back to me. "Get some sleep, but for your safety don't leave this room unless someone gets you." With that she left, shutting the door behind her.

I followed her to the door and peeked out, but she was already moving down the stairs. I shut the door and turned off the light. Not having a change of clothes, I just lay down on the bed as I was and tucked the blanket around me. I closed my eyes, trying to relax my mind enough to sleep, and hopefully not dream. The first howl startled me back awake and I rushed to the window, peering out into the night and seeing nothing. I wanted to go downstairs and see if everyone was down there, but I heeded the doctor's words and stayed in the room. Eventually I drifted off into a thankfully dreamless sleep.

Chapter 8

I woke up the next morning to the delicious aroma of coffee. I stretched, untangling myself from the blankets before I opened my eyes. Mark was sitting in a chair beside my bed wearing a pair of jeans and a Star Wars t-shirt, his hair looking freshly washed. He hadn't fully shaved, leaving a mustache and goatee around his mouth that I found incredibly sexy. The last few days he'd been completely scruffy, and before that he'd always been clean-shaven. I found myself liking this new look.

I sat up, looking around for the coffee I could smell. Mark smiled and grabbed a mug of coffee from the dresser behind him, handing it to me. I took a sip and sighed in pleasure. The coffee was delicious and sweetened with caramel-flavored creamer, just the way I liked it. I took another sip and peered over the rim of my mug at Mark. He seemed much more relaxed and his eyes were back to their usual chocolate brown.

"You can use the shower across the hall again," Mark said, standing up and moving to the door. "Mirabelle brought you some clothes; they're in the dresser. Come down and eat as soon as you're ready."

Mark left the room before I had a chance to respond, shutting the door behind him. I wasn't much of a morning person until I had been sufficiently caffeinated, so I drained my coffee before getting up and rifling through the dresser. The dresser was full of clothes that all seemed my size, including several bras and underwear. I definitely owed Mirabelle for this! I grabbed a matching bra and underwear along with jeans and a simple turquoise blue V-neck shirt before crossing the hall to the bathroom.

After I was showered and dressed, I went back to my bedroom and slipped on socks and a pair of tennis shoes before jogging down the stairs to the kitchen. I was in a fabulous mood, feeling much more like myself with underwear on! It also helped that I hadn't had any weird dreams the night before. I passed the dining room, which was empty, and carried my empty coffee mug into the kitchen. Mark and Beth were in the kitchen talking quietly when I walked in. Beth glanced at me, frowned, and quickly scurried out of the room without a word.

I refilled my coffee mug and opened the fridge, finding my favorite creamer inside. I fixed my coffee in silence and grabbed the plate of food Mark handed to me. At the far end of the kitchen, toward the back door, was a breakfast bar with four stools around it. I followed Mark's lead, sitting on a stool and silently eating my eggs and bacon. Mark watched me silently until I cleaned my plate.

"Do you want more?" he asked, grabbing my empty plate as soon as I finished.

I shook my head and stood up, refilling my coffee mug once more. "Where is everyone else?"

"Work mostly. It is Monday after all. The newer wolves are all in the barn with Jed. Full moon is tonight, so there's a lot of preparation going on."

"It's Monday?" I asked, so confused as to the days. "My students are supposed to be doing their Shakespearean presentations today."

"Well, I suppose they'll be doing their presentation for a substitute. I missed the wrestling tournament Saturday," Mark added glumly. "It was the first tournament of the season, and I wasn't there for them."

"Well, maybe we can be back for the next tournament. We should call the school and get this straightened out."

"We can't call anyone, Izzy. Hell, we can't even go out in public! There are pictures of us all over the news. Apparently we're being wanted for the murder of two security guards at The Pinkerton Hotel, as well as grand theft auto and an assortment of other crimes." Mark was pacing back and forth, but finally stopped in front of me. He sighed, running fingers through his hair. "The story on the news is that we quit our jobs at the local high school, ran away together, robbed a bank, stole a car, and killed the two security guards who were trying to apprehend us as we ran away with some little old lady's jewelry. We're very Bonnie and Clyde."

"You're kidding, right?"

"I may have embellished slightly, but basically that's what they're saying. We're on the most-wanted list, Izzy, and that's no joke."

I sat there dumbfounded. This was unreal. I'd never even had so much as a parking ticket, and now the police wanted me for murder! I stood up and carried my coffee with me into the living room, looking for a television. First thing I saw when I turned the TV on was a picture of Mark and me and a list of crimes we were wanted in connection with, including robbery, homicide, assault, and numerous others. I surfed through several channels, finding the same thing on every channel. The pictures flashing all over the news were our faculty yearbook pictures from the year before. I had shorter blonde hair curled conservatively and Mark was clean-shaven with short-cropped hair. I clicked off the TV after watching a segment of news showing what appeared to be the two of us robbing a bank.

"We may be responsible for stealing a car or two, but the rest of the crimes are ridiculous. Only one of those security guards had been killed, and not by me," Mark added angrily. "John's checking into things for us, but it doesn't look good."

"John?" I asked, "The big guy all in black leather?"

Mark nodded, smiling slightly as he sagged down into one of the plush black leather chairs. "Yeah, that's the one. He works for some high-tech security firm. He's looking into that bogus security footage of us robbing that bank. He's trying to track down the source. Hopefully if we can prove everything is made up, we can get our lives back... eventually."

I sat down and sipped my coffee, my thoughts drifting to my students, who must be so confused right now. I loved being a teacher, and I loved my students. I knew Mark felt the same way, especially about his wrestlers. Why was this happening to us? I felt like there was so much more going on than I knew. My friends would be confused, wondering what was going on. What about Justin? How would he find me now? "I need to find my brother," I said, although I had no idea how I was going to do that. I turned and looked at Mark, who sat slumped in his chair. "This has to be connected to him, and this vaccine."

Mark nodded but he didn't look at me. "I spoke to John about finding Justin, but I don't want you to get your hopes up. Justin has been hiding for months."

I agreed but didn't say anything. I had an idea of my own on how to find Justin, but I knew Mark wouldn't like it. All these months Justin had been missing and presumed dead with no contact except one phone call months ago and the email to Mark. Then I discovered that the world wasn't how I'd known it. This new world was full of vampires and werewolves. So far, I'd interacted with two vampires, both of whom had invaded my dreams. The man I tried not to think about, knowing to do so could put me into another dream that might kill me. The woman, on the other hand, had claimed she was helping me as repayment of a debt to Justin. What Justin had done for this vampire wasn't important right now. The fact was, she had known Justin and interacted with him. Maybe she knew where to find him.

"You're awfully quiet," Mark murmured, pulling me from my

contemplations.

I sipped my coffee, trying to reorganize my thoughts. "Just thinking," I replied. "How many werewolves are going to be here tonight?"

Mark shrugged and glanced out the window toward the barn. "The whole pack will probably be here. Beth, Michael and probably Frank will be in cages, along with the guy from last night."

"What's the story with that guy?"

"He says his name is Leon and that he's never had a pack. The guy claims he wants to be part of our pack, but Jed doesn't like inducting new wolves this close to the full moon. Jed caged him last night until we make a decision. He likes to get to know new wolves as humans first. Plus the circumstances are just odd around how he found us, and there's no doubt that he sought us out."

"The guy agreed to being caged?"

"No," Mark replied simply, still looking out the window. "We had to persuade him."

I remembered hearing wolves howling last night, and wondered about their method of persuasion. "So tonight the newer wolves get caged along with this Leon guy and everyone else runs around as a wolf?"

Mark turned his head and looked beyond me, toward the hallway. I started as Jed answered my question before strolling into the room. "No, not everyone runs around as a wolf." He looked pointedly at Mark before taking a seat across from me. "Mark, John and the twins will stay in human form tonight as a precaution. John will watch the caged wolves, and I'll take the rest of the pack up into the mountains."

"You don't just change here?" I asked, curious.

Jed smiled in what I assumed was meant to be a friendly manner, but there was just something about him that scared me no matter how nice he appeared to be. He sat at ease in denim jeans and cowboy boots. Today he wore a black and gray flannel shirt with the sleeves pushed up to his elbows. His dark eyes met mine as he spoke. "Normally we do just change here. I have a couple hundred acres of forest and that's usually enough, but the whole pack is meeting tonight and we need a bigger hunting ground."

"How big is the pack?"

Jed looked at me and I wondered if I shouldn't have asked such a question. Maybe I was prying too much. I was surprised when he answered me. "There are currently 62 members of my pack, including those who aren't active participants," he added the last with a look at Mark. "My territory covers most of Oregon and the south end of Washington, but the majority of the pack lives within a few hours' drive."

I wondered if 62 wolves was a large pack, but figured that might not be an appropriate question. Jed was answering my questions, but I didn't want to push my limits with him. "What did you mean by 'active participants'?" I asked. Mark shifted in his seat and I glanced at him out of the corner of my eye.

"Active participants are those who join in for meetings, the full moon, and a variety of other things that come up with the pack. The inactive participants like to pretend they're not wolves at all, living their lives as humans as much as possible. Most packs wouldn't tolerate such behavior, and would simply kick the wolf out of the pack, making him a rogue wolf. Fortunately, I am much more understanding than most Alphas." Jed smiled at me again, but I knew his speech was for Mark's benefit by the way his eyes slid toward him. "I currently only have one inactive wolf."

Mark's reluctance to talk about werewolves was starting to make sense. I wondered what had happened to pull Mark away from the pack. Mark shifted in his chair and glanced at me before quickly turning and staring out the window once more. His stance said loud and clear that he didn't want to talk about it. Jed, on the other hand, seemed to be forthcoming with answers right now. I just wasn't sure how much I should push and pry.

I took another drink of coffee before turning back toward Jed, who seemed to be waiting on my questions. "What's the difference between being a rogue wolf and being part of a pack?"

"Protection, for one," Jed replied. "As part of a pack we are sort of like a family. If one person has a problem, the whole pack works to help. This doesn't just apply to wolf problems either, but also with the occasional human problem as well. Of course, that's just my pack. Not all packs are the same. There are a lot of rules around packs, but suffice it to say wolves in a pack get extra benefits in general."

"So a rogue wolf doesn't get pack protection?"

Jed nodded his head and his eyes shifted quickly toward the window, and the barn beyond. "A pack is not just a group of werewolves. There's more to it. Werewolves didn't just burst into existence, and neither did vampires. Great magic long ago was involved in creating both species, and great magic surrounds us still. Unfortunately, we don't know as much as we'd like about the vampires. They guard their secrets as tightly as we guard our own."

I had a feeling he was still guarding a great many secrets, no matter that he seemed to be sharing information openly with me. I suspected I was only learning what I needed to know. Werewolf information was maybe limited, but I bet Jed would be open to spilling vampire secrets. "So what do we know about vampires? Mark explained a bit, like how to kill them. What I don't understand is these weird dreams. How do they work? Can I get rid of them?"

"You mean your strange connection to this vampire who invades your dreams?" Jed asked, and I nodded. Jed leaned back and was quiet for several moments before speaking. "We have our theories regarding that, but they are just theories. A vampire gives you his blood in some way and you develop a psychic bond, but it seems to be only temporary. The human gains healing abilities, again temporarily, and the vampire gains a servant to do his bidding. If the vampire gives the human his blood again, the bond deepens. The bond can also deepen if the vampire bites the human. Each physical connection with the vampire and the human increases the strength and duration of the bond. There are those humans around who have become almost vampires themselves, living for many years while remaining young looking. As long as they continue to drink vampire blood, they will continue to regenerate and therefore do not age like normal people."

"That's disgusting," I replied, wrinkling my nose.

Jed laughed and I heard a chuckle emanate from Mark as well. "Well, humans have always been obsessed with a search for the fountain of youth. That's how the vampire creation story goes. A young man obsessed with wanting eternal life sells his soul and becomes the first vampire. But this man didn't just sell his soul; he also sold the soul of everyone he turns. If you've ever spent time with a vampire you'd know, they have no souls. They are pure evil."

"You really think that?" I asked.

"Yes, I do. Sure, they can act the part of a human because they were human once, but it's just that, an act." Jed leaned forward, elbows on his knees. "Remember that when dealing with vampires, Isabella. Everything they do is for their own benefit. They cannot be trusted. They don't have morals like we do. They only think of thirst and power, and they will use humans in any way they can to achieve their goals."

My heart was thudding in my chest. "So how do I make sure they don't pop up in my head again? I was worried about sleeping last night, thinking I'd go into one of those dreams again."

Jed shrugged and leaned back, an intense look in his eyes. "We don't know. As I said before, vampires guard their secrets. I've heard various things over the years, but nothing more than rumor. No human linked to the world of vampires has shared its secrets. Maybe it's the nature of the bond, a sort of symbiosis. On the other hand, maybe the vampire has bound the human so they are unable to speak of such things. We just don't know, and there seem to be too many variables. Not all vampires are the same."

I thought about that while I finished my cup of coffee. Jed

went back outside to finish preparations for the full moon and Mark wandered off to brood somewhere. Left alone, I had nothing to do but think. Jed had warned me against trusting vampires, but maybe I could bargain with them. Of course, what would a vampire want or need, besides blood?

My thoughts ran dark as I thought about sitting here surrounded by werewolves, day after day. With the exception of Mark, these wolves didn't care about me and they certainly didn't care about my brother. Justin had answers, I was sure of it. Not just that, he was family. And I would go to the ends of the earth for my family, even if it meant dealing with vampires. Unfortunately, I didn't even know if this vampire, Patricia, knew where my brother was currently. Could she be trusted? Finding Justin, I decided, was worth the risk.

Chapter 2

I put my coffee mug away and decided to give myself a tour of the house. I wandered back through the first living room I'd been in and found another hallway. I passed a bathroom and a couple locked doors. The last door at the back of the house opened up to a huge room that looked like it had been taken straight out of a country-western bar. Along one wall were rows and rows of alcohol, with a long bar stretching the length of it. Several wooden tables were scattered around the room. Toward the back of the room were two pool tables, set up and ready for play. A small stage was in one corner with what I guessed was a dancing area in front of it. Moreover, the whole room was decorated with cowboy boots and antlers, including a huge antler rack chandelier right in the middle of the ceiling.

I wandered through the room, noting the worn wooden floor. It truly looked like someone had uprooted their whole bar and placed it smack dab in the middle of this house. On the other hand, maybe the bar had been the original structure, and the house had been built around it. Either way, it was pretty impressive. I ran my hand across the bar, feeling the smooth polished wood. Werewolves, I decided, were very strange.

I wandered back through the house and up the stairs, but just found several more bedrooms and a couple more locked doors. Probably one of the locked doors was Jed's bedroom. Prying into an

Alpha's personal business would be a very bad idea, so I quickly moved away from the locked doors. I stopped back in my bedroom and peered out the window, which opened up to a partial view of the barn, a vast field, and forest beyond. It was a beautiful view, but it felt very isolated. I supposed werewolves liked living in the great outdoors, away from cities so they could roam free like their wolf cousins.

I closed my bedroom door and lay down on my bed, closing my eyes. I took slow, deep breaths, debating the wisdom of what I was going to try. No werewolves were around to stop me. The house was, as far as I could tell, completely empty. "Patricia," I said softly, trying to somehow reach out with my mind and contact the woman vampire. This was probably a stupid idea. "Patricia."

Again and again I said her name. I tried saying her name aloud and in my head. I tried picturing her as she had appeared in my dream. I even got up off the bed and spun around in circles, chanting her name. Nothing happened. No voice. No dream. Nothing.

After about an hour of trying different things, I finally gave up. Maybe she couldn't answer during the day. Maybe she couldn't answer me at all. It was probably for the best that I hadn't been able to reach her. Despite that, I'd probably try again later tonight. If it still didn't work, I'd just have to think of another way to find my brother. I didn't think I'd be able to sit around and wait for the werewolves to find him on their own. They weren't motivated the way I was.

I wandered back downstairs to the kitchen, but didn't run into anyone. I was bored and didn't want to turn on the television again. The last thing I wanted to do was dwell on the fact that I was a wanted fugitive. I opened up the back door off the kitchen and started walking toward the barn. There was a crisp autumn breeze, but the sun was shining down enough to keep me comfortable in my short-sleeved shirt. I examined my surroundings, seeing nothing but fields or forest in every direction. I had no idea where we were, since I'd been in a weird dream-coma when Mark had driven us here, but we were obviously far from any city.

I approached the barn cautiously, peering around the corner before entering. The man from the other night, Leon, was sitting on a bed of hay in the second cage on the left. He lowered the book he'd been reading and looked up at me with yellow wolf eyes. I stared back at him for a beat before turning away. I glanced around the barn, but didn't see anyone else. This strange man was not who I wanted to converse with, so I quickly backed away from the barn and ambled back toward the house. Instead of going inside, I walked around the outside of the house, ogling at its vastness.

On the other side at the very back of the house was another door, which I guessed entered into the bar area. The door was locked, so I continued around. Several clotheslines were along the side of the house, already full of clothes. I'd also found Beth and Mark, who were chatting amicably as they hung damp clothes onto the lines. Beth giggled at something Mark said and patted him on the shoulder before she turned back to the laundry basket. Conversation suddenly ceased as I walked toward them. Mark turned and smiled at me, his eyes a soft brown and his demeanor seeming relaxed. Beth looked up at me and I watched the smile that had been on her face slip away. The new expression on her face was blank, but I felt an underlying menace there.

"I wondered where everyone went," I said, reaching toward the laundry basket to help.

Beth snagged the basket away before I could touch it, and I straightened up immediately. "You'll make the clothes smell," Beth snapped before turning and carrying the basket to another line of clothes, her short brown hair whipping fiercely in the wind. What did that mean? I smell?

Mark put his hand around my shoulder and steered me toward a side door in the house. We entered a large laundry room, which Mark quickly hurried me through into the hallway I'd explored earlier. I remembered checking the door to this room earlier, but it had been locked then. He closed the door behind us and turned toward me, grinning. "Sorry about that. Beth is very particular about the clothes having only wolf scent on them, especially right after the full moon. She washes them in a special scent-free detergent and then line dries them so the scents on them are more natural. Even Mirabelle isn't allowed to handle them. Don't take it personally."

Okay, that's different. I shrugged and walked down the hallway toward the bar, Mark following on my heels. "Does Beth live here?" I asked, trying to keep my voice even. I moved around the bar and looked at the various bottles of alcohol. The bar was fully stocked with more varieties of alcohol than I even knew existed.

"Yeah, she takes care of the house. Since Jed's wife died four years ago Beth has become the caretaker of the house."

"So, are they a couple?" I asked, confused.

He shook his head and settled onto one of the bar stools, leaning his elbows on the counter. "No, it's not like that. Think of her as a live-in housekeeper. Jed provides her with a safe place to live and pays her to keep the house in order. She also makes most of the meals and does the laundry."

I found a small refrigerator with soda and juices in it, and grabbed some orange juice, deciding to make myself a screwdriver. I didn't really know much about mixed drinks, but you couldn't really mess up vodka and orange juice. I grabbed a glass and mixed up the drink before sitting down at the bar beside Mark. He looked at my drink, but didn't comment on it despite the early hour.

"So she's been here for four years?" I asked and Mark nodded. "I thought she was a new wolf? Didn't you say the new wolves stayed caged until they could handle running around?"

Mark ran his hand through his hair and I groaned internally, watching his eyes dart around the room as though he was struggling to come up with a story for me. I drained my drink and stood up to get another. I must not have made the drink strong enough, because I hadn't even felt the telltale alcohol burn.

"New wolves do stay caged," Mark replied as soon as I had

turned my back on him.

I rolled my eyes and quickly made another drink, this time adding some rum and pineapple juice. I took a drink before turning to face Mark, trying to keep calm. "If you're not going to answer my questions honestly, I'll just go ask Jed. He seems to have no problem answering my questions."

"I didn't lie to you," Mark retorted angrily. "Why are you drinking so early?"

I felt my anger boiling at his remark, and his avoidance of my question once again. "Oh, you never lie *outright*. You just skirt the truth, or change the subject, like you did just now." I paused to take a drink and attempt to calm myself down again. I was irritable and Mark was pushing my buttons with his evasiveness. "Why do you keep avoiding my questions?" I asked.

Mark closed his eyes and took several slow, deep breaths. I waited for him to calm down, restraining the urge to tap my fingers on the counter impatiently. He finally opened his eyes and looked at me. "Beth isn't a new wolf, but she has issues controlling her wolf, so she chooses to stay caged. It's sort of a touchy subject, so please don't ask anyone else about it, especially Beth."

"Why didn't you just say that to begin with?"

"There are... reasons. It's too much to get into right now. Please, just drop it."

"Fine," I snapped, draining my drink and pouring myself another, this time with less juice and considerably more alcohol.

Mark put his hand on my arm, restraining me from taking another drink. "Are you all right? Did I do something?"

"I'm just peachy." I pulled my hand away from Mark and drained my third drink. What was with these drinks? Shouldn't I be getting at least a little tipsy by now? Was there actually alcohol in these bottles? I sniffed the rum. Yes, that smelled like rum. I put the vodka and rum away and started sorting through the different alcohols. I found a bottle of whiskey and grabbed a shot glass. It may taste gross, but I should be able to feel something.

"Izzy," Mark murmured quietly as I poured a shot and quickly downed it without looking up at him. It burned going down and I gasped for air for a couple seconds. That was disgusting, but at least I could feel the burn. I poured another, quickly drinking it as well. Then another. After five shots like that I finally stopped and looked up at Mark. Concern etched his face, but he wisely held his tongue.

"Remember the fight you had with those guys in the alley?" I asked as I began pulling drawers open. I pulled a small knife out and held it up, glancing at Mark. He nodded his head, his eyes glued on the knife. "When you broke that baseball bat some pieces went flying and embedded in my arm. When I pulled them out, they healed up instantly. I didn't really think about that before, until Jed mentioned the quick healing people receive from drinking vampire blood." I quickly pulled the knife across my hand just before Mark grabbed it out of my hand. I watched the blood well as Mark ran around the counter and grabbed a towel, pushing it against my hand.

I wiped the towel across my hand and inspected the wound. A lot of blood was on the towel, but my hand was flawless. Mark took my hand in his and examined it while I reached out awkwardly and grabbed another shot of whiskey. "I hardly even felt it," I muttered, downing the shot, "just like I don't feel this."

"You're not invincible, Izzy. And I'd be willing to bet you'd heal slower with a more serious wound," Mark replied, still holding my hand. "I'd rather not test the limits of this vaccine full of vampire blood."

"Well, I guess I should look on the bright side," I said, hefting the whiskey bottle. "I won't get drunk!"

Mark chuckled and took the bottle from my hand. "You won't get drunk for now. I hope that over time with no vamp contact the effects will leave your system. I think that's why the vaccine is supposed to be given in three injections, to stabilize the vampire connection for as long as possible. On the news they're talking about adding yearly booster shots."

"Yearly?" I asked, feeling my eyebrows rise in surprise. "Does that mean that three injections of vampire blood will last for a year? What about one injection, or two?"

He shook his head. "I don't know. I guess down the road we can do the alcohol test to find out how strong the connection is though," he adding, smiling. "I wouldn't suggest testing the connection by cutting yourself though."

"How do we sever the connection? I don't want to keep having these dreams for a year, Mark." I doubted I could resist the vampire for a year. He was amazing. I quickly turned my thoughts away and focused back on Mark.

"We kill the vampire, of course. If the vampire is gone, there's no connection to worry about."

We kill them? Was he crazy? I ground my teeth together and pulled my hand away from Mark. "And what about the fact that I probably have two vampires linked to me? Did you think about that? I know I did. Why else would I be dreaming of two different vamps? Or the fact that we don't know who these vampires are, or how to find them, let alone kill them! There has to be another way!"

"John is our resident vampire expert, and he thinks that because you have two different vampires fighting for control of you the connections are weaker. I'm not sure what would happen if we killed one vamp and not the other, though. It could strengthen the connection with the other vamp, or maybe it would do nothing. Perhaps it would sever all connections. We just don't know." He sighed and leaned against the bar. I wondered if Mark was as frustrated by all of this as I was.

"So he thinks my connection is weaker than if I had one full vampire in control? How would killing one of the vampires make this better? I almost died from this damn vampire shit already. What about everyone else out there, Mark?" I asked as I drummed my fingers on the smooth bar. How many people had gotten an injection already? How many people had gotten all three? "At least I know what's going on. What's happening to everyone else? Has anyone died from it? Are they turning into mindless vampire slaves? Are they having strange dreams that they can't explain?"

Mark shook his head. "If there have been deaths, I haven't heard. As for them turning into slaves, I don't think so. Even the humans who repeatedly drink vampire blood remain who they are. That's part of the problem with identifying who is under vampire control and who isn't. They talk and act completely normal, until they do something that isn't normal for them. They may not be mindless slaves, but we're not sure how much control they have over their actions. Jed has people looking into that already, including John."

"So, basically you don't know anything," I muttered sullenly.

"Sorry," he said softly. "We're doing our best."

"Did they give you the injection?" I asked suddenly, remembering the IVs that had been hooked up to his arms. The men in suits had captured him the same time as me, and whoever was in charge had been pretty set on making sure I received the vaccine. "Was that what that silvery stuff in your IV was? Have you had vamp dreams too, or is that just me?"

Mark smiled and shook his head. "Werewolves are immune to vampire blood. I'm pretty sure they had some sort of silver concoction in my IV. That's why I was so out of it when you found me. Werewolves are sort of allergic to silver. I couldn't turn into a wolf and escape with all that silver running through me."

"Maybe they were trying to find a way to give you the blood too. Worldwide vampire control won't work if you have a bunch of werewolves who are immune," I added.

Mark frowned in thought, taking in my words. "Perhaps," he said softly. "Well, if that was their plan it didn't work. I haven't had any weird issues or dreams or anything that would indicate a vampire connection."

"Okay, well that's good. I think having a bunch of werewolves under vampire control would be a bad idea."

Mark chuckled and nodded his head. "That would be bad. I don't even want to think about it. It's bad enough thinking about the entire human population being infected."

Could it actually happen? Could the entire human population become vampire slaves? How long would it take? Mark took my hands in his, pulling me out of my reverie.

"Thank you for rescuing me, Izzy," he said softly. I looked up into his soft brown eyes. "I should have thanked you earlier, but I guess a lot has been going on. I owe you my life. They may not have been able to inject me with their blood, but I'm sure they were keeping me alive for a reason and I doubt I would have liked it. So thank you, from the bottom of my heart."

"You saved me, too, so I'd say we're even," I replied, smiling back at him. "Thank you too, Mark."

He grinned and pulled me to him, releasing my hands and wrapping his arms around me in a fierce hug. I leaned my head on his chest, listening to his heart beat steadily as I wrapped my arms around his waist. We stayed like that for several minutes, and I felt some of the tension and anxiety I'd been feeling melt away. I'd needed this, I realized. I'd been seeking comfort in the wrong place. Alcohol may not work on me, but a hug from someone I care about sure did help me relax.

"Vanessa is here," Mark said suddenly. I pulled away and looked toward the door, but saw no one. "I heard the front door close, and I can smell her. Come on, I'll introduce you."

Mark grabbed my hand and we headed into the smaller living room, where a slender young woman with bright pink hair spiked up all over was standing. The girl appeared to be somewhere in her early twenties. She wore black combat boots, torn jeans and a black mesh tank top with nothing under it but a very visible bright pink bra. There were piercings on her ears, lip and eyebrow. She smiled broadly when we walked in and rushed at Mark. Mark released my hand as he and the woman hugged. "It is great to see you again, M-Dawg," she said, punching him on the shoulder.

Mark chuckled as he mussed her hair. "Great to see you too, Vanessa. I like the pink look. This is Izzy," he said, indicating me.

I smiled and held out my hand. "It's nice to meet you," I said. Instead of shaking my hand, Vanessa reached out and pulled me into a hug. I could hear her sniff the air around me as she held me.

"Any girl of Mark's is a friend of mine," she said, squeezing me tightly.

"I'm not Mark's girl," I said, pushing back on her gently.

Vanessa released me and stood back with her hands on her hips. She glanced at Mark and then back at me, a small frown on her face. "You're covered in his scent," she said certainly. "Plus you walked in here holding hands."

"That doesn't mean I'm his girl," I retorted. Dealing with werewolves and their heightened senses was getting on my nerves. "Don't I have your scent on me now, too?"

She held up her hands in surrender, grinning. "Okay, okay, no offense meant. You just seem to have a *lot* of his scent on you." She turned and skipped around the couch, opening a large case that was sitting on the coffee table. "Jed called me this morning and told me about you two being on the most-wanted list. I'm here to do a makeover! I can't do much for Mark, but I can definitely change your appearance enough. So, how do you want your hair?"

My eyebrows rose as I walked around the couch and glanced into the case. All sorts of hair salon products and tools were inside the large case. I glanced over to Mark, but he wasn't there. I looked around the room but couldn't find him anywhere. I looked back at Vanessa and her pink hair, then back to the case. My hand drifted of its own accord to my long blonde hair. I loved my hair! Other than a botched dye attempt when I was 15, I'd never had chemicals of any kind on my hair.

"You look kind of queasy," Vanessa said slowly as I sat down on the couch.

"I don't dye my hair," I said, stroking my long blonde tresses. "I don't cut it, either."

"Do a lot of people know that about you?"

I nodded. "When I was 15 I had a friend with beautiful red hair and flawless skin. She was popular and had a ton of boyfriends. I, on the other hand, was a skinny, quiet, flat-chested girl with horrible acne. I didn't know the first thing about styling my hair and never wore makeup. I also had never had a boyfriend. For some reason I got the bright idea that having red hair would change all that. So I went to the store, bought a box of hair color, and dyed my hair. It was the worst mistake ever."

"Didn't look too good, huh?" she asked.

I shook my head. "It was pretty much a disaster. It turned out this bright orange color. I looked like Ronald McDonald! I had to beg my dad to take me into a salon to fix it. Unfortunately we didn't have much money, and my dad didn't know any better. He took me to the barber shop he used." I shuddered, thinking about it. "On the upside, my hair wasn't orange any more, but a kind of weird brownish color that I could handle. The big problem was that I had fried my hair, so instead of Ronald McDonald, I looked like a brunette Einstein. I think I wore hats for three months before I ended up just chopping my hair off at my ears in a short bob. After that I vowed to never dye my hair again."

Vanessa chuckled and put a hand on my shoulder. "I am a professional and I promise you will like whatever I do," she said. "If everyone is looking for a woman with long, blonde hair..." she trailed off and I found myself nodding slowly. I really didn't want to be stuck in this house forever, and if a minor makeover could change my appearance enough it was worth a shot. I could handle a change, at least until we proved our innocence and were able to come out of hiding.

"What did you have in mind?"

Chapter 18

Several hours later, I was staring at a different person in the mirror. Never in a million years had I thought I would cut my hair, let alone dye it. Vanessa stood behind me, grinning widely. We had spent probably 30 minutes arguing back and forth about what to do, when Vanessa finally just said I had to trust her and let her do her thing. I had argued about just getting a perm or something, but she said that wasn't drastic enough, even if the perm had taken hold on my straight hair. I had laid down rules beforehand though. I wouldn't do some things. No haircuts above the chin and no red hair were the two items at the top of my list.

I ran a hand through my hair, marveling at how different I looked. I had to admit, it looked pretty amazing, and very different. My hair was still long, but with layers and side-swept bangs. The color was a chocolate brown with subtle highlighting to make it look natural and absolutely beautiful. Vanessa had also carefully dyed my eyebrows so it looked realistic. Just the color change had me looking like a completely different person. She had also promised that she could dye my hair back.

I shifted my eyes to Vanessa, who was bouncing in the mirror behind me. "Well?" she asked.

I took a deep breath and turned around to face her. "I love it," I said, smiling. "Although I do miss my blonde hair, I have to admit this is pretty amazing. I don't think anyone will recognize me like this. Honestly, I think my own brother would have to do a double-take."

"I knew it!" she cried, hugging me. "Mark's going to go ape-shit! You look down-right sexy as hell!"

I shook my head as she stepped away, glancing at myself once more in the mirror. The hairstyle was definitely sexy, but her comment had me cringing. Did I care what Mark thought? I wasn't sure what I felt concerning him. There were definitely feelings there, but I wasn't sure of the extent. So much had happened in the last few days that I hadn't really had time to examine my feelings. I was definitely attracted to him physically, but I always had been. Was that all there was to it? Did I want more?

"You okay?" Vanessa asked. "Your heart just sped way up and you look kind of pale."

I rolled my eyes and turned to Vanessa. "I'm fine," I muttered. "Quit using your werewolf powers on me."

She laughed softly, but her eyes were still very serious. "Okay, whatever you say," she replied, obviously not believing me but letting it go nonetheless. "Hair and makeup are done, so now it's time for clothes."

"What?" I exclaimed, glancing at Vanessa's poor excuse for a shirt. There was no way I was wearing a shirt like hers.

"Well, you can't run around in a t-shirt and jeans with sexy-as-hell hair. It just doesn't go together. I know Mirabelle bought you clothes, but her style is way too conservative."

"I like conservative," I muttered, crossing my arms.

Vanessa chuckled, nodding her head. "Yeah, I kind of figured you did. Remember, everyone will be looking for the blonde, conservative schoolteacher. Lucky for you, I brought a whole car full of clothes! Meet me in your room," she added, running out of the bathroom.

I groaned as I made my way upstairs to my room. I felt guilty that Mirabelle had already gone to such lengths to buy a dresser full of clothes. I opened the drawers and pawed through the clothes. They were very plain, consisting of t-shirts of various cuts and simple jeans. I supposed Vanessa had a point regarding clothing, but I wasn't sure about Vanessa's style. Wasn't a new dramatic hairstyle enough of a difference? Did I really have to change my wardrobe style as well? Even with all these changes, I somehow doubted Jed and the werewolves would let me go anywhere.

My bedroom door banged open and Vanessa came in with a huge box in her hands and a large suitcase on wheels rolling behind her. She dropped the box on the bed and hefted the suitcase up beside it, unzipping and opening it. I stepped forward, cautiously examining the contents. Vanessa pulled out several pairs of jeans first and I picked them up one by one, pleasantly surprised. While they seemed to be mostly skinny jeans, there were no strange holes anywhere. Next, Vanessa pulled out various tops in a variety of styles. They were definitely edgier, but nothing I was immediately opposed to wearing. I peered into the box, finding an assortment of dresses, shoes and lingerie.

Vanessa sorted through the clothes quickly and quietly, moving the clothes Mirabelle had bought to the back of the dresser and placing the ones she brought up front. As soon as she was done, she grabbed a pair of black skinny jeans and a low-cut black top and tossed them at me. "Put these on," she ordered.

I turned to go change in the bathroom, but Vanessa stopped me before I left the room. She thrust a set of matching black lacy bra and panties into my arms as well. "I'm already wearing underwear," I replied.

She shook her head. "You can't wear sexy clothes with ugly underwear. Besides, what if you're in a car accident and the EMT's have to cut off your clothes? Do you want to be wearing ugly underwear? You never know when you'll have an under clothes emergency. Trust me, put these on."

The underwear Mirabelle had brought was plain, but I didn't

think it was ugly. And if I couldn't leave the house, I really doubted I'd be in a car accident. I looked up at Vanessa, who had her arms crossed defiantly. She obviously wasn't taking no for an answer, so I took the clothes from her hand and walked across the hall to the bathroom. I quickly dressed in the outfit she had picked out, examining myself in the mirror. The top was see-through and cut in a V that showed considerable cleavage. I opened the bathroom door and made sure no one was around before scurrying back to the bedroom. I closed the door and turned for Vanessa to see the outfit. She oohed and clapped her hands, but I felt ridiculous.

"You can see my bra," I said slowly as I turned to look at myself in the mirror above the dresser. "I don't think I can do this."

Vanessa stared at me for a heartbeat, then sighed and nodded. "Okay, we can tone this down a bit. You have to feel comfortable in the clothes you wear, otherwise you'll be miserable."

Vanessa turned and rifled through the clothes and pulled out a black camisole and a long gray cable knit sweater. I exchanged tops and glanced in the mirror. The new outfit was much better. I still wasn't so sure about the black knee-high boots Vanessa thrust at me, but I let it go and pulled them on. The point of all this was so I could go out in public and no one would recognize me. My usual workday attire consisted of conventional long dresses or slacks, and this outfit was nothing like that. This outfit bordered the line of sexy, without going overboard.

"Well?" Vanessa asked. I glanced over at her and smiled, giving her two thumbs up. "Yes! Let's go downstairs and wow Mark!"

I rolled my eyes at her comment, but Vanessa didn't seem to notice. She skipped to the door and started downstairs, me on her heels. The house had filled up more while we'd been doing my hair and I heard several voices coming from the kitchen. Vanessa and I had snacked throughout the day, but the delicious smells coming from the kitchen made my stomach growl.

We peeked into the kitchen and I took in all the sights and

smells. Through the back window, Logan and Lucas appeared to be barbequing while Beth and Jed were preparing what looked like potato salad. Mark had the fridge open and several bottles of salad dressing in his hands. Vanessa cleared her throat loudly as we fully entered the kitchen and everyone turned simultaneously. A bottle of Thousand Island dressing slipped from Mark's hands and burst open, splattering the ground. Beth hurried with a wet towel to clean up the mess, but Mark stood still with his eyes glued on me. I shifted uncomfortably under the intense look and quickly turned and scurried out of the kitchen, through the dining room and into the large living room. I was breathing quickly and ready to bolt right back upstairs and change clothes.

John was entering the living room at the same time and I skidded to a halt. Today he wore a dark gray t-shirt, but everything else was black from the leather jacket to the boots and even the laptop he carried under one arm. He stopped in front of me, smiling as he held out his hand. "I'm John," he said simply. I stopped and shook his hand. "Weren't you a blonde yesterday?"

I laughed nervously, nodding my head. "Yes, I was. I'm Isabella Howerton," I replied.

He nodded and indicated we should sit down. I wanted to go back upstairs and change, but I obliged and followed him to the couch. He sat down and set the laptop he'd been carrying on his lap. "Mark asked me to do some digging for you today, and I came across a few things," he started as he opened his laptop and started keying things in. "I checked both your email and Mark's, as well as your cell phone number. Justin hasn't tried to contact you that I saw, but someone is monitoring all of your accounts. If he had tried, it would have been easy for someone to find him. I was able to track his last communication with Mark to a small town in Alberta, Canada. That was over a month ago, so Justin could very easily be in Oregon, if that was his destination."

"He did say he was coming to me," I replied, remembering

that frantic phone call so many months ago.

"Considering the difficulty I had trying to track his email, my guess is that he hasn't been found yet, at least not by whoever is doing the monitoring. There are a lot of other people out there trying to find your brother. I am curious how he's stayed under the radar for so long," John added, clicking on his computer again. "As for this manhunt on you and Mark, I found a fake surveillance video that has been released to the police regarding the murder at the hotel. It's going to take some time to find the source. I'm also trying to track down the original footage, but that's proving difficult as well. Here's the fake."

John turned the computer toward me and I watched a video of what looked like the hotel lobby. The video was black and white and appeared to be from the ceiling. The two security guards stood at the door, as they had been. I watched in fascination as the first guard moved toward Mark, but everything after that was different from what had happened. The video showed Mark grabbing the first man and tossing him, then shooting both guards. I shook my head in disbelief. "That's not what happened," I muttered.

John nodded his head and reversed the video clip to the moment after the guard moved to Mark, showing it in slow motion. "Watch closely," John said, pointing at Mark. "You can just make out the moment the video was altered."

I watched the video in slow motion and noticed how Mark seemed to jump to the side between one second and the next. I leaned in, looking at the new Mark. His back was to the camera, but the build and height were just slightly off. "They re-did the video with someone else?"

"That's what I think," John replied, pointing at the first security guard. "This guy has been changed too, but it's subtle. I'll need some more time, but I think we have a good shot at fixing this for you two."

I took a deep breath and let it out slowly. I felt a hand on my shoulder and I jumped, turning around. Mark stood behind me, holding his hands up in surrender. "Sorry, didn't mean to startle you. I was just listening to John."

Mark walked around the couch and sat next to me, his arm draped casually around my shoulder as he leaned in to look at the laptop. "I appreciate your help on this, John. Any ideas on how we find Izzy's brother?"

John closed the video down and began clicking on his computer again. "I'm looking for his associates," he said as he began typing on the computer, "but I haven't turned up anything yet. According to all reports, his whole team died."

"They're not all dead, or at least they weren't when Justin called me months ago. Kirk Daughtry and Jared Bushing were still alive last I heard."

"I'll look for them as well." John turned the computer toward me again, showing me a recent local news article. The article was about the vaccine and who had already received it. According to the article, everyone in government, law enforcement, health care and education were the first to receive the vaccine, and by now had received anywhere from one to three doses. The article also estimated that 60% of the population had already received at least one dose of the vaccine. The article touted the many redeeming qualities of the vaccine, particularly how it was curing sick children in hospitals.

I finished reading the article and sat back. John clicked on the computer again, displaying other websites from across the country that said the same thing. I glanced at headline after headline, all talking about the new wonder drug. The drug was also being sent to other countries as it became available. Petri Co. was producing the vaccine in mass quantities as fast as possible. From the sounds of it, government officials in various foreign countries from Europe to Asia were the first to receive the vaccine.

"This is happening fast," Mark muttered, his words echoing my thoughts.

John nodded his head. "They've run out of the vaccine in quite a few places, but they're basically saying if everyone gets at least one dose they should be fine for a month until they can get a second dose." He closed down the official news articles and opened up an internet blog. "Not everyone is running for the miracle cure, though."

Mark chuckled as we perused the blog, which warned people away from getting the vaccine. The author called everyone who got the vaccine, "sheep being led to the slaughter by Big Business" and pointed out how quickly the drug had gone through the certification process. The blog had many valid points, including speculation on the side effects, but in the end most people would dismiss this blog and others like it, because people tended to believe the official news over conspiracy news.

"This sounds like you," I said to Mark, glancing at him sideways, "talking about government conspiracies."

Mark chuckled again, shaking his head. "That's because it is Mark," John said. "He asked me to post this for him. Look at all the comments."

I glanced from John to Mark, then back to the computer screen. There was a stream of comments supporting Mark's article. "We're a community of bloggers," Mark said. "There are about ten of us who write for this blog, all under different names of course. With all that's going on, I knew I had to post this. If I can stop one person from getting the vaccine, then that's one less person under vampire control."

"When did you have time to write this?" I asked.

"Last night," he replied. "I gave it to John before he left."

John closed down his computer and stood up. "I'll work more on finding Justin tomorrow. If the vampires want your brother this badly, we want him more." John left the room, heading toward the delicious aromas coming from the kitchen.

Mark's arm was still around my shoulder, and now that we were alone it felt suddenly awkward. I scooted away a little, letting

Mark's arm drop. "I like the hair," he said softly. "Of course I like the blonde more, but this is nice too."

"I feel the same way. It definitely looks different."

"Well, at least on casual observation no one will immediately know it's you, and that was the idea."

I nodded my head, but I really wasn't thinking about my hair. I was thinking about how to find my brother. John was working the tech end of things, but all we'd learned was that Justin had been in Canada a few weeks ago. Maybe Kirk and Jared were with him. Looking for three people had to be easier than looking for just one. I was wringing my hands, wondering what to do next when Mark placed his hands on top of mine. I stopped and looked up into his chocolate eyes, noting the slight yellow cast to them that I'd be learning meant his wolf was close to the surface. Not too surprising since it would be a full moon tonight.

"Are you thinking about Justin?" he asked softly and I nodded my head, fighting back tears that were threatening to overwhelm me. "We'll find him, Izzy."

"I certainly hope so. I'm sure he's seen the news. He has to be wondering what's going on. I just hope he doesn't make a mistake trying to reach me," I added.

Mark's arms enveloped me, pulling me to him in a tight hug. Tears cascaded down my cheeks as I sobbed into his chest. I'd never needed my brother more than I did now, and not because of the vaccine or the fact that he might have vital information. No, I just needed my big brother to scare away the monsters for me like he did when we were little. Now here I was, hugging one of the monsters.

That thought stilled my tears and I pulled away from Mark, surreptitiously glancing around the room for a tissue. I spotted a box of tissues across the room and hurriedly grabbed several tissues, wiping my eyes and nose. Mark patiently waited until I was finished before moving across the room to stand behind me, his arms encircling my waist in a possessive way. I stilled, unsure what to do.

"Food is done," Mark whispered in my ear.

I nodded my head and surreptitiously pulled away. We moved into the dining room, where Jed, Beth, Vanessa, John, Michael, the twins and one other man introduced as Frank were all already seated and filling plates. The table was large but there were still two open spots. Mark and I sat down at the far end of the table and helped ourselves to steak, chicken, salad, potato salad and hot biscuits covered in jelly. There was little conversation while everyone ate. I quickly cleared my plate, but the men all went back for second helpings, particularly of the very raw steak.

When everyone had finished eating, and all food was gone, we moved into the living room for a quick meeting. I sat down in a chair at the edge of the room, feeling out of place. Jed stood, waiting for everyone to settle in before speaking. The sun was quickly drifting lower in the sky, and I guessed it would be dark in an hour. "I think everyone knows their places tonight, but I just want to go over a few things. I will be leaving shortly to meet the rest of the pack, but I want everyone here to remain on high alert. We still have a rogue wolf in the barn, as well as a developing vampire problem. After the attack and abduction of Mark and Isabella, I think it best to be cautious. I don't anticipate problems, but better safe than sorry."

"I'll be your runner," Vanessa said to the twins, bouncing in her seat. Her eyes were twinkling with excitement and the twins grinned back at her eagerly.

Jed nodded. "Yes, Vanessa has agreed to stay here in wolf form and act as the runner in case of trouble here. She's one of the fastest, so she should be able to get close enough to alert us quickly. I also have Erika with the remainder of the pack in the woods to act as runner, in case of trouble on our end. John will guard the interior of the barn and the cages. Mark, I want you to stay inside the house and monitor from the control room. Isabella can give you a hand with that. Logan and Lucas will monitor outside in human form. Keep walkie-talkies on but silent, unless there's a problem."

Everyone nodded his or her heads, plans in place. I wondered where the control room was, but figured I'd wait until after Jed left to ask. Jed glanced out the window at the setting sun and pulled his keys out of his pocket. "I'll see you all in the morning," he said, looking around the room with yellow wolf eyes. "Be safe."

Jed held a look with Mark before heading toward the front door. Mark stood and followed him, returning a few minutes later with a somber look on his face. Michael was bouncing on his feet, growling, and John quickly led him out to the barn, followed by Frank. Vanessa's eyes had turned bright yellow already. She gave me a quick hug before hurrying outside, presumably to change into wolf form. The twins went into the kitchen to clean up the food and start coffee before beginning their rounds. The only ones left in the living room were Beth, Mark and me.

Mark moved to the large window, staring out past the barn and the setting sun. I sat awkwardly on the large couch, with Beth at the other end. Beth cast a quick glance at me before she got up and walked over to Mark. She wrapped her arms around his waist, hugging him from behind exactly as Mark had hugged me just before dinner. I felt a pang of jealousy as Mark wrapped an arm around her shoulder and pulled her to him in a side hug. I watched them as she stood up on her tiptoes and whispered something into Mark's ear. He smiled and murmured something back to her that I couldn't hear. She smiled back up at him and kissed him on the cheek before she turned and walked toward the kitchen. She stopped at the kitchen entrance and turned back toward me. Her eyes were bright yellow and the look on her face was deadly. She left the room and I heard the kitchen door bang closed a moment later. I watched out the window as she sauntered to the barn, swaying her hips with each step. My eyes moved to Mark, noting that he, too, watched her walk away.

Chapter 11

Mark led me to one of the locked doors I'd come across earlier, just across from the bar room. The door opened to a closet full of coats and shoes and I wondered briefly what we were doing there and why a closet needed a lock. Mark moved the coats out of the way and pressed his hand against a section of the wall, revealing a control panel. Mark punched in the numbers 1843 and the back wall of the closet slid open, revealing a staircase leading down. We stepped on the stairs and Mark tapped the matching control panel, causing the door to close quietly behind us.

Dim bulbs lit the way along the narrow staircase walls, leading us underneath the house. At the bottom of the stairs there was a short hallway with four doors. Mark showed me the first two, which were a bathroom and a storeroom full of canned food and emergency supplies. The third room was full of cots, blankets and clothes. Mark turned toward the last room, which also had a control panel. He punched in 0815 and the door clicked open, revealing a room full of computers and monitor screens.

I followed Mark inside and looked at the monitors, which showed various views around the exterior of the house and barn. Mark pulled a chair out and I followed suit, sitting down on his right. He clicked a few buttons on the main computer and the views switched so that each monitor showed several locations, now including the inside of the barn and house. There must be cameras all over the place! I hadn't noticed any before, but then again I hadn't been looking for them.

I examined the monitors in the house, seeing the empty living rooms, kitchen, dining room, bar and hallways. "Are these all the cameras in the house?" I asked, pointing at the screen.

"Bedrooms and bathrooms are off limits for cameras," Mark responded.

A flicker of movement caught my eye on another screen and I turned toward it. A lone wolf was loping across the field behind the house and I stared in fascination. "Is that Vanessa?" I asked, watching the black and white screen with interest.

Mark looked where I was pointing and nodded. "Yes, beautiful isn't she? The infrared cameras don't pick up the colors of her wolf, but she is a magnificent almost silver color."

I watched the wolf run across several cameras, making a tour around the house and barn before disappearing into the field. "So this is the control room. Are there any other hidden gems in this house?"

"No, I think you've seen it all. Jed built this shelter here years ago, but just added the computers when John joined the pack about fifteen years ago. This room gets more updates than anything else in the house." Mark pointed to another monitor that showed a long stretch of road. "The property is too big to have cameras everywhere, but they cover the closest areas around the house and a good mile of the road leading in."

I tried watching all the monitors on my side of the room, but it was impossible to do so. I glanced behind me at the monitors on Mark's side of the room, which showed the interior and exterior of the barn, as well as the shop. Logan was walking around the exterior of the shop, while Lucas patrolled down the road.

A flicker of movement caught my eye and the screens showing the barn suddenly transfixed me. There were several monitors showing the cages in the barn. John stood watching the cages, hand resting on the gun at his hip. Three of the cages contained wolves, two dark colored, one light, but all with distinct size differences. What had caught my eye was movement in the fourth cage, where Beth was changing into a wolf before my eyes. She was on the floor of the cage with her head down, as her whole body seemed to shake. Her hair grew longer and fur soon covered her arms. Arms and legs seemed to move and shift into odd angles, warping until they were no longer human shaped. I winced, watching what appeared to be a violent and painful transformation. I wasn't sure how long it took, but soon a wolf was where Beth had just been, shaking off the tattered remnants of her clothes.

I felt Mark's eyes on me, watching my reaction. I schooled my face as best I could, but I'm sure something between awe, horror and disgust was probably etched clear as day on my face. I moved my chair so I was facing only the screens on my side of the room with my back to Mark. Goosebumps rose across my skin, and I shivered uncontrollably.

"It's not always so violent," Mark said softly, moving his chair beside mine. "I wish you'd seen Vanessa change. Her transformation is easily the most beautiful and graceful. She embraces every moment of her transformation and her time as a wolf. She was born a wolf, so perhaps that's why it's different for her."

"Vanessa was born like this? Is that common?" I turned to look at Mark.

"Oh, no," Mark replied, shaking his head. "There are only four natural born wolves in our pack; Vanessa, Thomas, Alexander and Jed. The rest of us are made by the bite of another."

"Does it hurt?" I asked, my eyes drifting back to the barn monitor on Mark's side of the room.

Mark turned away from me, his focus back on the monitors. "We need to pay attention to these," he said, pointing at the screens.

I turned my chair back toward my bank of screens, watching for movement. After several minutes, Mark spoke again. "It can hurt," he began softly. "It's different for everyone. If you embrace the wolf it can be magical and painless, but if you fight it..." he trailed off.

"Beth doesn't embrace it?" I asked timidly, risking a glance at Mark over my shoulder. "Is that why she is still caged?"

Mark sighed loudly before responding. "She's trying to accept what she is. That's why she's here, with Jed. He's helping her cope with what happened to her."

"Was she attacked?"

"It was an accident," he said quietly, the pain in his voice obvious. I waited for him to elaborate, but he never did.

After a couple hours of watching monitors, I went upstairs and made a pot of coffee. It was going to be a long night. Mark didn't expect me to stay up all night watching the monitors with him, but I figured I'd try if I could. The moment the coffee was finished, Lucas walked in through the back door. He was dressed casually in jeans and a denim jacket.

"I smelled coffee," he said as he sauntered over to me. "Any way I can get a thermos to go?"

"Sure," I replied, as I started opening cabinets, looking for a thermos. I found a large metal one and filled it with coffee before handing it to Lucas.

I started another pot of coffee while Lucas stood hovering behind me. As soon as the coffee started brewing, I turned around and faced him. "Do you need something else?" I asked, looking into his yellow wolf eyes.

He took a deep breath and angled his body toward me. I instinctively backed up into the counter and crossed my arms. He chuckled and cocked his head, his eyes roaming over my body. "I could use a distraction," he said, his voice husky.

"Well, that's what the coffee is for," I retorted. "Shouldn't you be patrolling?"

The back door opened and Logan entered, looking very similar to his brother in jeans and a flannel coat. Logan marched up behind his brother, his yellow eyes glaring fiercely. "Get back on patrol," he growled, shoving Lucas toward the back door.

Lucas grabbed the thermos and laughed as Logan ushered him out the door. I breathed a sigh of relief when they were both gone. When the coffee was done brewing, I filled another thermos full and started a third batch before carrying the thermos and two mugs back downstairs to Mark. I was at the control panel in the closet when I heard what sounded like a woman's voice saying my name. I stopped and waited, listening for the voice. After several minutes of hearing nothing, I entered the code into the control panel and went downstairs.

Mark glanced at me when I entered the control room, his eyes now yellow even though they'd been normal brown when I'd left. I set the thermos and mugs down and turned back toward the door.

"Where are you going?" Mark asked.

"I couldn't carry the creamer too," I replied, glancing back at him over my shoulder.

"You stopped at the top of the stars. What were you doing?"

I shrugged my shoulders. "I thought I heard something."

Mark frowned and waved a hand at the monitors. "I haven't seen anything or anyone, except the twins. Was Lucas harassing you?" he asked in a growl. I wondered if watching Lucas on the monitor had been what brought the yellow to Mark's eyes, or just the fact that it was a full moon.

"Nothing to worry about," I replied as I walked toward the stairs. "Be right back with the good creamer."

I hurried up the stairs and into the kitchen, wrenching open the fridge to grab the bottle of creamer out. As I closed the refrigerator door, I heard the voice again. I looked around the room, spinning in a circle. There was a loud bang outside the back door, as though something had slammed into the wall, and I rushed to the window to peer out. I could just make out a form lying on the back porch. I moved toward the door, but Mark was running past me in a blur before my hand touched the handle.

"Get into the control room!" he yelled as he yanked open the door.

I followed Mark to the door, watching as he knelt over Logan. Blood had stained Logan's shirt red, but he was awake and struggling to stand upright. Mark helped Logan up and looked back at me, his eyes a golden yellow color. "Get into the control room, now!" he shouted.

I shut the door and peeked out the window in time to see Logan and Mark both stand up and race off into the night. Logan obviously wasn't too injured. I heeded Mark's words and rushed through the house, fear pumping the adrenaline through my body. Something was out there and whatever it was had injured a werewolf. I ran past the front door and skidded to a halt when I heard the soft knock on the door. I stopped and faced the door, breathing hard.

Knock, knock, knock. I slowly walked toward the door and peered out the peephole. Standing on the front step was the same woman who had been in my dream. She smiled and waved at me through the peephole, her flawless pale skin almost glowing in the porch light. My heart sped up and I debated the wisdom of opening the door. If she truly was a vampire, she couldn't enter the house uninvited. Or was that just a vampire myth?

"Open the door, Isabella," the woman's voice seemed to echo through the house and I found myself walking toward the door and turning the handle.

The woman was as beautiful and flawless as she had appeared in my dream. Her pale skin was perfect and her long chestnut hair cascaded across her shoulders in soft waves. Her eyes were just a normal brown though, not black as I had remembered. I studied her outfit, which was an almost carbon copy of my own, except the sweater she wore was red and low cut and paired with a belt. She smiled at me warmly and I found myself smiling back automatically.

"It is so nice to finally meet you while you're awake. And I must say, I absolutely love the hair," she said, holding out her hand to shake mine. "I'm Patricia."

I shook her hand, which felt surprisingly warm. I'd always thought vampires were supposed to be cold. "What are you doing here?"

She laughed softly, shaking her head. "What am I doing here? You called me, my dear," she replied. "And I'm so glad you did."

Realization dawned on me then and I felt a momentary panic. I had wanted to get in touch with her, but I didn't think she'd actually show up here. I didn't even know where here was, so how did she know? I heard a wolf howl and my heart sped up as another howl answered it. "What's happening?"

She waved her hand in the air, as though dismissing my question. "Nothing, dear, nothing," she replied. "Shall we go now?"

"Go? I'm not going anywhere with you!"

She crossed her arms and pouted with her glossy red lips, looking like a petulant child. The look might work on a man, but it did nothing but irritate me. "Oh, you're going to be difficult aren't you?"

I stared at her, hands on my hips. "People are getting hurt out there!"

"Oh, no one will die," she retorted, as though that would make me feel better. "I gave my boys their orders. They are just a distraction, and a temporary one at that. We really must be going."

I backed up into the house more, partially closing the door. "I don't think I want to go with you."

"Is that any way to treat me after all I've done for you? I took a great risk switching the vaccines for you. You have no idea," she said menacingly, her nice façade dripping away. "You want to find your brother, and I'm going to help you before the wrong person does. Trust me; this is mutually beneficial. I can order you if I must, Isabella, but I'd much rather have you come along willingly."

I swallowed hard as I heard her words echo inside my head. There was definitely a connection there, but I was beginning to wonder how strong it really was. Could she really order me around, or was that just a ruse? "What would happen if I shut this door and walked away?"

She tsked and leaned toward me, tapping her lacquered nails on the door frame. "That wouldn't be a very wise idea, for your brother or your werewolf friends."

I wondered how far away the rest of the pack was. If I stalled long enough would they arrive to save the day? Another howl ripped through the night and I shuddered at the sound, thinking how much it sounded like an animal in pain. Someone was being hurt right now. "What exactly do you want me for?"

She smiled widely, showing brilliant white teeth, complete with two sharp fangs on the top row. "I need your help reaching Justin. I know generally where he is, but I can't access him. You help me, and I help you."

"What do you want with Justin?"

"He has something that I want," she replied, shrugging as though it was inconsequential. "I have no plans to hurt you, or your brother. I can actually help you, if you'll let me."

Help me with what, I wondered. I was chewing my bottom lip, actually debating on going with her. I was desperate to find Justin, and I knew when I'd attempted to contact her earlier that it was probably a bad idea. Okay, it was definitely a bad idea, but did I have a choice?

"If I go with you…" I began.

She held up a hand, cutting me off. "My boys will back off and leave your little werewolf friends alone. I will not harm you or your brother. I promise."

I wondered how much I could trust a vampire with a promise. Probably not at all, but it was already too late. I had already made the decision that I would do anything for my brother, even if it meant putting my trust in a creature of evil. I closed the door behind me and followed the vampire into the night, with the echo of wolf howls ringing in my ears.

Chapter 12

Patricia drove a large black Hummer. I was completely surprised when she led me to the Hummer parked in the driveway of Jed's house. I pictured her as the fancy red sports car type of woman, not the big tank sort. I climbed in the passenger side, buckling in as she turned the truck around and sped down the driveway with the headlights still off. A mile down the road she finally flipped the lights on and pulled out a cell phone.

"Call the boys back," she said simply into the phone. She listened briefly to the voice on the other line, then dropped the phone back onto the seat and turned to me. She didn't look very happy. "Your wolf friends are all fine, but they killed Roberto."

I didn't know who Roberto was, and I didn't care. One less vampire in the world was fine by me, but I wasn't going to say that to her face. I may be acting foolishly, but I didn't have a death wish. "So where is my brother?"

"Somewhere near Walla Walla," she said frankly.

We sped down winding roads, the Hummer handling better than I expected. I saw no signs indicating where we were, but I kept an eye out so I could find my way back. We eventually merged onto I-84 heading east towards Walla Walla, and the Hummer roared as speeds reached into the 90's. Patricia seemed relaxed, leaning back in her seat as she drove with one hand casually draped over the steering wheel.

After a couple hours of driving, Patricia pulled off to get gas and I took the opportunity to get out and stretch my legs. The clock on the dash said it was almost midnight, but there were still quite a few people on the road. A bleary-eyed gas attendant came out to pump the gas. Patricia chatted with him while I wandered into the mini mart, browsing the snacks. I grabbed a variety of food and drinks and placed them on the counter before using the bathroom.

When I came out Patricia was paying for the gas and food and I wordlessly followed her back to the truck, my arms full of snacks. I sat back in the Hummer and pawed through the snacks, pulling out a bag of beef jerky. Patricia started the truck, but she only drove to the edge of the parking lot.

I felt her eyes on me as I gnawed on a particularly tough piece of jerky. "What?" I snapped, glancing at her.

"I'm thirsty," she said softly.

My heart sped up at her words and I purposely looked down and away from her face. I was pretty sure she wasn't talking about water. I took a couple deep breaths, and then grinned, putting on a brave face. I reached into the bag and pulled out a bottle of Coke, handing it to her. "Here you go," I said, daring to look at her.

She smiled and took the soda from my hand. I watched as she opened the bottle and took a long drink. "That's nice," she said softly. "I love the way the bubbles tickle my tongue."

I was staring at her with my mouth hanging open. Apparently vampires could drink things other than blood. I guess you do learn something new every day. I was still watching her in fascination when she reached out and grabbed my chin, pulling my face close to hers. I found myself staring straight into her eyes, which shifted and changed until they appeared as two dark black coals.

"I am going to drink from you, my dear, and you're going to let me. You're even going to like it," she said softly, her words echoing in my head. "You *want* to feed me, dear Isabella."

She moved her hands across my face, tilting my head to the side. I felt a sharp pain in my neck, like a pinprick, and then there was only pleasure. She was right; I did like it. I had no cares in the world except to please this beautiful creature. She needed what my body could provide her. I would replenish my blood, so why shouldn't I share it with her? She wouldn't hurt me anyway.

Time seemed to stand still while Patricia drank from my neck. With each pull of blood, I felt pure pleasure coarse through my body. I'd never felt anything like it. It was pure ecstasy. She finally stopped and ran her tongue across my neck, lapping up the blood. Then she bit her wrist and held it in front of my face. I was still wallowing in the pleasure as I stared at the blood pooling on her wrist. I knew she wanted me to drink it, and I wanted to please her. I took her hand in mine and leaned my face close to her wrist, but I couldn't do it.

I shook my head and pushed her hand away. "I don't drink blood," I muttered. Why was I saying that? She wanted me to drink, so I should just do it. I looked at the blood again, but it turned my stomach. Blood was not appealing.

Patricia made a sound in her throat and grabbed my chin, forcing me to look at her again. "You need to nourish yourself. You won't heal if you don't drink, my dear. Don't you want to please me?" she asked and I nodded my head eagerly. Of course I wanted to please her! "I want you to drink my blood. That would please me. Will you do it, for me?"

I nodded my head and she smiled, releasing my head and holding her wrist in front of me again. Without thought, I had my mouth around her wrist, sucking in the blood. It tasted salty on my tongue but I drank until she pulled her wrist away. She smiled at me and I smiled in return, wiping my mouth with the back of my hand. "Eat some food, dear, and make sure you drink some juice," she said.

I happily complied, digging through the bag and pulling out an orange juice I hadn't remembered buying. Patricia must have gotten it for me. How thoughtful of her. I drank the juice down quickly and munched on a candy bar as she drove us back out onto the highway. After some time I felt my eyes growing heavy and I curled up in my seat. I didn't have a care in the world as I drifted off to sleep.

The man of gold and fire was waiting for me in my dreams, seated upon a lavish throne made of crushed red velvet and dark wood. He wore dark wash denim jeans and nothing else. His bare feet were spread before him on a thick bearskin rug that still had the bear's head attached. I stood at the edge of that rug, my bare feet tickling the edge of the fur.

"Well, well, well," he said, and I started at the sound of his voice. He'd never spoken in my previous dreams. His voice was deep with an odd European accent that I couldn't place. I wasn't sure if it was Scandinavian, German, or something completely different. "Patricia sure has taken a liking to you, hasn't she?"

I felt my heart flutter in a panic as I thought of Patricia. She wouldn't like me talking to this man. I turned away, meaning to leave, but there was nowhere to go. The room we were in was circular, with no doors or windows. Light was coming from somewhere overhead, but when I looked up all I saw were stars twinkling high above. This is a dream, I reminded myself.

"You can't leave until I let you go," he said and I turned back, my blonde hair whipping my face.

I looked down at myself, taking in the blonde hair and the pale blue see through gown I wore. I imagined I was wearing jeans and a t-shirt, and within seconds my clothing changed to reflect my thoughts. That's better, I thought, running a hand across my clothes before I looked back up at the man.

He was smiling at me as though I amused him deeply. A plush chair appeared before him and he beckoned me to sit down. "Please," he said softly.

I crossed my arms, but decided it wouldn't hurt to comply. I moved to the chair and sat down. He angled his body, relaxing back in his throne and casually draping one leg over the arm of the chair.

"Patricia is certainly pushing her limits," he said conversationally. "Did you willingly drink her blood?"

"She asked me to," I responded automatically.

"Did she?" he asked, raising his eyebrows. "Was this before or after she drank your blood?"

"What does that matter?"

"Humor me."

I shrugged, not sure why he was asking me all these questions. "After," I responded.

He smiled and nodded, though I was sure he knew the answer before he asked. "She's trying to control you. Did you know that?"

I immediately shook my head. "She wouldn't do that."

He laughed, but there was no humor in it. "Oh, yes she would. At first, I knew something was strange about our connection, but it wasn't until just moments ago that I realized what it was. Patricia has been giving you her blood, and biting you. She's a bold one." I was shaking my head as he spoke. "She's addled your thoughts. Let me help you think more clearly."

"I don't think that's a good idea," I responded immediately. Did he think I would trust him? I didn't even know who he was.

He leaned forward, suddenly holding out a mirror to me. I frowned, but took the mirror from him and held it up to my face. My reflection seemed as it usually did, except with my former blonde hair. I suppose I still thought of myself as a blonde in my dreams. I ran a hand through my hair and turned my head to the side. That's when I noticed the blood on my neck. I ran my hand over my neck, feeling the two holes in my skin. Blood seeped down my neck, and I realized it had been pouring across my shoulder and down my shirt, soaking it quickly in blood.

The man was suddenly standing before me, lowering the mirror so I was staring at his muscular body. "Who are you?" I asked, staring up at his chest.

The muscles in his stomach contracted and flexed with his

laughter. "Donovan, Henri Donovan," he replied in a very good James Bond impression. "And you are?"

I smiled in spite of myself and looked up at his face. He was incredibly handsome, with piercing blue eyes. "Isabella," I said softly.

He brushed his blond hair back out of his face as he looked down at me, a smile playing at his lips. "You're not like the others," he muttered. He seemed pleased, but I had no idea why.

I was holding my hand to my neck still, trying to stop the bleeding. This was a dream, but I couldn't seem to stop the flow of blood no matter how much I concentrated on trying to stop it. Henri reached out and pulled my hand away from my neck, examining the puncture marks. Blood flowed faster and I realized my top was now completely soaked. I closed my eyes and tried to imagine myself wearing a new, dry shirt. When I opened my eyes I was indeed wearing a different t-shirt, purple this time, but it was already soaked with blood.

"Patricia is trying to gain control of you, but she's not powerful enough, so she will continue to drink your blood until you are dead. Listen carefully to me," he said as he leaned toward me. "I will give you the power to resist her, but you must do as I say. Do not drink her blood again. Do not tell her of our encounter. And if the opportunity presents itself, kill her."

I shuddered at his words, wondering why I would do such a thing to my Patricia. Patricia only wanted the best for me. Yes, Patricia loved me. She cared for me. I would be safe with her and no one else.

"No you will not be safe with her," Henri growled, and I realized I had been speaking aloud.

"Why do you care?" I asked slowly, my thoughts coming slowly. "Patricia loves me."

"I *don't* care, but neither does she."

No, that wasn't true. My Patricia would care for me and take care of me. She would help me find my brother. I must not listen to this man. I felt Patricia's voice in my mind, whispering soothing words to me. Yes, my Patricia loved me and would take care of me forever. Yes, forever.

"Look at me!" Henri roared, and my eyes jerked up to his face. I felt the blood flow faster down my neck and I was growing quickly light-headed. "You will die! Is that what you want?" I shook my head automatically. Of course I didn't want to die. Why was he asking such a question?

He nodded his head and in the blink of an eye he pressed his mouth against my neck, drinking deeply from the blood that poured freely down my neck. I felt faint, as though I was going to pass out. How was that possible, if this was a dream? Henri licked my neck, sending a shiver of pleasure down my spine. He held his bleeding wrist in front of my face, urging me to drink without saying a word. The room was growing dark and suddenly I knew that I was dying. His blood would save me from death. I grasped his wrist and drank the blood, wondering briefly if I was damning myself.

I woke with a jerk, grasping my neck in a panic. The sky was still dark and I was still in the Hummer, but it was no longer moving. Patricia was leaning over me, her chin dripping blood. I scooted away from her, backing into the door of the truck. Wet blood covered the front of my shirt and the memory of my dream was quickly coming back to me. "Do not tell her of our encounter," Henri's voice echoed in my mind.

"Who was it?" Patricia asked, her voice dripping with menace. She grabbed my face, forcing me to look into her pitch black eyes. "I know there is another. Tell me who! Who was in your dream? Answer me truthfully."

I felt a tug at my mind and felt the urge to answer her, to tell her everything, but I managed to bite back the answer. "What?" I squeaked out.

She leaned away from me, frowning. "Who was in your dream?"

I shook my head and frowned back at her. "I don't remember any dream," I lied, the words coming swiftly from my lips. I felt as though I had been in a fog and it was suddenly clearing. "What happened to my shirt?"

"Don't worry about that, dear," she responded, smiling as she brushed a hand across my cheek. I fought the urge to pull away from her, knowing that I needed to play along. I had a feeling that my life depended on it. "Go get cleaned up in the bathroom," she ordered.

I opened the door to the Hummer and walked toward the bathrooms. We were in a rest area and the only sound was that of a semi-truck idling nearby. I walked into the bathroom and winced at the fluorescent lights. I hurriedly emptied my bladder before moving to the sink to clean myself up. I was pale and almost green looking, with blood drying my neck and shoulder. How close to death had I been?

I was pulling the sweater off over my head when Patricia walked in behind me. Her face was clean of blood and her eyes were once more a normal brown color. A clean black shirt was draped over one arm. She took the blood-soaked sweater from my hands, and I pulled off the camisole as well and handed it to her. I washed quickly in the sink, using paper towels to get all the dried blood off my skin before putting the clean shirt on.

I tried not to look too closely at myself with Patricia staring at me, but I did notice two sets of bite marks on my neck. There were four holes in my neck! I was not happy about that at all, but I pretended there was nothing wrong, smiling happily at Patricia in the mirror. Patricia patted me on the head as though I was a pet, and ushered me back to the Hummer.

I climbed in and waited for Patricia to start the truck. The clock on the dash said it was a quarter after four in the morning. "Where are we?" I asked as we pulled out onto the road.

"Eastern Washington," she responded.

"I thought my brother was in Walla Walla."

She shook her head, but her eyes remained on the road. "No, I said your brother was *near* Walla Walla. We drove through Walla Walla over an hour ago. We're close to him now though. I can feel it."

I didn't respond to her comment, but it bugged me. What did that mean that she could feel it? Had she fed off my brother as well? Considering what she'd done to me, I could hardly be surprised. Jed had warned me not to trust vampires, and what did I do? I got in a vehicle with the first vampire I met. Then I let her bite me. Stupid, I thought, very stupid.

My thoughts drifted to my brother. I wondered what Patricia wanted from him. I knew she wasn't going to tell me, so I'd just have to wait until I saw Justin and ask him myself. The Hummer slowed down and I peered out into the darkness, but all I saw were what looked like fields. Patricia suddenly veered off the road and I had to grab the door handle to steady myself. She slowed the truck as we skidded down a stretch of gravel road, bouncing with the many potholes. There didn't seem to be markers of any kind indicating where we were.

After about ten minutes of driving Patricia veered the truck off the road, her headlights illuminating nothing but dead grass. We bounced over rocks and uneven ground and my seatbelt jerked tight around me. Several minutes later she pulled the Hummer to a stop in front of an old rundown farmhouse. A barn stood several feet from the house, half its roof caved in. Weeds and bushes were growing up through the dilapidated porch of the house and it looked like no one had lived there in quite some time.

Patricia turned off the engine and sat tapping her fingernails on the steering wheel. She looked at me thoughtfully and reached into the back seat, pulling out a thick black vest. She tossed the vest into my lap and I grunted with the weight of it. I undid my seatbelt and hefted the vest, looking at it closely in the dim light the headlights provided.

"Is this what I think it is?" I asked as I pulled the vest around my shoulders and began cinching it together.

"Kevlar," she replied simply.

As soon as I had the vest on, Patricia handed me a black duffel bag. I unzipped it and reached into the bag. I pulled the first item out and felt my heart thud faster in my chest. "Why do I need a gun and a bullet proof vest?" I asked.

"I sense your brother is near, but he's not alone. This is just a precaution," she replied, before turning to face me fully, her eyes going black. "You will not shoot me or harm me in any way. You will guard me with your life. You will attack only on my command. Do you understand?"

I nodded, feeling a strange pressure on my head. I had a bizarre urge to strap the gun to my side and jump in front of bullets to protect Patricia. No, I wasn't going to do that. I am my own person. I control me, no one else. I swallowed hard and put the gun holster on across my shoulders, feeling odd as I placed the gun under my arm. I had shot a few guns, but I wasn't very comfortable with them.

I reached back into the bag and pulled out the last item, a long knife. The knife was in a leather holster of some kind that had long ties coming off it. "It's a blessed knife," Patricia said as I examined the rough leather-bound handle and slowly pulled the knife out of its holster. "It's very old, and also very sharp. Strap it to your leg and do not remove it unless my life is in danger."

I slid the knife back into the holster and held the knife against my right leg, wrapping the ties around my thigh and cinching them tight. What were we getting into that I needed a knife, a gun and a bulletproof vest? I glanced over at Patricia, who was staring out into the night. I looked where she was looking, but I could see nothing beyond the glow of our headlights.

Patricia flipped off the headlights and I blinked at the sudden darkness. "Let's go find your brother, dear," she said softly as she jumped out of the Hummer.

I followed suit a moment later, quietly shutting the door

behind me. I glanced around nervously, wondering if I should be carrying the gun in my hand or leave it in the holster. I'd never imagined myself in such a situation. Patricia's precautions were making me nervous, and I shivered involuntarily. I had a very bad feeling about this.

Chapter 13

Patricia walked toward the farmhouse and I scurried behind her. She'd gone to the effort to put a vest on me, so I guessed Patricia wanted to keep me alive, for now. Of course, she'd also ordered me to protect her with my life, so maybe she just wanted me to stay alive long enough for her to get out. No matter, Patricia was a vampire and could likely handle whatever it was that might be out here.

I shivered again as a cold chill ran up my spine and Patricia stopped in her tracks, turning to look behind me. I felt a hand on my shoulder and I whipped around, stumbling back into Patricia. Two men stood side by side, smiling widely to show off their sharp fangs. I stared at the men for several seconds, realizing I recognized one of them.

"Jin?" I asked the shorter man. "Jin Hao?"

He turned his black eyes to me, and smiled suddenly in recognition. "Izzy, it's so good to see you. Your brother has been worried sick about you."

"Justin? Where is he?" I asked, scanning the area nervously.

"Oh, he's off with Sarah. You know how those two are," he replied with a grin.

Justin said Sarah was gone, which I had figured meant dead. I glanced at Patricia, wondering if she could shed light on what was happening, but she had her eyes focused solely on the two vampires. I turned my attention back to them as I slowly backed up. "So Justin is around here?"

"He's close. We can take you to him," Jin replied as he took a step toward me.

Patricia took a step forward and pushed me behind her. "You're not taking her anywhere. Who are you working for?" Patricia asked.

Jin glanced at the other man, who stood still with his arms crossed. The other man looked military, with a short buzz cut and black cargo pants. He also carried a gun in a holster similar to mine. Unlike me, this guy probably knew how to use his gun. Not that he needed it, being a vampire.

"We work for NuvaDrug," Jin replied with a shrug. "Mitch here works security. Izzy can tell you all about it. I'm a researcher working with Justin. He and I are in the middle of a very important project, but that's strictly classified."

Patricia shook her head in front of me. I was pretty sure she was looking for a different answer. "Let us try again, shall we? Who *made* you?"

Jin frowned thoughtfully, stroking his chin as though he was in serious thought. "Well, that's quite the philosophical question. I don't know if we have time to answer that before the sun comes up. I suppose it depends on your personal beliefs. Do you believe in God?"

"That is not what I'm asking, and you know it," Patricia snapped. I took an extra step backward. I didn't want to be anywhere near an angry vampire. "What vampire turned you?" she asked, biting off each word.

"Oh, that's what you want to know. Sorry, but I'm not allowed to say. I don't believe you're on the approved list. I'll have to check. What was your name?"

"I am Patricia Von Deeten, and even a newbie such as you should know my name."

Mitch flinched visibly at Patricia's words and cast a worried glance at Jin. Obviously Mitch had heard of Patricia, and by the way he was fingering the butt of his gun, I guessed it was not favorable. Jin was smiling and flipping an imaginary notepad in his hands, seeming oblivious to Mitch's concerned looks.

He ran a finger down his palm and then shook his head. "Sorry, there's no Patricia Von Deeten on my list," he replied, still staring at his hand. He closed his imaginary notepad and smiled back at Patricia. "I'll have to ask my supervisor."

"Who is your supervisor?" Patricia asked sweetly.

"Sarah, of course," he replied, pulling out a cell phone.

"Jin was the lead researcher," I whispered under my breath to Patricia, hoping she'd hear me and the other vampires would not. "He was in charge of all the others, including Sarah and Justin."

"Vampire hierarchy trumps human," she replied softly without turning to look at me.

Jin wandered off, talking animatedly into the cell phone. I stared at Mitch, trying to place him. I knew most of the people Justin worked with, but I didn't remember meeting him. The only members of security for NuvaDrug I had met were Kirk and Jared, but they had been friends of Justin's before joining the company. Most of the other people I had met were researchers, or students finishing up their PhDs, like Sarah had been.

"Where's Justin?" I whispered back to Patricia.

There were no lights on in the house behind us, but that didn't mean he wasn't in there. "He's somewhere behind us," she replied, glancing over her shoulder at me. "He's been moving steadily away from us."

Why was Justin moving away from us? I turned with the intention of going after Justin, but Patricia put a restraining hand on my arm. "He's moving too fast for you to catch up. Do not worry so much, my dear. We will find him."

I turned back around, watching Jin impatiently. Patricia seemed calm and relaxed, but I was on edge. The sky was beginning to lighten and I wondered what the vampires were going to do when the sun rose. Jin finally got off the phone and stuffed it into his pocket. With each passing moment I was able to see more details as the early pre-dawn light illuminated the sky. Jin looked yellow to me, almost jaundiced. His eyes were two black spheres and his lips were gray. Mitch looked pretty much normal to me, except for slightly paler than usual skin, black eyes, and of course a nice set of fangs.

"Well, I spoke with the boss," Jin said as he bounced back to us. "Sarah wants Izzy here alive, but she said she didn't care if you lived or died."

Patricia nodded her head as though she had expected it. I backed up a couple more steps, wanting to put some space between me and the vampires. "Isabella, come back here," Patricia ordered.

I stopped in my tracks, feeling that strange tug at my brain. My left foot took a step forward and I silently cursed under my breath. I could feel her power moving me forward, but I was aware of it. Whatever had happened with Henri Donovan in my dream had given me a measure of control against the vampire influence, but it wasn't perfect. My feet slowly shuffled forward of their own volition, moving up beside Patricia. Damn, this wasn't good. Patricia was going to use me as a shield, I just knew it.

I had barely reached Patricia when I felt a gust of wind as Jin and Mitch suddenly moved. I'd never seen anything like it. It was like watching two tornadoes collide. There was a swirl of dust and a blur of colors as all three vampires moved. Mitch was suddenly beside me, pulling me back toward the house. I stumbled backward, my eyes transfixed on the sight before me as Mitch tugged me behind him. He dropped me onto the porch of the house and pulled out his gun.

All I could see were streaks of red from Patricia's sweater, mixed with streaks of black from Jin's clothes. Jin suddenly went flying through the air, crashing into the house beside us. Patricia stalked toward him at a normal pace, looking perfect as usual. Gun shots rang in my ears, and I ducked down, putting my hands over my head as Mitch emptied his clip beside me. I cautiously peeked up when the gunfire stopped.

Patricia was littered with bullet holes and blood oozed from her chest, leaving dark streaks on her vibrant red sweater. She glared at Mitch in annoyance, but was quickly distracted when Jin leaped at her. She moved quickly, flinging him through the air once more to land several feet from the Hummer. Mitch had already put another clip in his gun and began firing rounds into Patricia once more.

Ignoring Mitch, Patricia sped after Jin once more. Jin bounced to his feet, took a quick look at Patricia and then sped straight toward me. The wind was knocked out of me as Jin rammed his body into mine. He had one arm around my waist as he dragged me past the house at an intense speed. My eyes began to water as my hair whipped into my eyes. I couldn't see where he was taking me, but I could see a blur of red and another blur of black following behind us.

The red blur suddenly overtook us and I was catapulted out of Jin's grasp, flailing my arms frantically to no avail. The ground was suddenly before me and I braced my arms out instinctively. There was a loud snap as I hit the ground, but I felt nothing as I scrambled to my feet and began running back toward the house and the Hummer.

We had run quite a ways, but the adrenaline coursing through my body spurred me on at speeds I was usually incapable of. The dilapidated back of the house was in view and I made a beeline toward it, stumbling over rocks. I crawled up the back steps and pulled the door open, glancing behind me briefly. I couldn't see any of the vampires, so I slammed the door behind me and sagged to the floor in relief.

As the adrenaline left me quickly, I began to feel the pain. It was primarily in my right arm, but I could feel aches all over. I looked down at myself, assessing my injuries. Dirt covered my pants and there was a hole in one knee, with a bit of drying blood on it. The pain in my legs was quickly dissipating, but the pain in my arm was growing more intense.

My right wrist throbbed and there seemed to be an extra bend in my arm below the elbow. I gingerly touched my arm, wincing in pain. There was considerable bruising, but most of it was already beginning to fade as my body healed. All that vampire blood must have been healing my body extremely quickly.

I sat back and closed my eyes while I waited for my body to heal. After a few minutes I looked at my arm again. The bone wasn't miraculously straightening out, but all the other smaller wounds were healing. Cuts and scrapes were now completely gone, leaving streaks of dried blood. I took a deep breath, knowing what must be done. I had to set the break so it would heal properly. I grabbed my arm and attempted to put my bone back in alignment, but all my attempts were futile. I didn't know what I was doing and I was just a human. Even though I may have vampire blood coursing through my body, I wasn't full of vampire strength.

Tears coursed down my face as I attempted again and again to realign my broken arm to no avail. Every time I attempted it, the pain would intensify. I picked myself up off the floor and started pacing around the house, unsure what to do. The pain in my arm was unbearable, but I obviously wasn't going to be able to do anything about it. For now I just needed to get my mind off the pain in my arm.

I had run to the house instead of the Hummer for one reason: Justin. If Justin had been in this house, then maybe there were clues as to where he went. I went from room to room, searching. The house appeared to have been vacant for a long time and had little to no remaining furniture. One bedroom had a bed with rumpled sheets thrown on it, and a makeshift bed made on the floor. I searched through the room, but came up empty-handed.

The quick search through the whole house was futile. I made my way to the front door and pulled it open slowly, revealing a stream of sunlight. I walked onto the porch and blinked in the early morning light before making my way to the Hummer. Climbing in the truck was a chore with my broken arm, but I managed to pull myself with minimal added pain. I adjusted the seat and reached for the ignition, but there was no key. What had Patricia done with the key? I didn't remember her taking it. I rifled through the truck looking for the key, but came up empty-handed. Damn it! I got out of the truck and began walking toward the barn. I'd already scoured the house, so I may as well search the barn too.

I wondered what had happened to the vampires. According to the werewolves, sunlight would kill a vampire and the sun was shining down brightly now. I entered the barn cautiously, staying away from the section of roof that had caved in. The barn still had hay bales stacked along one wall, although from the smell of mildew they appeared to have been there for some time. I walked around the hay bales and stopped in my tracks.

Mitch was sitting on the ground wedged between stacks of hay bales. Several boards were over his head, protecting him from any sunlight that might make its way through the broken barn roof. His eyes were closed and he didn't appear to be moving. I glanced around the rest of the barn and spotted Patricia on the far side. She was sitting down in a dark corner of the barn, watching me. A beam of sunlight bathed the center of the barn, separating me from the vampires.

I cautiously took two steps forward until I was directly in the light, unsure what to do next. The vampires seemed trapped by the sunlight and I figured I was probably safe for the moment. I glanced at Mitch again, but he seemed to be asleep. Patricia, on the other hand, was very much awake.

"Come here, my dear," Patricia said sweetly.

I felt the tug on my mind and involuntarily took a step forward. I shook my head as I tried to fight her off, even as my other foot moved forward a step. I needed a distraction before I got out of the sunlight. "What's with him?" I asked, pointing at the other vampire.

"So young," Patricia replied sweetly.

I paused, still in the ring of light. "What does that mean?"

She shrugged, ignoring my question. "Come to me, Isabella." Her words tugged at my brain and my right foot moved forward again. I never should have looked in the barn. What was she going to do to me?

"Where's Jin?" I asked, trying to distract myself from moving closer to her. It seemed to be working. I was able to pause when I thought of other things, but the moment I let go of those thoughts I moved forward again.

She shrugged again, a simple lifting of her shoulders. "He took off. He may have another place he can hide from the sun. Or, perhaps he burned up. Who knows?"

I desperately didn't want to go to her, but my feet moved once more against my will. While unable to control my body when she commanded, I at least retained my own thoughts. I remembered my thoughts of reverence for Patricia and how I had idolized her. It may have been brief, but I absolutely did not want to repeat that.

"You're fighting me," she said suddenly, her voice angry. "How are you fighting me?"

My heart began thudding in my chest as I remembered the warning Henri had given me in my dream. I must not let her know anything had happened. She already suspected someone had been in my dreams. I needed to distract her. I took another step forward, thinking fast. "My arm," I said suddenly, pointing at the unnatural bend between my elbow and wrist.

Patricia's eyes transfixed on my arm and her face relaxed. "Oh no, you're injured," she said sweetly, her voice dripping with compassion. "Let me fix that for you, my dear."

I had already walked across most of the barn at a slow but steady pace, trying to keep to the sunlight. I stopped just in front of her in the last ray of sunlight glinting through the broken roof of the barn. She moved quicker than I could see, so she was suddenly standing in front of me. Her arms were out to her sides in a welcoming gesture. I took a deep breath and took the last steps into the darkness.

Patricia grasped my broken arm in her hands as soon as I was out of the sunlight, and with a quick movement realigned the break. I screamed out as pain coursed through my body. Patricia let go of my arm and I stumbled back into the sunlight before dropping to my knees, cradling my arm to my chest. I felt drained and exhausted. The room was spinning round, and I felt a wave of nausea tear through my stomach. I curled into a ball on the dirt floor of the barn, resting my forehead on the cool ground as darkness overtook me.

Chapter 14

I'm not sure how long I was unconscious for, but the sun had gained more ground inside the barn when I finally woke. I slowly sat up and wiped the dust off my face. I moved my right arm cautiously, marveling at how perfect it looked. There was no longer any pain, or even a sign that it had been broken. I used my arms to lever myself up to a standing position, thankful for a vampire fixing my arm. Of course it was because of a vampire that my arm had broken in the first place.

I looked over at the vampire in question. Patricia was still in the same general location, but was now lying under a tarp with her eyes closed. Her chest wasn't moving, but I had no idea if vampires actually breathed or not. I glanced around, noting that the other vampire was exactly as he had appeared when I had entered the barn. Was he asleep? I quietly backed away from Patricia, hoping I wouldn't wake her.

When I had made my way out of the barn I breathed a sigh of relief. None of the vampires had stirred in the slightest. Perhaps they were down for the day. I felt my neck, making sure I hadn't been snacked on while I'd been out. I didn't feel any new marks, so I guessed I'd been okay since I'd been in the sunlight. I also hadn't been visited in my sleep by any vamps, so I took that as a good sign as well.

Now what should I do? I could go back into the barn and

search Patricia for the keys to the Hummer. What if she wasn't really out? What if she was only sleeping, and the moment I got out of the sunlight and into the darkness she'd grab me? I didn't want to be under the power of the vampire again, but she was also my key to finding Justin. I debated briefly, but it wasn't worth the risk. Patricia still had enough control over me as it was and I didn't want to give her the chance to gain more.

I only knew the general direction Justin had gone, but what were my options? I could wait for night and the vampires to wake up, or I could go try and find my brother on my own, on foot. Neither was a good option, but I didn't think there was really much of a decision.

I hurried back to the Hummer and did a thorough search for supplies. I grabbed the small duffel bag and loaded it with the snacks and drinks that I had left. The Kevlar vest was heavy to wear, but I decided to leave it on anyway. Better to be safe I supposed, even though it would only prevent bullets. I also left the gun and knife in place, not that they'd do me any good. My instincts always told me to run, but the gun would at least make people think twice before messing with me. That was my hope anyway.

I looped the duffel bag around my shoulders and carried it slung across my back. I marched quickly around the house and the barn, heading in the direction Jin had been dragging me and Patricia had indicated my brother was travelling. I hiked through a field until I came to a forested area with thick blackberry bushes making the way nearly impassable. I found a narrow animal trail and made my way through, my clothes getting caught repeatedly on the blackberry thorns. The berries had died already, so I didn't have any to munch on as I pushed my way through.

Trees that had been sparse before began to thicken, and I soon found myself in an old forest. I glanced behind me, but could no longer see the house or the barn. I had attempted to travel in a straight line, but the trails had twisted and turned already numerous times and I wondered if I was going the right way. Justin had taken me hiking with him numerous times, but he had always guided the way. He'd also always carried a GPS or a compass at the very least. I had nothing but an animal trail and a desire to find my brother before the vampires found me. That may have been good motivation, but it didn't improve my navigation skills any.

    I continued to wander on, stopping periodically to take a drink of water or nibble on the jerky and granola I still had in my bag. The sun had long since passed its midpoint in the sky when I finally came out on a dirt road. I wasn't sure if it was an actual road or a driveway, but it was a sign of civilization either way. A fence with a hotwire across the top ran along the far side of the road, barring entry into the vast field. I walked onto the road, looking at the tire tracks visible. The tracks looked clean and new to my eyes, and I took hope that they would lead me in the right direction.

    I stopped briefly to eat the last of my beef jerky and rest. I didn't have much food remaining in my bag, but the jerky helped stop the growling in my stomach. After finishing off the jerky I rifled through the bag, finding only a candy bar and a granola bar remaining. I took out the candy bar and ate that as I started walking down the road.

    Travel was much easier and quicker when I didn't have to zigzag through blackberry bushes or climb over downed trees. I followed the road up and down hills and around bends. I could see cows in the field to my right and the promise of humans urged me on faster. I topped another crest and came to a fork in the road. The left fork angled up into a dark, forested area, while the right fork ran along the edge of the fenced field. The tire tracks led into the forested area, but every instinct in me urged me to go right, toward what was surely civilization.

    Indecision shook me as I looked from one path to the other. Had I been a stronger or more confident person, I'd have surely taken the path to the left. But I was not confident. I was scared and confused and wanted nothing more than to see another human, and the large forest to the left was far too dark for my liking. I turned toward the right, following the well-kept road that ran along the field of cows. After what must have been only 15 minutes I began to smell smoke. I hurried down the road faster and spotted a small blue house in the distance, with a trail of smoke coming from the chimney.

I wanted to run to the house, but my exhausted body could only move at a quick walk. An old green pickup truck was parked beside the house and I had a moment of indecision as I walked up to the porch. I had just placed my foot on the first step of the porch when the front door opened and an old man walked out, holding a shotgun leveled at my chest.

"Please, don't shoot," I said, holding up my arms and backing down the step. Maybe I should have taken off the gun and vest before I got this close to the house. That probably would have been a smarter way to go. On the other hand, if he shot me at least I was wearing a bullet-proof vest.

The old man wore a tattered red flannel shirt, blue jeans complete with suspenders and mud-covered work boots. What remaining gray hair he had stuck up at odd angles and a pair of wire-rimmed glasses hung off the bridge of his overly large nose. He sized me up, holding the shotgun steady. A woman came up behind him, wearing a pale blue shirt covered with tiny white flowers. Her long graying brown hair hung in a braid over one shoulder. She smiled down at me and placed a hand on the old man's arm, lowering the shotgun to the ground.

I blew out a breath of relief and slowly lowered my arms, careful to make no sudden movements. "Who are you? What are you doing here?" the old man asked in a clipped tone.

"My name is Isabella. I'm looking for my brother," I replied. The sun was beginning to set and I felt a shiver of fear. The vampires would be out soon. "Has anyone come by recently?"

"This is all our property," he replied, pointing with the shotgun toward the field of cows. "No one comes here."

"I heard a truck last night," the woman said and the old man hushed her, turning around to whisper angrily at her.

The woman shook her head and pushed past the old man, stepping onto the porch. "Phil was asleep, but something had woken me up in the middle of the night. I got up to get a drink of water and I heard what sounded like a truck crashing. I looked outside and swear I saw headlights way off yonder," she replied, pointing back toward the fork in the road. "I figured maybe someone finally bought the old place up the road."

"There was no truck," the old man, Phil, stated. "I took a walk down there this morning, and didn't see nothing. No sign of any truck crash either. I tell you, you was dreaming, woman."

"So there's a house that way?" I asked, pointing back toward the fork in the road.

"The house is about two miles down the road, where it splits," the woman replied.

I turned to Phil. "Did you go down to the house?"

Phil shook his head. "No, I didn't go down to the house. And I don't suggest you do either. If your brother is missing you just march into town and go report it to the police. They can search the house. Probably it was just some young kids partying anyway."

"I'll take you to the house," the woman said, and Phil grabbed her arm.

"What's gotten into you, woman? You're not taking her to that house, and that's final. If she is fool enough to go, then that's her own problem."

"Isabella," I heard Patricia's voice in my head and I shivered suddenly. She was awake and the sun was almost set. I wondered how long it would take Patricia to find me. Hopefully she couldn't control me from a distance.

The woman spoke again and I turned my attention back to her. "I'll take you to the house."

"Damn it, Elsie, no!" Phil said again, yanking on the woman's arm. "Get back in the house."

Elsie shook off Phil's hand and smacked him hard across the face. I winced at the sound and backed up a couple more steps. Phil cautiously put a hand to his reddened cheek, his eyes wide in surprise. Elsie turned her back on him and walked down the porch steps to me. "I'll take you to the house," she said again.

Elsie walked over and climbed into the truck, starting it a moment later. I looked from the truck to Phil. Tears swam in the old man's eyes, and my heart ached for him. "Why don't you want her to take me to the house?" I asked softly.

He shook his head, turning away from me to wipe at his eyes. "If you want to go, go, but leave my wife out of it."

"Please, tell me why," I urged him again.

He turned back to me, the rim of his eyes red. "The place is haunted, if you believe those tales."

"You believe it's haunted?"

He shook his head, his eyes going back to the truck his wife sat in. "Strange things have been happening lately. Maybe it's haunted, maybe not. Probably it's just kids causing problems. Either way, we don't go there."

I shivered, my instincts telling me to listen to the old man. Elsie backed the truck up and pulled up beside me, rolling down the window. "Let's go," she said.

I took one last look at Phil before turning and climbing into the truck with Elsie. She drove off quickly, leaving a cloud of dust behind us. We quickly reached the fork in the road and Elsie turned the truck down the tree-lined path. We crested a hill and I saw the sun setting in the distance, painting the sky a beautiful red color as the last bright rays dipped below the horizon. The road dipped down and we were soon enveloped in darkness as the trees thickened on either side of the road. After a few minutes Elsie pulled the truck to a stop in front of an older large white house with lights on inside. Someone was definitely home.

A black Suburban was parked in front of the house next to a hot pink Corvette. I stared at the house, wondering what sort of people were inside. I turned to Elsie to thank her but she sat staring straight ahead. She hadn't said a word during the short ride here, and I was growing nervous.

"Elsie, do you know who's here?" I asked. Elsie continued to stare straight ahead, hardly blinking. I touched her arm, shaking her gently. "Elsie?"

Elsie's eyes closed and she slumped in her seat, breathing softly. I shook her arm, but she didn't wake up. I shook her again, saying her name over and over again to no avail. She snored softly. Maybe she was narcoleptic. After all the strange things that had been happening, I didn't believe it for a second.

I quietly opened the passenger door and ran around to the driver's side, pulling open the door. I pushed Elsie over onto the passenger side and climbed into the driver's seat. I reached over to pull the door closed behind me and stopped. Holding the truck door open was Sarah, my brother's old girlfriend.

Sarah smiled up at me, flashing fangs around her bright pink lips. Her blonde hair was big and wavy and she wore a hot pink dress and matching high-heels. The pink corvette suddenly made sense now. Pink had always been her color, and vampirism obviously hadn't changed that. It also hadn't changed her looks much, with the exception of making her paler than before. Sarah was as beautiful as ever, with a heart-shaped face and a perfect physique that made the guys drool and the girls envious.

"Oh, darlin' Izzy, so good to see you," Sarah said in a thick southern accent. "Please come in. We've been expecting you."

"What about her?" I asked, pointing at Elsie.

Sarah waved her arm and Jin was suddenly at her side. He grinned up at me and I couldn't help but stare at the blood at the corner of his mouth. "Jin will take Elsie home," Sarah said as she stepped back and indicated I should get out of the truck.

I deliberated briefly, but knew I couldn't do anything against one vampire, let alone two. I grabbed my duffle bag off the seat and slid out, jumping to the ground. "Don't hurt her," I said as Jin took my place in the driver's seat.

Jin giggled at my words and I looked back at Sarah. "Jin, do not touch the woman or harm her in any way. That is an order," Sarah said forcefully, glaring at Jin. "No biting."

"Or her husband," I added.

Sarah glanced at me briefly, irritation clear on her face before she turned back to Jin. "Do not harm her husband either, in any way. They are not food, Jin. Am I clear?"

Jin bobbed his head. "I understand. I won't touch them." He slammed the truck door shut and turned the truck around, heading back toward Phil and Elsie's house. I crossed my fingers, hoping the older couple would be all right, but helpless to do anything about it.

"Come into the house," Sarah said as she placed a hand on my arm. Her nails were filed into long pink-painted points that dug into my flesh, drawing a thin line of blood.

I let Sarah lead me to the house and she finally let go of my arm when she opened the door. I rubbed the spot on my arm that she had been holding, wiping away the blood that remained to see perfect unbroken skin once more. The front door opened into a living room that was lit with numerous candles. An older gray recliner with a pink blanket placed over the seat sat at the far end of the room, but that was the only furniture to be seen. Two men stood on either side of the recliner, looking very much like bodyguards in all black with hands crossed behind their backs and guns at their hips.

Sarah moved toward the recliner and sat down, smoothing the skirt of her dress. "Thomas, bring me my pets," Sarah called.

I stood by the front door, ready to bolt at any moment. Not that I could outrun vampires, but that didn't stop my instincts from looking for the first escape route. Two men wearing only hot pink boxer shorts shuffled in with their heads bowed, followed closely by another man wearing a tailored suit that looked like something out of a mobster movie. The man had slicked back black hair and an unlit cigar clenched between fangs.

I turned my attention back to the two men in boxers, noting the red welts across their backs and the telltale bite marks on their necks. Humans, I guessed. Their backs were to me as they knelt on the floor in front of Sarah, heads bowed and arms held out in front of them. One of the men had a cast on his arm that looked dirty and appeared to be covered in dried blood. The mobster vampire who I guessed was Thomas moved back to stand beside me, leaning casually against the wall.

Sarah's eyes flicked up to me so fast I wasn't sure if it actually happened. She leaned back dramatically and lifted her feet into the air. The man with the splint on his arm immediately shuffled forward and Sarah dropped her feet onto his back, using him as a foot stool. "Come here, pet," she said sweetly, motioning to the other man.

The other man stood stiffly and walked to Sarah, standing before her with his head down. From his posture I could guess he wasn't happy to be there. Sarah's eyes flicked to me again and I realized she was putting on a show for me. I was still unsure of what the purpose was though.

"Fido, make a chair for our guest," Sarah said, pointing at me.

The man turned to look at me, and I sucked in some air. I knew this man. His name was Jared Bushing and he was a friend of my brother's. He'd also been on the expedition with Justin as a guide and translator. He was ex-military and had always kept his hair cut short, but now it was grown out past his ears. I wasn't sure if he recognized me or not in the brief look he had given me before he dropped to his hands and knees beside Sarah's chair.

Sarah looked directly at me and pointed to the man on his hands and knees. "Sit down, Isabella." There was no mistaking it was an order and not a request.

I tentatively moved into the center of the room, stopping

when I reached Jared on his hands and knees. I glanced up at Sarah and the look on her face had me scurrying to perch on Jared's back. I tried not to rest my weight on him, but he was tall and I couldn't sit on his back fully and keep my feet still on the ground. Sarah made an angry growling noise and my head jerked up to look at her.

"Get up, Isabella," she instructed, and I happily complied. "Fido, position 12," she ordered.

Jared hurried to comply, re-arranging himself so he sat cross-legged on the ground with his arms out to his sides. Sarah pointed from me to him, indicating I should sit in his lap. I slowly sat down, with my legs spread out awkwardly in front of me. I wouldn't be able to get up easily from this position.

From this angle I was forced to look upward at Sarah, so she sat as though seated on a throne. She seemed to be making a show of getting comfortable, rearranging her feet on the other man's back. It took me a moment to realize why she was doing it. From this new angle so close to the floor, I could clearly see the other man's face. I knew the rough angles of his jaw, the small scar above his eyebrow, and the hazel eyes that looked at the ground.

Sarah obviously noticed my recognition and plastered a pleased smile across her face. "So, Isabella, what do you think of my pets? This here is Rover. Can you say hello to our guest, Rover?"

Rover, who Sarah was using as a footstool, wouldn't turn and look at me but he did mutter a quiet hello. My heart wrenched at the sound of his voice and I clenched my fists in anger. "Shh," Jared whispered behind me so quietly I wasn't sure I had heard it or not. His hand moved discreetly, squeezing my thigh in warning. I had started to stand up, but I really needed to calm down.

I took a deep breath and settled back against Jared before looking back up at Sarah. "I came for my brother," I said confidently.

Sarah sat up, moving her feet off her human pet's back and stroking his sandy brown hair lightly. "Oh, dear, I don't know if I can help you with that," she mused. "Your brother is involved in a very special project for our company. He's doing some very vital research. Jin was supposed to be in charge of it, but, well, his mind is not what it used to be. Perhaps we can come to an arrangement."

I felt Jared jerk at her words and I figured I wasn't going to like any arrangement Sarah devised. I still had the gun and knife, along with a bullet-proof vest on. No one had bothered to take them from me, but I supposed no one thought of me as any sort of threat. The sad part is they were probably right. My experience with guns was limited to .22s and my experience with knives was limited to the kitchen. Jared, on the other hand, definitely knew how to handle a gun.

"I'd like to speak with my brother," I replied, thinking fast. If Jared could somehow get my gun, maybe we'd have a chance to shoot our way out. Bullets hadn't seemed to slow Patricia down, but maybe they'd work on newer vampires.

At the thought of Patricia I felt a pressure in my head before I heard her voice. "Get out," she said.

"What about my brother?" I asked back in my head.

Sarah spoke, distracting me from my internal conversation with Patricia. "Your brother is out on a project, darlin'. I can take you to him, though," she drawled sweetly.

"Where is Justin?" I asked both Sarah and Patricia in my head.

Patricia's voice came back quickly, but she seemed distracted. "Not here," was her clipped response.

Sarah smiled at me; still petting the man she called Rover. "I had to send him away, but I can take you to him. Justin has been… petulant. I think having you near will help him concentrate more on his work."

"Help him concentrate?" I muttered, more to myself than to the vampire before me, but she responded nevertheless.

"I have tried numerous ways to motivate your brother, but he has been willful thus far. We figure you can be a good influence on him."

I caught the "we" reference and I had a feeling it didn't refer to her and Jin. My guess is it had to do with whoever was in control of this company she referred to earlier, whether it was still NuvaDrug or something else entirely. I looked around the room, wondering again how I could possibly escape. The mobster vampire still stood near the door, so I'd have to get past him to get out. But then what? Vampires were too fast to try and outrun.

The front door opened and Jin entered, bleeding from several wounds. "That Patricia woman attacked me. I hurt her and she took off," he said simply. Jin moved into the room, his black eyes turned toward me. "I need a drink."

My heart began pounding as I quickly realized he meant to drink from me. Jin moved forward, leaving a trail of blood on the carpeted floor behind him. "Get your own snack," Sarah snapped and Jin's eyes turned angrily on Sarah.

"I'm hungry and you already have your two pets! Let me have her!" he cried, stamping his foot on the ground.

Jared moved, wrapping his arms tightly around me as he scooted us backward and away from the vampires in front of us. Sarah continued to pet Rover, leaning back in her chair as though she had no care in the world. The two men on either side of her stepped forward though, pulling guns out simultaneously and aiming them at Jin.

Jin seemed oblivious to anything happening around him. He continued to stamp his foot and yell. "I'm hungry! I'm hungry! I'm hungry!"

"Jin, stop it now!" Sarah ordered, pointing a finger at Jin. He stopped yelling and pouted out his lower lip. He crossed his arms and I thought I saw a tear roll down his cheek. "Thomas will take you to get a snack, won't you Thomas?"

The gangster vamp moved from his spot by the front door, the unlit cigar still in his teeth. "I suppose I can take him into town," he replied, shrugging his shoulders. "Just don't blame me for the mess he's bound to make."

Sarah glared at Thomas and bared her fangs. A hiss escaped her lips and I shuddered as I watched her face contort with anger. Seeing this new side of Sarah made me realize all too quickly that she was not the same person I once knew. "You *will* keep him under control," she ordered of Thomas.

Thomas pulled the cigar out of his teeth and stepped up behind Jin, his eyes glued on Sarah. He was obviously not cowed by her look of rage. "You forget I don't work for you," he responded, pointing at Sarah with his cigar. "I'll take Jin to town, but you're responsible for him, not me."

Thomas put a hand on Jin's arm and led him out the door, while Sarah seethed angrily from her chair. Her two bodyguards returned the guns to their holsters and settled back in on either side of her chair. Sarah turned to face me and I shrunk back into Jared, not happy to be the focus of her anger. I watched her eyes turn black and felt a flutter of panic. I stared at her for a beat, wondering what I could possibly do. I shifted minutely and slowly reached for my gun.

Sarah moved faster than I could blink, ripping the gun from my hand before it had even cleared its holster. I heard the gun skid across the floor but I had no chance to go after it. In the blink of an eye she had hauled me up by my vest so that my feet dangled a good foot above the ground. She pulled me toward her, so my face was inches from her own. I stared at her mouth, not wanting to look into the black pits that her eyes had become. Suddenly I was flying through the air, flailing my arms in a desperate attempt to catch myself on something. I slammed into a wall, coughing as sheetrock rained down around me. The pain was immediate throughout my body, but not severe. I struggled to regain my footing as Sarah stalked toward me. I quickly blinked away the sheetrock dust and rolled out of the wall, but a second later I was being pulled up by my ankle and flung across the room once more. I instinctually covered my face with my hands before I flew into the opposite wall and crashed to the floor.

I was lying on the floor staring up at the ceiling as a pair of pink high-heeled shoes came into view. Sarah's yanked me up by my vest again and spun me around and around, my hair whipping into my face and stinging my eyes. My stomach churned and I felt like I was going to throw up. Before my stomach could heave, I was flying through the air once more. I watched the ceiling come quickly into view and I had just enough time to close my eyes and cover my face before I hit and burst through the ceiling.

The ceiling shattered around me and I dropped back to the floor just before the rest of the ceiling broke apart on top of me. I coughed and struggled to breathe, but each breath was pure pain. The room had grown dark and there was a loud ringing in my ears. I felt no pain, just lightheadedness as darkness began to descend rapidly.

In that moment I knew I was dying. My mother's face was above me, serene and smiling, softly caressing my face. Something grabbed my arm and I was flying, but I couldn't see anything. I felt an impact again and heard someone yelling, but spots danced before my eyes, obscuring my vision. The pain was gone now and I felt peace envelop me. I closed my eyes as I soared through the air once more. There were so many noises around me, but they were muffled and distant.

I shivered suddenly as darkness enveloped me and my last thoughts drifted to my brother. The peace that had been surrounding me was no longer a comfort, because I was a failure. My brother was still missing and being coerced by vampires. Would he survive? Was he being treated well, or being tortured? What would happen when the vampires were done with him? Would they make him a vampire as well, or just kill him? Either way, I had failed to save him. Would he know that I had tried? Did it matter since it had only resulted in failure? What was I, but a useless woman amidst the monsters of the world? I was useless, powerless. I was a failure.

Chapter 15

I opened my eyes, but all I saw was darkness. Was this the end? I was curled in a ball, lying on my side on something cold. I tried to sit up, but my feet hit a wall. I felt around with my hands, feeling only cold metal below and around me, like a cage. My heart began pounding as I struggled to move, but I was trapped and only able to get myself into a crouched sitting position.

I had died, and now I was being punished. There was nothing but the darkness and my small cage. Was this how I would spend eternity? Was this the punishment for my failure?

There was a sensation of movement and the cage rocked back and forth. It was too dark to see anything, but I could use my other senses. I ached all over. I tried to stretch and loosen my cramped muscles. Do the dead get cramped muscles? I was also freezing cold. I ran my hands across my body. My Kevlar vest was gone, as were my shoes and socks, but the rest of my clothes remained. The knife Patricia had given me was surprisingly still strapped to my side. Would I still have a blessed knife in the Underworld?

The cage bounced again, and I guessed I was in a vehicle of some kind. I could hear a low rumble that could be an engine of some kind, although it was distant sounding. My cage rested on more metal and I reached through the bars, feeling metal on one side of my cage and nothing but open air on the other sides. I moved my hands around the cage until I came to the door, feeling for a latch. I could feel the latch, but it wouldn't budge. Something clinked and I moved my hands up, feeling a thick chain around the cage as well. I trailed my hands around it until I came to a padlock.

Too bad I didn't have any bobby pins or paperclips to try and pick the lock with. Not that I knew how to pick a lock anyway. I fumbled at the sheath on my side, carefully pulling the knife out. I held the blade against the edge of the cage and attempted to swing my arm. I had little room to move and the blade did nothing but make a loud cling when it hit the cage. I sighed in frustration and sat back against the edge of the cage, trying to stretch my legs as far as possible. Probably the knife was useless and that's why I still had it. It was just another symbol of how pathetic I was. I put the knife carefully back in the sheath. Useless or not, the knife made me feel better.

"Damn it!" I muttered angrily, slamming my hand into the cage. "Damn, shit, damn, fucking piece of crap!" Again and again I slammed my fist into the cage, muttering obscenities under my breath with each punch. My fist hurt and I felt blood, but it quickly healed and dried on my knuckles. I punched the cage again, releasing my anger and frustration as tears began pouring down my face.

"Are you about done? Some of us are trying to sleep?"

I sniffled and wiped at the tears on my face. "Jared?"

"Yeah, it's me. Kirk is here too, in another cage. I must say, I'm surprised you're still alive with the way Sarah flung you all over the place," Jared's voice replied from somewhere to my left.

I wasn't sure if it was better to be alive and in this cage, or dead. The vampire blood I had drunk must still be prevalent in my system. That was the only explanation for me still being alive. "I've been dosed with a fair amount of vampire blood," was my muttered response.

"Really?" he asked, sounding surprised. "By who?"

"A vampire named Patricia. She's the one that Jin was talking about fighting with. I also got dosed with that vaccine." I ached, but it was mostly from being cramped and unable to change positions. I scooted my butt back into the corner of the cage and put my feet in the far opposite corner, and I still couldn't stretch out completely.

"Sarah made it clear that none of the vampires are to give us blood. None of us got the vaccine either." I heard shuffling and assumed Jared was trying to get comfortable in his own cage.

"That's strange. I thought the vampires were giving the vaccine to everyone." I pulled my knees to my chest and tucked the bottom of my jeans around my toes. It helped, but I still shivered from the cold.

"They're mass producing it for the general public, yes. We've been kept as Sarah's pets, and she said she doesn't want to use her powers to break us," Jared remarked angrily. "We aren't special enough to be rewarded with the healing effects of vampire blood." I looked toward his voice, straining to see anything in the darkness. He sounded angry, but I was glad he hadn't been given vampire blood. He was still his own person, for now.

"What about my brother?"

"I don't know," Jared replied. "We saw him every once in a while, but he was never allowed to talk to us. Sarah took care of him, though. She needs him for something, so I don't think he's been injured."

That was comforting news, for my brother at least. "How long have you been her...pet?"

Jared laughed, but it was humorless. "I've lost track of time. She wasn't always the one in control. When she first turned we had her contained, but she was growing stronger each day. Then one day she just disappeared." He stopped talking and cleared his throat loudly before continuing. "When she returned she had vampires with her, under her control, and we were helpless to stop her. I filled her body with bullets, but they did no good. It just made her angry. That's when she took over, and made us her pets. Jin was originally one of her pets too, but he broke too quickly. After that she turned him into a vampire."

"Jin does seem off," I remarked.

Jared laughed again. "He's a fruit cake! Something went wrong when she changed him. Maybe it was because he'd already gone nuts beforehand. Sarah's not the same person she was as a human, either. I'm sure you noticed that. She's cruel and power-hungry, and even the other vamps are scared of her."

I thought about that, and I had to wonder about the changes vampirism seemed to have. Sarah had been ambitious before but never cruel. And her love of pink seemed to have multiplied. Maybe being dead would be better. "Where's Kirk? I thought you said he was in here too?" I asked suddenly, looking around as though I might see him.

"Hey, Rover, wake up," Jared said suddenly.

"I'm awake," Kirk's voice responded quietly.

"Kirk, are you okay?" I asked.

I waited, but he didn't answer. "He only responds to Rover now," Jared commented. "Hey, Rover, Isabella is here. Do you remember her?"

"No," Kirk answered simply.

"Rover, you remember Isabella. She was your girlfriend. You used to talk about her nonstop."

"No," Kirk answered again.

I fought back tears that threatened to overwhelm me. My voice still came out strained. "Kirk, uh, Rover, don't you remember me?"

"You're Muffin," he responded.

"I'm what?"

Jared answered, and it sounded as though he was trying not to laugh. "Sarah had a hard time coming up with a name for you. It was a big debate between Muffin, Oreo, Cocoa and Pumpkin." He suddenly stopped chuckling, all humor gone. "I'd be concerned about her choice of name. She was convinced your new pet name had to be some sort of food."

Oh, great, she was going to use me for a snack. I pushed the thought away. "Kirk, please, you have to remember me. You're not a pet, you're a person. I'm Izzy and you're Kirk, not Rover."

"Master told us to sleep," Kirk responded simply and I heard shuffling from his direction. What had she done to him? This was not the man I remembered.

"He's gone Izzy," Jared whispered softly and I heard the pain in his voice. "You don't know what it's like. Not yet, anyway. She'll break you too, eventually."

I shook my head even though no one could see it. "She hasn't broken you," I replied.

He sighed loudly. "Almost," he said softly. "I'm glad you showed up when you did, although I'm sorry you're stuck here with us. I was close, Izzy, so close. It'd be easier to just give in instead of fighting her all the time. She's incredibly inventive in her methods of persuasion."

"She tortures you," I stated, remember the welts that marred his back.

"Sometimes," he responded. "Sometimes she gives pleasure, sometimes pain. You never know what's going to happen. She locked herself up with Jin for two weeks straight, and when he came out he was completely nuts. I don't know what she did to him, but I could hear his screams for days."

"What did she do to Kirk?" I asked, wanting to know and afraid to find out at the same time. Kirk had always been strong and arrogant even. I found it hard to wrap my mind around the way he was acting.

Jared was quiet for a long time, and I thought he wasn't going to answer. When he did speak, his voice was quiet and resigned. I wondered how much of him had given up already and how much fight he still had left in him. "Kirk fought a long time, Izzy. I hope you understand that. It wasn't like one day he was normal and the next he wasn't. It's all a game to Sarah. She has all these memories of her life as a human, and she used those memories to warp and twist things. She'd make up these stories about all of us, twisting them for her own purposes. She made us memorize them, so that we'd start to think they were reality. I don't know what's real and what she made up half the time. To top it off she only calls us by the names she gave us, and you are punished if you answer to your real name. And the punishments..." he trailed off and didn't say any more.

"I'm so sorry, Jared." It wasn't enough, but it was all I could say. There was obviously a lot more, but I didn't think Jared was in a place to talk about it. I'd heard enough for now anyway.

"We should sleep," he said, abruptly changing the subject. "Rest when you can, Izzy. Trust me on this."

I curled back up on the floor of my cage, still shivering from the cold. I cried again, softly this time so I didn't disturb Jared. But this time I cried not for myself, but for Kirk and Jared. I even cried for Jin and the torture he must have endured before going completely insane. Finally as my tears subsided I fell asleep.

I was thankful for my dream this time, because at least I was warm. I woke up on a soft bed, covered in thick blankets with a fire blazing from a giant hearth. The blond vampire, Henri, lounged in a chair beside the fire, watching me intently. He was dressed in only a pair of pink silk boxer shorts. I peeked under the blankets and rolled my eyes. I was wearing absolutely nothing. I quickly imagined myself wearing a pair of my favorite thick black sweats and a sweatshirt before I crawled out of bed.

"Nice shorts," I commented, pointing at the pink boxers.

He shrugged. "This is your dream. I am here because you wish me here, wearing what you wish me to wear."

I tried imagining him wearing jeans, but the pink boxers remained. "You're lying," I retorted.

He laughed as he leaned forward and casually rested his

elbows on his legs. "Am I?" he asked, his eyes crinkling with mirth.

"Yes," I responded adamantly.

Henri laughed again and stood up, moving close beside me. "Things have changed," he mused softly, trailing a hand across my cheek.

I backed away from him and moved toward the fire, relishing the warmth. Henri moved up beside me, mimicking my movements as I warmed my hands in front of the fire. I cast a sideways glance at him, but he stared straight at the fire. I shivered and imagined a thick blanket around my shoulders and a cup of hot chocolate in my hands. The items appeared and I sipped at my hot chocolate, but I still couldn't seem to get warm.

"It must be cold wherever your body is," Henri commented. "I'd love to warm you, but I can only do so much in a dream."

"Why is it that sometimes I sleep and it's just a normal night of sleep, and then other times you're here?" I asked, looking directly at Henri.

Henri smiled and turned toward me, his eyes a brilliant blue color that looked amazing with his pale golden hair. I'd never been this close to him and just admired his face. He smiled warmly at me, and the difference made him seem almost human. "We have a connection. You need me and here I am. You want me here."

I didn't want him here, did I? I shook my head. "I have a connection with Patricia too, but she doesn't invade my dreams constantly."

"Dreams are my realm. I have power here that others do not."

I shivered again and sipped at the hot chocolate. It tasted delicious, but I knew it was only illusion. "If you have power in dreams, can't you make me warm?"

"I could make you believe you're warm, but so could you. Your body is cold, so it reflects in your dreams because your mind is translating that information, making you shiver. If you wish to ignore it in your dream, then do so. Try it," he said softly.

I closed my eyes and imagined away the hot chocolate and the blanket. I removed everything from the room, including Henri. When I opened my eyes I was in a small cage in what looked like a cargo trailer. I had a moment of panic as I felt the walls of my cage. Then I noticed Henri standing in the trailer, looking down at me with a frown on his face.

"This is not what I meant," he said softly, looking around the trailer at the other two cages that contained sleeping forms of Jared and Kirk. "This is where you are?"

I nodded as I curled myself into a ball, shivering more than before. "It's completely dark though. I guess this is what I imagine it looks like."

"Well, this won't do at all," Henri muttered and suddenly I was lying on a beach with the hot sun scorching my skin.

I sat up and looked around, marveling at the white sandy beach that ran on for miles next to a brilliantly blue ocean. My skin looked sun-kissed already and I once again had my long blonde hair. I was wearing a very tiny teal bikini and was sitting in a lounge chair with a tropical drink of some kind in my hand. I glanced to my left and saw Henri lounging similarly to me, wearing a pair of tight teal swim shorts that left little to the imagination.

My eyes trailed across his defined chest and arm muscles. He smiled over at me smugly and took a sip of his drink before setting it down. "Isn't this better?" he asked, and I grinned in spite of myself.

"I have to admit it is definitely an improvement." I took a sip of the drink, letting the tropical flavors tingle over my tongue as the alcohol warmed me. "At some point I'm going to wake up though. You helped with the Patricia situation. Can you help me with this?"

"You're willingly asking me for help?" he laughed, his deep voice rumbling.

"Yes," I responded testily.

"Unfortunately my physical body is a considerable distance from your own, and our connection is not very strong. My ability to help is limited. Perhaps if you gave me some insight into your circumstance..." he trailed off, motioning to me.

"I'm being held by a vampire named Sarah Ellister. She has a penchant for pink and last I knew we were somewhere in southeastern Washington."

He raised an eyebrow at me. "I know the vampire you speak of. She's a recent addition, and not one of mine."

"What do you mean she's not one of yours?"

"She is not of my line." He shrugged. "I could contact her, but I do not know how she would respond. You would be better off with Patricia."

"I thought you didn't like Patricia."

He smiled humorlessly and shook his head. "Patricia has been disobedient of late, but if she is still in close proximity to you she may help. You need help in the physical form."

"What about my brother? Do you know where he is?"

"Who is your brother?"

"Justin Howerton," I replied.

I was watching Henri closely when I mentioned my brother's name, looking for a reaction. He looked directly at me and pursed his lips minutely. "That explains the interest in you. I had wondered before why Patricia chose to give you her blood, despite orders to the contrary."

"What do you mean? What orders?"

He waved off my question and stood up, walking toward the water. I set my drink down and hurried to catch up with him. The sun that had been bright overhead just moments before was now setting, painting the sky beautiful colors. We walked into the waves, letting the cool water lap over our feet. Henri stared out at the sea and I stood beside him, waiting and hoping for answers before I woke up.

"You are just a pawn in a vast game of chess," Henri said suddenly, startling me.

"And what are you?" I asked, looking at his handsome profile.

"I am a king, of course," he replied, looking at me directly now. "But in this game there are many kings, all fighting for control of the board and of the pieces. Your brother is just another piece, albeit an important one."

"Why is he so important?"

"Because," Henri replied softly, "he started this game."

I didn't know what to say. A thousand questions raced through my head, but I couldn't pick just one to ask. Henri moved suddenly, banishing all thought as his mouth met mine in a kiss that startled me with its intensity. His arms wrapped around my body, holding me to him as his tongue explored my mouth.

After several moments he finally stopped kissing me and moved his face back so he could look at me. "I will do what I can to help you, my dear Isabella, but you must help me in return."

"What could I possibly do to help you?"

"Oh, I'm sure I will think of something. Just know that you owe me," he said, and I felt a shiver of fear at his words.

"How will you help me?"

"I will give you strength, as I did before. And a small portion of my powers. Embrace the strength I give you, and it will help you survive. Then, when I call, you will come to me."

"I don't understand."

Henri shook his head. "You don't need to. Just trust me."

Trust a vampire again. Was I crazy? Henri was different though, I told myself. Of course, I hadn't met him in the real world yet. He seemed to want to help me, but he did ask for something in return, and that bothered me. "What am I going to owe you? I need to know before I agree to anything."

"You will die without my help, and still you waver in accepting." He laughed at that before turning his beautiful face toward mine. He leaned forward and kissed me again, and I found myself responding to his kisses eagerly. He pulled away and looked down at me with his piercing blue eyes. "I do not know precisely what

I will require of you in the future, but I promise it will not involve hurting or killing any humans. Does that help?"

"Add werewolves to that as well. And no sex! I'm not a prostitute."

He scoffed at that. "I would never treat you as such. When you give your body to me, it will be completely willingly."

"Werewolves?"

"I will not ask you to hurt or kill any werewolves either, Isabella. Anything of the sort you do will be your choice alone. Does that suffice?" I nodded and he smiled as though he had just won a great victory. "Now we share blood."

"But, this is just a dream."

"And I am the Master of Dreams," he responded just before he bit me.

The pain in my neck was sharp and immediate, but it quickly changed until I felt light and euphoric. It was as though I was floating without a care in the world. One of Henri's hands held my head tightly while his other trailed down my body, increasing the pleasure I felt from his bite with each caress. I felt as though I was teetering on the edge of a precipice and the slightest breeze would topple me over the side. There was no pain or worry, just a feeling of bliss.

Henri stopped drinking after just a few moments and kissed me lightly across my neck. I was still floating without a care in the world when he bit his wrist. Two small beads of blood had formed on his wrist and he held it before me, waiting for me to take it willingly. I grabbed his wrist, closed my eyes and licked his skin. I swallowed the salty taste of his blood and felt a rush to my head, as though I was drunk. Henri pressed his wrist close to my mouth, urging me to drink more.

I sucked at his wrist, coercing the blood to continue to flow into my mouth. Henri made a sound of pleasure and I opened my eyes to look at him. His eyes were open and staring at me like twin black coals and my blood had tinted his lips red. He gently pulled my hand away from his wrist and stole a quick kiss.

"Sleep, my dear, sleep," he said softly. My eyes grew heavy and I floated down into a peaceful, dreamless sleep.

Chapter 16

I was freezing again. I opened my eyes slowly, wondering what had woken me. We had stopped, I thought, noting the lack of movement immediately. The rumbling sound of the motor suddenly ceased and I squirmed around in my cage until I was in a sitting position. I heard the sound of metal scraping, and a door opened, letting a beam of light into the trailer.

I looked around, quickly trying to take note of my surroundings. Jared and Kirk were in cages near mine, curled up and wearing the same pink boxers still and nothing else. Jared was awake and looking at me, while Kirk snored softly. The trailer was mostly filled with empty cages, although there were several boxes stacked at the very back.

The other trailer door opened and I focused my attention there, watching as Jin leaped into the trailer easily, followed by the two bodyguards. "I'll take the girl," Jin said as he began unhooking my cage from the side of the trailer.

I sat poised, ready to leap out the moment the cage door opened, but Jin simply hefted my cage up and carried me out of the trailer. I looked behind me in time to see the bodyguards grabbing Jared and Kirk in the same manner. So much for getting out of the cage, I thought.

We were parked in what looked like an old warehouse

building of some kind. My cage rocked with each step as Jin carried me through the warehouse, past Sarah's car and through a door into a large room filled with cubicles. We continued through the room, meandering past several sets of doors and down a hallway at the back of the room. Jin carried me to the end of the hallway and opened the last door on the left. He deposited my cage unceremoniously on the floor and quickly left the room.

The room looked like an old office, with tacky brown carpeting and beige walls that looked like they may have once been white but had discolored over time. The only furniture in the room was a metal chair, a small table and a large filing cabinet that took up most of one wall. There was no window, but since the offices were in the middle of a building I wasn't really surprised.

Moments after Jin had left, the other two bodyguards came in carrying Kirk and Jared. They deposited their cages on either side of mine and left, shutting the door behind them. They hadn't turned a light on, so the only light was the dim light coming from under the door. It wasn't much of an improvement from the trailer, but it was considerably warmer.

Kirk was making whimpering noises and I tentatively reached through the bars of my cage toward his. "Kirk, er... Rover, are you okay?"

"We've been here before," Jared said from the other side of me.

I turned and looked at Jared, but he sat curled up with his head on his knees. Kirk whimpered again and I strained to reach him through the bars, my fingers just touching the edge of his cage. "Rover, it's okay. It's okay," I said in my most soothing voice.

I moved my whole body, scooting my cage closer to Kirk's until the cages were almost touching. I reached through once more and my fingers just brushed his shoulder. Kirk stiffened and looked at me with wide eyes. Tears were streaked down his face and I thought I saw a glimmer of recognition before he turned his face away. I touched his shoulder again and he leaned back against the cage, giving me better access to his body. He was still bowed over, the one arm with the cast on curled against his chest.

I heard a noise from behind me, and turned to see Jared scooting his cage next to mine as well. I smiled as his cage slammed into mine and he reached his fingers through the bars. I reached my hand out as well, grasping his fingers with my own. Despite the circumstances, I felt better with human contact.

Kirk's tears trailed off and he finally turned and looked at me, his hazel eyes red-rimmed. He leaned his head against my fingertips, letting me caress his cheek. "Kirk," I murmured softly.

Kirk looked at me, a small frown marring his face. "Izzy?" he asked tentatively.

I heard Jared jump up in the cage beside mine, but I ignored him and kept my focus on Kirk. "Yes, Kirk, it's me," I said. Jared squeezed my fingers, encouraging me to continue. "Kirk, please, talk to me."

Kirk swallowed visibly, his eyes darting around the room before resting on mine once more. "Can't... can't call me that."

"Yes, I can. You are Kirk, I am Izzy, and that is Jared. We are not animals, no matter what Sarah says. Please, Kirk, you have to hold on."

"She hurts us here," he whispered, his face pressed against the cage.

"Here?"

"We've been here before, Izzy. This exact room, actually," Jared said quietly, his voice thick with emotion. "This is one of her torture rooms."

The words hung in the air and I felt a shiver of fear. My body may heal quickly, but I still felt pain. Sarah had already broken Jin and turned him mad before making him a vampire. Kirk seemed to be quickly on the way to madness himself. Jared seemed stronger, but if Kirk could break I doubted I would last very long.

The door opened suddenly and all three of us scooted to the backs of our cages as the hallway light illuminated Sarah in all her pink glory. She carried a large candle with her that had three lit wicks and smelled of lavender. She strutted into the room and kicked the door closed behind her. Sarah wore a long pink trench coat and pink high-heels that had to be 4 inches tall. She sashayed across the room, swinging her hips as she held the candle to her face.

Kirk was curled into a ball, whimpering once more when Sarah stopped in front of his cage. "Stop that, Rover. No crying," Sarah ordered, and Kirk's whimpers immediately ceased. Sarah smiled, looking up at me while she spoke. "There's a good boy."

She walked up to my cage and I watched her eyes turn to black instantaneously. "You will obey me and call me Master," she ordered me. I felt a pressure like I had before when Patricia had tried to control me, but it had no effect on me. I wondered if this was part of Henri's power to me. "Who am I?"

"You're a sick, twisted bitch," I replied.

Sarah's face contorted with rage and she looked at me once more with her black eyes. "I am Master. You obey me."

"You're a fucking bitch. Now let me out!" I screamed back at her. I grabbed the bars of the cage, trying in vain to bend them. Apparently the strength Henri gave me wasn't the physical kind. I was just as weak as I'd always been.

"It seems I'll have to break you the old-fashioned way. Good thing I have been practicing," Sarah said softly. She backed up quickly and stopped at Jared's cage, holding the candle above his cage as she peered down at him. The candle light illuminated the sadistic smile on her face and I cringed as Jared scooted back in his cage. She set the candle down on the small table and pulled a key out of her pocket, tapping it in her hand as though in contemplation. She moved to Jared's cage and put the key into the padlock, unwinding the chain that was around his cage. She moved to each of our cages in turn, pulling the chains off.

The cage doors were still locked and now she pulled a second key out, twirling it dramatically in her fingers. She moved in front of me and picked the cage up easily, carrying it to the other side of the room. "I want you to have a good view," she said softly to me as she lowered my cage to the floor opposite the others. "Will it hurt you more to watch me break Jared, who has hung on for so long? Or will it hurt more for you to watch me with your old flame, Kirk? Does your heart still yearn for him? I know his still yearns for yours. Or, it *did* anyway. Oh, choices, choices. What shall I do?"

I looked at Jared and Kirk across the room and saw the fear in their eyes. Sarah opened Jared's cage and pulled him out, tossing him across the room as though he were a ragdoll. He rolled onto his feet quickly, but Sarah was quicker. In a flash she grabbed Jared by the neck and seated him in the metal chair, wrapping one of the discarded chains around his body and securing it with a padlock.

Sarah reached out and grabbed the candle, holding it above Jared and letting hot wax drip slowly onto his chest where it solidified quickly. He didn't move or make a sound until she reached out and ripped his shorts off. His eyes darted back and forth in panic as Sarah lowered the candle and dripped hot wax across his manhood. He winced and looked away, his eyes settling on mine.

I held Jared's eyes the best I could as she peeled the dry wax off and set the candle down. Sarah glanced at me, smiling widely as she moved to the filing cabinet and opened the top drawer. "Burns are some of the worst pain. Don't you agree, Isabella?" she asked.

I ignored her, my eyes trained on Jared's. I was his lifeline in this moment. I couldn't escape or stop the torture, but I could hold his eyes and comfort him the best I could. I heard the tell-tale sound of a match striking. I looked up in time to see Sarah drop a lit match in my cage. I winced as the match hit my arm before the fire went out.

"Oops," she said, smiling down at me. She turned back to Jared and sprinkled lighter fluid over his body in a couple small splashes. She lit another match, this time holding it up to Jared's skin until the flame spread across his chest from the fluid. The flame went out and she lit another match, pressing this one against his thigh until the fire caught. Jared winced in pain, but held still until she put the fire out. I sensed her pleasure at his reaction, and she continued to light matches and flick the lighter fluid randomly across his body.

She lit three matches at once and set them on Jared's thighs, watching him squirm and wriggle away as she held the bottle of lighter fluid up dramatically. She cast a glance at me over her shoulder and the smile on her face had me cringing. Then she turned and squirted the lighter fluid across his lap. Jared screamed and flung himself around, trying desperately to put out the flame that spread across the most sensitive part of his body. His eyes darted around the room, seeking escape.

"Stop it, Sarah!" I shouted and her eyes turned angrily on me.

"Hmm, no more fire I think," Sarah commented as she swiftly put the fire out. Jared's skin was blistered and red, but Sarah just moved across the room to the filing cabinet. "It's just too slow."

She pulled a metal clamp out of the cabinet and held it up, examining it briefly before stuffing it back in the drawer. Next she pulled a hammer and a handful of nails out, turning dramatically toward Jared. He shook his head back and forth, struggling in vain to free himself. I could only imagine the pain he was already in. Sarah turned back to the drawer and grabbed several tools before walking back to Jared and setting them on the table for him to see.

"Stop," I pleaded and she turned her eyes to me. "You already hurt him enough. Please, just leave him alone."

I shrunk back as she walked to my cage, her black eyes flashing angrily. "You want me to stop playing with my pet? He is my pet! I will do whatever I want to him!"

Fear coursed through me at her words. She stood in front of my cage holding a small knife. "Please," I murmured as I darted a look back to Jared. He wouldn't be able to take much more. Would he break like Kirk or would Sarah kill him first?

"Hmm, I like seeing you plead with me. I did have plans for Fido though. He's really not a very obedient pet, but I suppose if he promises to behave I can be more lenient." She glanced at Jared, who was nodding his head furiously. Sarah turned and walked back to the table and set the knife down before walking back to the filing cabinet purposefully. She rifled through the drawer and quickly came out with a container full of sewing pins. Sarah moved back to Jared and quickly slammed a pin into his thigh to the tip. He cried out at the suddenness and Sarah smiled wickedly before shoving hundreds of pins into his body from head to toe in the blink of an eye.

Sarah stood back, admiring her work. Jared looked like a sewing lesson gone wrong, covered as he was with pearl-tipped pins. The pins were sticking out everywhere, particularly in the most sensitive areas of his body where painful burn blisters already covered his body. His face was the only place on his body that was free of pins. Jared's eyes were wild with pain, darting around the room before finally settling on mine once more.

"If you're a good boy, maybe I'll take the pins out," she said to Jared as she caressed his cheek. "I might even treat your burns."

Sarah unwound the chains from around Jared and grabbed his arms, pushing some of the pins in deeper and drawing a cry from him. She moved him backward, dragging him as he struggled to gain his footing. She reached up and grabbed something from the ceiling that I couldn't make out in the dim light, attaching his arm to it. She moved to his other arm and did the same thing, so he stood with his arms up above his head and his feet barely brushing the floor.

Sarah turned and opened Kirk's cage, ordering him out of it. He complied, crawling out of the cage and squatting at Sarah's feet. Sarah moved across the room until she stood in front of me. "If I were Fido, I wouldn't move a muscle," she commented, casting a glance over her shoulder at Jared. She turned back to me, leaning down close so she could whisper to me alone. "I hope you know that what I do is your fault. I need your brother to cooperate..." she trailed off as she sauntered over to Kirk.

"I can be a generous master as well, Isabella. It doesn't have to be all pain. Learn to obey me quickly, and the rewards can be great."

She untied her trench coat, letting it fall to the ground at her feet. She was completely naked, except for the high-heels. "Come, Rover," she called to Kirk.

Kirk stood and walked to her, head bowed and shoulders hunched. Sarah turned the chair around so it faced Jared and sat down. She spread her legs out wide and beckoned to Kirk. I was wide-eyed and transfixed, wanting to look away but unable. Kirk stopped before her, his eyes catching mine briefly. The quick glimpse was noticed by Sarah as well, and she smacked him hard across the face, producing a brilliant red welt across his cheek.

"I give you pleasure, Rover," she said, pointedly using his pet name. "You will keep all your attention on me. Now, take off the shorts and show me what you've got."

Kirk slipped the shorts off, his eyes focused solely on Sarah. I averted my eyes when he began kissing and touching her, but it was hard to ignore with them just a few feet away. She moaned loudly and I cast a glance upwards at Jared, catching the strained look on his face. Small dots of blood littered his skin from the pins and his eyes were wild.

I looked directly at Jared, trying to draw his attention. The moans grew louder and I cast a quick glance at Sarah and Kirk before quickly looking away. This was a show Sarah was putting on for me, and I imagined this was only the beginning. It seemed to last forever until Sarah screamed loudly, Kirk making noises in return. Jared had closed his eyes and was singing softly to himself, trying to distract himself from what was happening.

I was hunched over with my head down when Sarah's shoes came into view. She knelt and opened my cage. I backed up and reached for the knife at my side, but Sarah was too fast and grabbed me by the leg, tossing me across the room. I skidded into the chair and scrambled to my feet, but Sarah's hands were on my arms in a flash. I couldn't compete with her speed or strength. In the blink of an eye I was seated in the metal chair, one of the chains wrapped around my body.

She turned around so her back was to me, but I could see her playing with the items she had placed on the table. I wiggled against the chains, but they held tight. My arms were held against my sides and I wriggled my fingers, trying in vain to reach the knife strapped to my thigh. She hadn't strapped my legs down, so I pulled my legs up as far as I could. I waited for her to turn around, my legs coiled for attack.

"I wouldn't try anything stupid," Sarah mused as she picked up the small knife I'd seen her with earlier.

She turned around and I thrust out with my legs, aiming for her chest. She easily caught my legs with her hand and pushed me backwards with such force that my chair tipped over and I skidded into Jared. She stalked toward me and I wiggled and squirmed, managing to free one arm just as she reached my chair. Sarah lifted my chair with one hand, holding me in front of her briefly before she dropped me down. My teeth jarred together with the impact. I moved my hand toward the knife, but had no chance to grab it as Sarah screamed and sliced the knife across my arm.

I screamed out at the sudden pain and watched as blood began pouring down my arm. "Now look what you made me do!" Sarah screeched as she sliced another line on my other arm.

The pain was sharp and immediate, but the blood flow stopped quickly as the wound began closing up. Sarah watched the wound heal and a smile spread across her face. I was more fearful in that moment than ever before.

"Hmm," she mused.

She turned around and set the knife on the table before grabbing the candle and holding it in front of me. I thought she was going to drip the wax like she had with Jared, but instead she grabbed my arm that had come free and held it over the flame. I tried moving my arm away from the heat, but she held me tight. The pain was slow to build, not as startling as the cuts had been. She flipped my arm over and examined the burnt skin as the other side burned.

"Fascinating," she said as she flipped my arm over once more. The smell of burnt skin and hair began filling the room and I grit my teeth against the pain, determined not to cry out.

Sarah looked at my face and I imagined she was disappointed by my lack of reaction, because she removed the candle and began looking through her table of tools. She picked up the lighter fluid, but thankfully set it back down. Instead she picked up a pair of pliers and grabbed my hand, grasping one of the fingers with the pliers. I stared at Sarah's face, knowing what was coming and trying to prepare for it. She grinned wickedly just before she broke my finger and I screamed out at the sudden sharp pain. She grabbed my hand, watching as the finger adjusted and realigned. My broken arm hadn't realigned before, but whatever Henri had done to me was making me heal better and faster.

The pain subsided before the finger had fully healed, but I had no rest as Sarah grabbed my hand and broke all the fingers in quick succession. Since my fingers weren't enough she grabbed my free arm as well, popping it backwards at the elbow. I was screaming and crying but she paid me no mind as she turned away and set the pliers down.

It took longer this time for my fingers to heal, and even longer for my elbow. As soon as I was healed once more, Sarah removed the chain holding me to the chair. I had no fight left in me as I slumped in the chair, thankful for it to be over. Sarah's hands grabbed my upper arms and pulled me into a standing position. In her heels, Sarah towered over me by a good foot.

"We still have a little time left," she mused softly and I gasped as she grabbed me and pulled me across the room.

Manacles were hanging from the ceiling and I got a much

better view as Sarah grabbed my wrists and forced me into a set. I was short and my feet hung several inches above the ground. She picked up the tools off the table and carted them back to the cabinet. She pulled open the bottom drawer of the cabinet and pulled something out.

My arms were already aching at my shoulders from hanging, and the manacles dug into my wrists. Jared was hanging across from me and I caught the look of fear on his face as he watched Sarah. I turned my attention back to her as she stroked the item in her hands. It was a small whip all in black that was maybe as long as my leg. Sarah flicked the whip out quickly, the end digging into the flesh of Jared's thigh and leaving a bright red welt. Jared jerked but didn't cry out. I guess I knew what had caused the welts all over Jared and Kirk now.

Sarah turned back and sashayed toward me. She moved her body in close to mine, trailing the end of the whip over my shoulders as she circled behind me. I tried bracing for the pain, but it was like nothing I'd ever felt. The first whip lash came across my shoulders, causing me to cry out in surprise. I was more mentally prepared for the second whip and stifled my cry as it slashed across my lower back. The pain from the first blow still stung as she lashed out several more times, pulling small whimpers from my mouth.

I felt her moving my shirt around, probably examining the welts as they healed. The pain receded quickly while I waited for another strike. Several moments passed while she stood behind me silently. My breathing returned to normal and the pain was nothing but a memory when she struck out again, the whip slicing across the side of my stomach and pulling a scream from my mouth.

Sarah moved into my line of sight, watching the wound she had inflicted with keen interest. As soon as the wound healed she struck out again, slicing across the front of my stomach. I closed my eyes as she hit me again across the chest, the end of the whip biting into my collar. She flicked the whip out once more and it struck me across the cheek lightly.

Tears welled in my eyes and I opened them to see Sarah's face inches from my own. "Don't close your eyes," she ordered as she flicked the whip across my other cheek lightly, making me flinch.

The whip sliced across my face again in two consecutive movements, harder this time. I screamed as she hit me repeatedly without stop, the whip slicing across my body. She moved around me, dancing, as she flicked the whip out with varying degrees of strength. Sometimes the whip barely touched me and other times she used such force I could instantly feel the blood flowing from it.

Over and over the whip flung out, I screamed, Sarah smiled, and the pattern continued. Every time I began to lose consciousness Sarah would stop the torture, waiting until my body healed enough for her to begin again. She spoke very little, only commenting now and then about how she was going to break a new record on the number of times one person could be whipped.

Time was immeasurable. It slowed down and it sped up. The pain would grow until I could hardly stand it, and then Sarah would take a break so I could heal. Then her torture would resume worse than before. Eventually I stopped crying out, my throat hoarse from screaming as she whipped me repeatedly for what felt like hours. Then the torture suddenly stopped. I thought it was another of the breaks where she'd let me heal, but when I looked up she was at the cabinet putting the whip away. I tried to focus on her, but darkness was threatening to take hold of me.

"You did very well," she said as she moved in front of me. "1000 lashes and you're still alive. That's a new record. Next time we'll try for 2000."

Chapter 17

"Izzy," Jared said softly.

I struggled to open my eyes. Where was I? My hands hurt and my shoulders ached. Damn it; I had lost consciousness again. This was beginning to be a very bad habit for me.

I blinked, waiting for my eyes to focus. The room was dim and smelled lightly of lavender. Slowly, Jared came into focus across from me and I jerked against the restraints still holding me. Jared was still hanging as well, but the pins had all been removed and he now had small dots of dried blood all over his body. Nasty red blisters also covered his body from his stomach to his knees from the burns. The pain he must have been in was unimaginable, since he had no vampire blood in his system to heal him.

The pain from Sarah's whipping was thankfully gone already. I tried to look around, but it was hard to see anything while hanging from the ceiling. I looked down at my body, but all I saw was red blood staining my clothes and dripping onto the floor below me. I looked up at my hands, seeing dried blood across my wrists. I wriggled around and fresh blood flowed from my wrists. I didn't seem to be healing very quickly any more, and my wrists and shoulders ached with each movement.

I couldn't see much else in the room from my position, but Kirk and Jared's empty cages were both in my line of sight. "Where's

Kirk?" I asked Jared, my voice still hoarse.

"He's on the floor behind you," Jared replied. "Hey, Rover, can I get a little help here?"

I didn't hear a response and I looked worriedly at Jared. "Is he all right?"

Jared was glaring down at the floor behind me. "She ordered him to go to sleep and he just curled up and did so."

"Is she coming back?"

"No, I don't think so. She usually leaves when the sun comes up and comes back when the sun goes down."

"So we're stuck here like this until the sun sets?" I screeched, wriggling around in panic. Blood wasn't circulating through my body properly anymore and my arms were tingling. I swung myself to the side, where I could just see the chair. Each swing brought fresh blood from my wrists, but I didn't care. There was no way I was just going to hang here all day waiting for Sarah to come back and resume her torture. Vampire blood in my system or not, I doubted I would survive another session.

I swung back and forth, kicking my legs out until I grabbed the chair with my feet. I held on and pulled the chair closer, until I could stand on it. I smiled victoriously at Jared as I put my weight on the chair. I was able to relax my arms a little and I could see that the manacles I was hanging from were coming from holes in the ceiling. It was too dim to see anything beyond that.

I turned in my chair so I could see more of the room. Sarah had left the tools on the table, as well as the keys. She was apparently confident we weren't going anywhere. This only made me angrier. I turned the other direction and was able to see Kirk lying on the floor, his uninjured arm curled under his head. He was completely naked and devoid of any apparent injuries.

"Kirk, wake up!" I said in a loud stage whisper. "Kirk! Kirk! Wake up! Kirk!"

"Try Rover," Jared offered.

I glanced over at Jared, wondering if he was serious, before I turned back to Kirk and said, "Rover, wake up!" Kirk stirred, but simply rolled over so his back was to me. I tried again several more times, but he never moved.

"I think Kirk has left the building," Jared mumbled.

"Well then, we're just going to have to rescue ourselves. If it's daytime then the vamps are asleep, right?"

"Mostly."

I didn't ask him to elaborate. Mostly was good enough for me. I didn't really see many options at this point. I turned my body again so I could see the table. Carefully, I stood on one foot and reached out with my other foot toward the table. My foot rested on the table and I stretched out, trying to reach the keys. They were just out of reach, but if I swung out, I might be able to bring them closer.

I adjusted the footing on the chair, leaned back and swung out. The pain in my wrists was immediate and sharp, but I tried to ignore it as I kicked my feet out and put my foot on the table. I was almost standing on the small table, leaning sideways because of my manacled hands. I picked my left foot up and put it farther onto the table, but I lost my balance and swung backwards off the table, the manacles digging into my wrists as my body jerked against them. I gasped at the pain in my wrists and made the mistake of looking up as blood dripped down my arms and into my eyes.

"Are you okay?" Jared asked, concern etching his voice.

There wasn't really anything to say, so I just ignored Jared and tried again, blinking and shaking my head to clear the blood from my eyes. I wasn't as lucky the second time. My feet had barely touched the table when I fell backward again, immediately feeling the sting of the manacles biting into my flesh. The third time I made sure I had repositioned myself on the chair before I swung out. I tried a new tactic this time and grabbed the top section of the table leg. I braced both my feet around it and pulled.

The table was heavy and laden with a variety of tools, but I managed to scoot it a tiny bit closer before I lost my grip. I took a breather, resting briefly on the chair before I tried again. I managed to get a better grip on the table and scooted it a couple inches closer before I tired and had to take a break again.

After several more tries I had managed to scoot the table close enough to stand on. The candle was still sitting on the table, but it had scooted to the edge with each jarring of the table. As precariously close as the candle was to falling, I figured I shouldn't take any more chances moving the table. I slid some of the tools out of the way with my feet and concentrated on the key ring. It was small, holding just three keys. I used both my feet to lift the edge of the ring up and slide it over my toe.

I was relieved at my first victory and I very carefully lifted my foot up as high as I could. Unfortunately, I wasn't very limber and only managed to get the ring to shoulder-height. With my hands chained so close to the ceiling, I couldn't reach down to grab the ring. I lowered my foot and carefully pushed the key ring further onto my toe before I turned toward Jared. We were several feet away from each other, but I was fairly certain if I swung out I could reach him with my feet.

"I'm not flexible enough to reach my hands, but I think I can reach yours," I said to Jared.

He nodded and wriggled his fingers and hands, trying to get the blood flowing. "I've lost a lot of feeling in my hands from holding them above my head so long," he said solemnly. He looked over at me with a large grin plastered on his face. "But, after all you just did, I think I can do my part to help out. Just don't drop the key!"

"Right."

I carefully stepped off the table and onto the chair so I was closer. After double-checking that the key ring was all the way onto my big toe, I took a deep breath and swung with all my might. I didn't have enough momentum to reach Jared's shoulders, so I had to swing back and forth several times. My wrists hurt with each movement, but

I did my best to ignore them as I kicked my legs up and out.

After several swings, I manage to make contact with Jared, hitting him in the face with my left foot. Fortunately, I managed to get my right foot, which held the key, up onto his shoulder. He closed his eyes and licked his swelling lips. "Ow," he muttered.

"Sorry," I replied as I strategically placed both my legs onto his shoulders.

The manacles on my arms were straining to pull me backwards, so I knew we needed to move fast. I used my left leg to hold onto Jared as I lifted my right leg up toward his hand. My body was shaking with the effort, but I managed to get my foot up to his fingers. Jared reached out, feeling along my toe until he reached the ring. He slowly pulled the ring off, holding it tightly in his hand.

I lowered my right foot onto his shoulder before I let myself fall backwards, trying to minimize the pain. The manacles jerked against my arms again and I heard a loud pop as pain radiated from my shoulder. "Damn it," I muttered, guessing that I had just dislocated my shoulder.

I ignored it, focusing on Jared, who was fumbling with the keys. "I can't see them," he said, turning to me. "Can you scoot the chair over here so I can stand on it?"

I nodded and grabbed the chair with my feet, simply swinging it over to him. Jared grabbed it with his feet and stood on it, his head almost touching the ceiling. The first key Jared tried unlocked the manacles, and he quickly undid the other one as well, rubbing his wrists as he climbed down.

Jared grabbed the chair and pulled it close to me, so he and I could both stand on it. He shook his hands out, trying to return feeling so he could unlock me. He reached overhead and undid the first clasp and I nearly fell off the chair. Jared quickly grabbed me, keeping me from falling. I pulled myself close to him while he undid the second manacle.

As soon as I was free, we both climbed off the chair and

collapsed to the floor. My arms tingled as the blood began flowing normally through my arms. My shoulder was definitely out of socket, and still throbbed. I waited until I had feeling back in my arms before I spoke.

"Jared."

"Yeah?"

"Would you put my arm back in its socket?"

"Crap," he said, sitting up and looking at me. He took my arm in his hands, feeling carefully along my shoulder. His eyes held mine. "This is going to hurt."

"What's new?" I muttered in reply. "Just do it."

The words had barely left my mouth when he wrenched my arm, jerking it back into place. I cried out at the sudden pain and cradled my arm to my chest, lying back on the floor. After several minutes the pain subsided and I sat up, examining my wounds. Dried blood caked my wrists and I moved them gingerly, wincing at the pain. Fresh blood flowed as I moved my wrists. I watched the wounds, waiting for them to heal. I'd noticed that I seemed to be healing slower and I wondered if that meant the vampire blood was leaving my system. I wiped at my wrists so I could see the wounds better, and breathed a sigh of relief as the wounds slowly closed up. Even though I didn't want to be linked to any vampires, the fast healing was a welcome side effect.

I moved on to examining the rest of my body for injuries. My legs had been mostly untouched, while my entire upper body had been whipped repeatedly. I had long ago lost my shirt, and my bra was dangling by one strap. I took it off and examined it briefly before tossing it aside as a lost cause. Under normal circumstances I'd be covering my nakedness, but now wasn't the time to worry about modesty. Dried blood covered my body. I licked my finger and tried wiping away at a spot, revealing unblemished skin below. I ran my hands over my skin, but I didn't feel any welts and there was no more pain.

Jared had stood up and was moving around, stretching his arms. He didn't have vampire blood in him to help him heal, so he was moving gingerly. His wrists were red, but not bleeding since he hadn't been swinging around the way I had. Burn marks littered his body, along with the tiny dots of blood from the pins. One angry red welt stood out on his stomach, but he didn't seem to be in a lot of pain any more. On the other hand, perhaps he was just very good at hiding it.

I stood up and walked over to Kirk, who was still sleeping on the floor. Sarah's coat was pulled around him and I jerked it off him angrily. He woke up immediately and stared up at me as I pulled the coat on. The thought of wearing her coat gave me chills, but it was better than running around topless. I buttoned the coat up and turned toward the door, determined to leave this place.

Jared followed me quickly, putting a hand against the door before I could open it. "We need a plan first," he whispered.

I sucked in a breath and nodded. He was right; I needed to stop and think first. I looked over at Kirk, who was sitting on the floor where I'd left him. "Rover, come here," I ordered briskly. Kirk quickly stood and walked over to me, his head bowed. I was surprised that he had listened to me so quickly, sharing a startled look with Jared. That was something to figure out later. "You said you'd been here before. Can you get us out of here?"

"If it really is daytime, we can probably walk out the front door," Jared replied, a small smile playing at his lips.

"How?"

Jared leaned back against the door and scratched at his beard. "The young vamps pass out first and they don't move until the sun has set. I'm not sure if they're dead for the day or they just don't move when they sleep, but either way you could probably have a marching band walk past and they wouldn't stir. The rooms back here are for Sarah's human pets, but I think we're all that's left. Justin was always housed somewhere else, but I'm not sure where or even if he's here now. Another set of rooms looks like they were living quarters at some point. That's where Sarah and her bodyguards always stayed."

"What do you propose?"

"I'm sure there's a watch here somewhere, so we can find out the time," Jared commented as he moved back into the room and picked up the candle. He moved to the filing cabinet and began rifling through the drawers. A minute later he came back with a large rusty knife, but no watch.

"Whether it's daytime or not, we can't just stay here. Let's take a look," I said, pointing at the door.

"Wait," Jared said, holding his knife up with one hand, the candle with his other. "You should grab a weapon, just in case. There's a hammer on the table."

"I have a knife right here," I said, pulling the knife out of the sheath still on my side.

Jared's eyes were wide as he held the candle up to my thigh, where the sheath was. "Where did that come from?"

"What do you mean? I've had the knife on my side this whole time," I responded. "That vampire, Patricia, gave it to me. She said it was blessed."

Jared held the candle close to me, looking at the knife with interest. "Blessed, huh? That could be handy." He set the candle down on the floor. "I'll go first."

Jared moved in front of me, holding his knife with one hand while he slowly turned the door knob. He opened the door slightly, peering out into the hallway. After a second he opened the door farther and moved into the hallway. I trailed behind him, holding my knife in a death grip. Jared moved swiftly to the door across the hall and pressed his ear to it briefly before opening it and peering inside.

Jared shook his head and moved down the hallway, opening the next door. I followed quietly behind Jared, my eyes trained down the hallway. Kirk followed me like a silent shadow, mimicking my movements. There was no one in any of the rooms we found, so we quietly crept back the way we'd come in, moving stealthily through the giant room of cubicles in a crouched position.

We moved slowly and it seemed to take forever for us to reach the door that entered into the rest of the warehouse. There was a window in the door that Jared quickly peeked through, his eyes searching for any signs of vampires. He squatted back down and motioned for me to come closer. I shuffled up beside him and he leaned his head close to mine so he could whisper.

"I don't see anyone," he said softly. He motioned with his hands as he spoke, pinpointing locations for me. "Over there is where Sarah and her lackeys sleep. I always saw Justin being carted off somewhere past the cars, so if we move back that direction we can look for him on our way out of this place. I don't know if the vamps are asleep yet or not though. It's pretty open between here and the cars, so we're taking a big risk. I think we should wait here just a little while longer. I think it's close to sunrise."

"How do you know?"

He shrugged and looked at Kirk, who was crouched down beside me. "Kirk was better at telling time than me, but I was getting pretty good at knowing when the sun rose and set. I guess when you're life depends on it you pay more attention. Ask Kirk what time it is."

I turned to Kirk. "Kirk, what time is it?" I asked, and although Kirk was looking right at me, he didn't respond. "Rover, what time is it?"

"Master is asleep," Kirk responded quietly.

"Master?"

Kirk bobbed his head. "Master Sarah," he responded.

"That means it's after sunrise," Jared surmised. "The bodyguards and Jin will be asleep, but I don't know when the old gangster sleeps. He always seemed to be up longer."

"I say we go for it," I replied softly. I was antsy to get out of there. "Is there any cover?"

Jared shook his head. "No, not really. Are you sure about this?"

I nodded my head and held up my knife, indicating I was ready to go. "I'll go first. You follow with Kirk. Stay down and move fast."

Jared peeked through the window in the door once more before inching the door open. I scooted behind him and peered out as Jared ran at a crouch along the wall. I grabbed Kirk's hand and pulled him behind me as I followed Jared's path beside the wall. Jared waited until we had reached him before he darted across the warehouse, stopping next to Sarah's pink car. He hunkered down and moved around the car, looking for any signs of danger. After he had decided the coast was clear, he turned and waved to us. I grabbed Kirk's hand again and pulled him behind me as I ran at a crouch to meet Jared.

"I remember seeing them lead Justin through there," Jared whispered, pointing to a set of doors on the far side of the warehouse. He pointed back past the truck and trailer we had come in to a set of large roll-up doors. "That way will take us out of here."

There was little debate in my head as to which way to go. My brother could be just on the other side of those doors. I pointed across the warehouse and Jared nodded his head, not looking surprised at all by my choice. Once again, Jared ran ahead, his bare feet slapping softly against the concrete floor.

Kirk and I followed quickly behind Jared, who wasted no time before opening the door. We moved into a large room that had several filing cabinets in rows behind a long counter. It looked like a reception area, with a small waiting room on the other side of the counter. Banks of windows lined one wall, letting in a stream of early morning sunshine. We had still been moving hunched over, hiding behind any cover we could find, until we saw the sunlight.

Jared stood first, walking around the counter to stand before the windows until he was bathed in pale yellow light. I followed him more cautiously, looking in every direction. I spotted one door leading outside and another door in the waiting room that I pointed to with my knife. Jared nodded and walked to the door, opening it with a quick movement. He peered into the room and turned to look at me, shaking his head. I moved up beside him and looked in as well, seeing only a toilet and small sink.

I moved back to the windows and looked outside. We appeared to be in an old industrial complex, judging by the various brick and concrete buildings I could see. None of the buildings looked to be in use any more. Weeds had grown up around the structures, winding their ways through windows and doors that had long ago fallen off their hinges. Signs for various businesses still hung here and there in various states of disrepair. The building immediately beside the one we were in had an old sign for an auto repair shop lying on the ground in two pieces.

"If they took Justin out this door, then maybe they're using one of these other buildings as well," I said as Jared came up beside me. I pointed at the auto repair shop. "Let's check in there. It's the closest."

Jared sighed loudly before looking at me. "We don't even know if Justin is anywhere near here, or what might be lurking in these other buildings. In case you didn't notice, Kirk and I aren't exactly dressed for exploration. I say we put as much distance between us and this place as possible."

"Sarah kept Justin close, didn't she?"

"Yes," Jared replied shortly.

"Please, Jared, let's just look in this one building. Maybe we'll find some clothes. We need money, clothes, a vehicle, a phone," I began, ticking items off on my fingers before Jared grabbed my hand and stopped me.

"Okay, Izzy, you win. We'll check this building, but quickly and we keep to the sunlight."

I nodded immediately. "That's fine," I agreed, quickly moving to the door. Kirk was standing in the middle of the room, staring out the window. "Kirk, uh Rover, follow me and be quiet."

"Yes, Master," Kirk said as he moved up behind me. My heart fluttered at Kirk's words and I cast a worried glance at Jared, who simply shrugged. One worry at a time, I supposed.

Jared led the way once more, but this time I stayed right behind him as we ran across the parking lot to the next building. Jared pulled the door open, leading us into a small office area with a single desk and two chairs that had been chewed up by mice. He quickly opened the blinds on the window, letting the sun illuminate the room fully.

An open doorway led into the shop area, but the sunlight only illuminated a small space in the doorway. Jared took a few steps into the shop and surprised me when he left the circle of sunlight. I stayed by the doorway, watching Jared race across the shop to a set of chains hanging on the wall. He grabbed the chains and pulled. I winced at the loud grinding noises coming from the top of the chain pulley, until I noticed the sunlight peeking through the bottom of the set of roll-up doors that was slowly lifting.

Once I realized what he was doing, I ran to join Jared. I sheathed my dagger and pulled on the chain. Slowly, we raised the door until the shop interior was fully bathed in sunlight. I looked around, taking stock of the place. Tools were scattered here and there and I absently wondered if Sarah had gotten her torture tools from this abandoned shop. A set of coveralls was lying on top of a cabinet. I smiled to myself as I walked over and pulled the coveralls off, turning to show them to Jared. He grinned and walked over to me, snatching the coveralls out of my hand and quickly pulling them on. I searched through the cabinet, but couldn't find any more clothes for Kirk.

"Justin's not here," Jared said as we finished searching the shop. "I found a bunch of keys though. Maybe there's a car."

I nodded my head, fighting back the tears that threatened as I worried about the fate of my brother. Was he close? Jared led the way out of the shop and around the building, where we came to a gravel lot with two cars in it. Jared held a handful of keys, sorting through the key tags to find the appropriate keys. "Here, try the Blazer," he said, handing me a key ring. "I'll try the station wagon."

I ran over to the dirty white Chevy Blazer and unlocked the door, climbing into the driver's seat. I turned the engine over and smiled when it started right up. I left it running and jumped out of the truck, waving to Jared who seemed to be having no luck with the station wagon. Jared walked around the Blazer, examining it and kicking at the tires. He stopped by the open driver's side door and grinned.

"Looks good enough," Jared said as he pulled himself into the driver's seat, setting the knife he still carried onto the center console beside him.

I walked around and opened the passenger door, pulling the seat forward for Kirk. "Get in," I ordered, standing back while Kirk climbed in. As soon as was he seated, I pushed the seat back and climbed in, slamming the door behind me.

Jared drove the truck out to the main road and looked both directions before pulling out and driving west. After a few minutes we entered the rest of the town, which had few cars on the road yet. Jared pulled into a gas station and parked at the far edge of the parking lot. "Is there any money in there?" Jared asked, pointing at the glove box. "We have a little less than half a tank of gas."

I opened the glove box and began rifling through it as Jared searched the center console. I found $1.25 in quarters and handed it to Jared before I climbed into the back seat, where Kirk was curled up with his arms wrapped around his legs. I looked over the back seat and saw a small, dirty blanket. I reached out and grabbed it, shaking the dust off before I pulled the blanket over Kirk.

There wasn't much in the truck. The back of the truck was mostly empty, consisting of tools for changing a flat tire and a couple pieces of garbage. I moved my hand between the seat cushions and came up with a lot of garbage and a little more loose change, which I handed to Jared.

Kirk sat where I'd left him, with the blanket thrown over his legs and not doing much to cover his nakedness. I moved him around into a normal sitting position and pulled the blanket over his lap before buckling him into a seatbelt. He stared at me with utter devotion on his face, not saying a word as I maneuvered him around. I felt tears well in my eyes as I looked at the man I had once loved. There was no recognition on his face, just blank adoration.

"We have a total of $2.18 in change," Jared said suddenly.

I quickly wiped at my eyes and turned around, sitting next to Kirk. "That won't even get us a gallon of gas," I replied.

Jared sighed, nodding his head. "I know. I'll run inside and see if I can get directions and maybe some food. We'll just have to make do with the gas we have already in the tank."

Jared was back in five minutes carrying two large fountain drinks and a bag. He slid into the seat and turned to me. "There are some day old burritos and I don't know what else in there. They just opened up and the manager was going to toss them, so he said I could just have them."

"That was nice of him. Did you get directions?"

He nodded. "We're in Idaho, but there aren't many options at this point. We can just go west through Washington and back down into Oregon, but we're not going to get far on the little gas left in this gas hog. We can get maybe 100 miles, 150 if we're lucky. And you know when the sun goes down we'll have vampires after our asses."

"Then maybe we should call for help," I mused. "Be right back."

"Wait," Jared said, grabbing my arm as I started to climb into the front seat. "You might want to wipe your face off a little first."

I pulled the visor down and examined myself in the small mirror. My hair was a mess and I had blood streaked across my face. I remembered blood dripping down my wrists and onto my face. I had wiped it off, but it had just left a streak of dried blood. Jared handed me a napkin, and I spit on it before rubbing it across my face. When the blood was cleaned off I ran my fingers through my hair in an attempt to make myself more presentable.

"Better?" I asked, turning toward Jared.

Jared grinned, but nodded. "Sorry to say you won't win any pageants today, but you look mostly normal."

"Thanks," I muttered acerbically before jumping out of the truck.

I ran into the store and found the manager directing a pimple-faced young man in proper cleanup of a spill. The manager, an older man in black slacks and a tan polo, looked me up and down, taking in my bare feet. I smiled timidly and waited until he approached me.

"Do you need something, miss?" he asked politely.

"I need to call someone in Oregon," I replied softly.

"You're with the other young man, in the coveralls." It was a statement not a question, but I nodded anyway. "You two in some trouble?" His eyes drifted to my bare feet once more.

I nodded again. "I have friends in Oregon who can help, but I'm not sure how to find them. I have a name and I think he lives south of Portland, near Estacada. I'm afraid I lost my cell phone and I don't have his number."

The manager stared at me for a moment before he motioned for me to follow him to an office at the back. He sat down at a computer and turned it on. "What's the name you're looking for?"

"Jed Harris," I responded, leaning over the desk to peer at the monitor.

The manager typed the name into the search directory. There was one person listed as Jed Harris and several as J. Harris near Estacada. In addition, there were another 98 matches in the Portland surrounding area. I had my fingers crossed that luck was on my side today. The manager picked up a phone and dialed the number on the first listing, handing the phone over to me as it began ringing.

A man answered on the second ring. "Hello?" I didn't immediately recognize the voice, and my heart sunk.

"Jed?" I asked. "Jed Harris?"

"Jed's out back. Who is this?" the man asked.

I took a deep breath, praying I had the right number. "It's Isabella Howerton."

"Isabella?" the man exclaimed and I heard shuffling noises and talking in the background.

"Izzy," Mark's voice said over the line.

Utter relief filled me at Mark's familiar voice. "Yes, it's me. Oh, Mark." I stopped talking as tears began flowing down my cheeks.

"Izzy, it's okay. It's okay."

"No, it's not okay," I replied, trying to stifle my tears. I took a couple deep breaths before I was able to speak coherently. "I need your help. I'm heading back to Oregon, but I won't be able to make it all the way. Can you and some of your friends meet me somewhere?"

"Caller ID says you're at a gas station in Idaho."

I nodded, even though he couldn't see me. "Yes, we can get maybe 100 miles on the gas we have."

"I'll give you a credit card number and you can fill your tank up. It'll take you most of the day, but you should be able to make it here tonight with few stops."

I thought about that, and while it sounded like it would work there was a nagging worry in the back of my mind. What if we were still on the road after dark? Would Sarah and her goons come after us? Patricia was still out there somewhere, and then there was the worry about my brother. Was I leaving him behind? What would Sarah do to him? Would she take her anger out on him?

I turned to the manager. "My friend is in the Blazer. If I give you a credit card number can you run it and fill our tank?" The manager paused briefly before nodding his head. Mark relayed the credit card info and I wrote it down on a scrap of paper and handed it to the manager, who left to go fill our truck.

As soon as the manager was out of the office, I ran around the desk and sat down at the computer. I pulled up a map of our location, and eyed the best route. "How quickly can you get to Walla Walla?" I asked Mark.

"What's going on Izzy?"

"I don't have time to talk about it, but we need to get out of this town and somewhere safe. I don't know if we could make it back before it's fully dark, and I don't want to take that risk," I felt the tears threatening again. Was there anywhere even safe? I knew I'd feel safe with Mark and the werewolves around, but was I leading them into more danger?

Mark sighed loudly into the phone. "You just disappeared, Izzy. Vampires attacked us and suddenly you were gone. I thought..." he trailed off, and I felt a pang of guilt at the pain I had caused him.

"I don't have time to explain it all, but I think my brother is here. I'd just stay here and wait for you, but there are others with me and they need help. Besides, I really don't want to be caught alone after dark."

Mark was quiet on the other line for several moments. "Vampires," he muttered angrily. "We can be in Walla Walla by 3:00 pm; 2:00 pm if we hurry. Meet me at the first hotel you see when you enter town. I'll find you there."

"We're in an older white Chevy Blazer," I replied just as the manager entered the office. "I have to go. See you soon."

"Be safe," Mark replied and I hung up the phone. I quickly scribbled Jed's number on a paper and thanked the manager before rushing back to the Blazer to hopefully put some distance between the vampires and us.

Chapter 18

I jumped in the truck and quickly buckled in, outlining the plan to Jared as he drove us out onto the highway. I sipped on one of the sodas and rifled through the bag, pulling out a couple burritos. I handed one to Jared and reached back to hand another to Kirk. Kirk was sitting exactly as I'd left him, with his head bowed. I waved the food under his nose, but he didn't move.

I sighed in frustration and put Kirk's burrito back in the bag. There were potato wedges, over-cooked chicken strips and a couple corn dogs in the bag as well. I grabbed the chicken strips, swallowing drinks of soda in between each bite of the dry chicken. The food was barely edible, but I ate it anyway. As soon as I was finished, I climbed into the back seat and buckled myself in next to Kirk.

"Kirk, you need to eat," I said, grabbing the burrito out again and handing it to him.

Kirk stayed as he was with his head bowed. I put the burrito into his lap and grabbed the soda, holding it up to his mouth. "Drink," I said, again getting no response. "Rover, drink."

Kirk tipped his head up and grabbed the soda, sucking the drink down quickly. I pulled it away from him before he drank it all gone and picked the burrito up again. "Rover, eat," I ordered. I cringed internally as he complied immediately.

I looked away from Kirk as he ate, my eyes meeting Jared's in the rearview mirror. "If anyone can bring him back, it's you Izzy," Jared said. "You almost had him before."

I nodded absently and turned my attention back to Kirk as he finished the burrito. He was so different from the Kirk I had known. Kirk could be a jerk at times, but he had always been strong and confident. Timidly, I reached out and put an arm around his shoulders. He flinched as though I had struck him, but settled down quickly.

"Rover," I whispered and his head came up eagerly.

Kirk stared at me, not moving. I could only compare his expression to that of a dog, waiting for his master to acknowledge him. "Do you know who I am?" I asked softly, and was relieved when Kirk nodded his head. "Who am I?"

"Master," he replied.

It felt like someone had punched me in the gut. No, he hadn't said what I thought he'd said. I tried again. "What is my name?"

He frowned just before he turned his head away from me. "Master," he said again softly.

"What is your name?"

"Rover," was his quick response.

"No, your name is Kirk. Tell me, what is your name?"

"Rover."

"Damn it, look at me!" I screamed and Kirk's head jerked toward me; fear evident on his face. "Your name is Kirk and my name is Isabella. Don't you remember?"

He shook his head, his eyes wide with fear. What was I going to do now? I wrapped my arms around him and pulled him to me. He was stiff at first, but eventually he relaxed against me and laid his head on my shoulder while I stroked his hair. Tears poured down my face and I let myself cry, releasing all the anger, fear and frustration that was inside me. I felt an aching despair, as though I was doing everything wrong. I was failing Kirk, just as I was failing my brother.

Kirk snaked an arm around my waist, startling me as he

squeezed me gently. His head nuzzled against my shoulder and he snuggled himself tighter to me. My heart sped up. "What is your name?" I asked again softly, holding my breath while I waited for his response.

"Kirk?" he asked and I let out my breath.

I smiled and nodded my head, moving back slightly so I could look at Kirk's face. "Yes, you're Kirk and I'm Isabella."

"Isabella," he said softly. I grinned, feeling a weight begin to lift off my shoulders until he spoke again. "Master Isabella."

"No, Kirk, just Isabella. Look at me," I said. Kirk immediately lifted his head up, his brown eyes wide as he stared at me. "Do you remember me?"

He frowned, his eyes searching my face. I thought I saw recognition flare briefly, then his eyes fell and tears welled in his eyes as he shook his head. "No," he muttered so softly I could barely hear him.

"Kirk, I know you remember me. We were together for five years!" I yelled, and quickly regretted it. Kirk winced and huddled against himself, shaking.

"She warped his memory of you," Jared said from the front seat. "Try another tactic. Make him remember something good."

I met Jared's eyes briefly and nodded my head. Okay, new tactic. "You were in love with a girl with long, blonde hair. She was a teacher. Her name was Isabella. You were going to marry this girl." I stopped, not sure how to continue because the rest of the story didn't have a happy ending. There was no fairytale wedding. I'd broken off the engagement three months before the wedding. I took a deep breath and tried again, this time thinking of a specific memory.

"Do you remember that snow skiing trip we took?" I asked, pulling my arms tight around Kirk until he relaxed into my body. "We'd been dating for about four months and you wanted to show off your moves. I'd never been skiing and never went again after that trip." I chuckled, remembering. "You tried teaching me to ski and decided I was good enough to go up on the big lift. You practically had to push me off at the top. Then one of my boots came out of the ski halfway down the hill and I couldn't stomp it back in. You tried coming back up to help me and ended up sliding down the hill backwards, while I slid down on my butt with one ski on my foot and the other ski sliding beside me.

"By the time we made it back to the lodge we had a dozen bruises and snow in a variety of unmentionable places." I paused and leaned close to Kirk, whispering in his ear. "That was also our first night together. I was shivering from the cold and you so gallantly offered to warm me up. And you most definitely did warm me up, all night long."

I pushed Kirk up and grabbed his face, turning him until he was looking directly at me. He looked at me in return and reached a tentative hand up to stroke my cheek. "Izzy," he said softly, "What happened to your hair?"

I laughed and wrapped my arms around him, hugging him fiercely. "You remember me?"

He pulled his arms tight around me then leaned back, searching my face again. "You're my fiancée, Isabella Howerton."

I hadn't been his fiancée for several years now, but I couldn't say anything. I was treading dangerous water here. "What do you remember, Kirk?"

He frowned and looked around the truck, confusion evident on his face. "What's going on? Why am I naked?" He started breathing quickly and I feared he was about to have a panic attack. He looked down at his arm that still had the dirty cast on and his breathing quickened again.

"Kirk, please, look at me. It's all going to be all right. Everything is fine, just calm down please." I took Kirk's face in my hands again and forced him to look at me. "Focus on me, Kirk. You know me. I'm here for you. You're safe now. Everything is going to be okay. I promise."

His eyes were wild and darted back and forth, but I kept my face right in front of his until he focused on me. His breathing began to slow as he stared at me. "Izzy, why did you leave me?"

"What?" I asked automatically, confused. He opened his mouth to reply and I quickly covered it with my hand. "Shh, please don't worry, Kirk. I'm here for you now. I'm not going anywhere."

He eased at my words and caressed my cheek again, a small smile playing at his lips. "My Iz-a-belly," he said softly just before he kissed me.

I wasn't sure what to do, so I just kissed him back. The kiss was slow at first and gentle. Then the kiss began to grow as Kirk opened my mouth with his tongue. His uninjured hand moved from my face and found my stomach where the coat opened slightly. Warmth flowed across my stomach at his touch and his kisses grew more insistent. Within seconds his hand had found its way upward and he was pushing me back on the seat.

Jared cleared his throat loudly and I jerked up, pushing Kirk off me. The blanket I had placed over Kirk's lap had fallen onto the floor, showing me just how happy Kirk was to see me. He reached for me again, grabbing at the buttons of the coat. "Kirk, stop," I said, pulling the ties tight on the coat and pushing him back again.

"Why?"

"We're in the back of a truck and we have an audience, that's why," I replied quickly.

Kirk looked around, seemingly noticing Jared and the truck for the first time. I picked the blanket up off the floor and placed it on Kirk's lap, adjusting his seatbelt to hold it in place better. "Where are we? What's going on?" Kirk asked, and I heard the panic in his voice again.

"Kirk, it's all right. We're just driving somewhere safe," I replied as I adjusted my clothes.

Kirk didn't respond with words, but he curled his legs up under him on the seat and buried his face against his knees. I took a deep breath before putting a hand on his back, patting him softly. Scars crisscrossed his back mixed with newer, angry red welts. I leaned into him and he jerked away, sending me a quick glance. "Master?" he muttered.

Two steps forward, one step back, as the old saying goes. I wasn't sure if I'd made any progress or not. "Isabella," I said, taking Kirk's face in my hands and forcing him to look at me again. "You know me. I'm Isabella. You're Kirk."

"Master Isabella," he said again. "Master Isabella."

Over and over he muttered the same thing and I couldn't take it anymore. I was mentally drained. I unbuckled myself and climbed into the front seat. I had briefly regained a part of Kirk and had just as quickly lost it. Jared kept glancing at me, but I stared straight ahead, not wanting the judgment I was sure I'd see in his eyes.

After about ten minutes, Jared finally spoke. "So if I forget who I am will you help me remember by a little make out session? Maybe a lap dance would help?"

I turned and glared at Jared and got a laugh out of him. "Very funny," I muttered.

"Don't beat yourself up so much, Izzy. You had him back for a while. I'd say that's a sign he's not completely gone. Just give him some time."

I nodded my head but I wasn't so sure. I looked into the back seat. Kirk had curled up and appeared to be sleeping. He was so different from the man I had known, mentally and physically. His body was still muscular, but thinner than I remembered. Kirk had always been confident, good-looking and a smooth talker. His confident attitude had been one of the things that had drawn me to him in the first place, and one of the things that drove us apart. He was a ladies-man when I met him and I found out far too late that he never stopped being a ladies-man.

I never told him I had found out about his infidelity. One day I just gave him his ring back and moved my stuff out of his place. Even after five years together, I had never completely moved in with him. I think a part of me knew we weren't right for each other and I always had my apartment as a backup. Kirk had tried for months to win me back, but I shut him down and told no one of my reasoning, including my brother. Justin and Kirk had been friends for far too long for me to ruin their friendship, and I wanted to keep the peace. That's what I told myself, but in reality I didn't want to admit that maybe I hadn't been enough for him. The shame that I felt was too overwhelming for me to ever admit that Kirk had sought pleasure from the company of another woman.

The truck jerked, bringing me out of my reverie. I cast a worried glance at Jared as the engine groaned again and thick smoke began coming up from under the hood. We drove for another mile until the smoke was so thick and dark we could hardly see. Jared steered the truck off the road and stopped, shutting off the motor.

I sat in the truck as Jared popped the hood and looked over the engine. I decided to use this time to stretch my legs. We were on a vast open stretch of highway with a small forest on our side of the road and fields everywhere else. I walked around and stretched before coming to stand next to Jared.

The smoke had dissipated quite a bit, but I had no idea what I was looking at. "Is it overheating?" I asked.

Jared glanced at me then stared back at the truck, hands on his hips. "I don't have a clue," he said. "Radiator is full. Oil is empty though. I guess that could do it. The hoses all look hooked up right. No obvious leaks."

"Do you know anything about engines?"

"Not a damn thing."

I laughed, looking at Jared in his stolen mechanics overalls. "What do you propose?"

"Let it cool down and try again. There's a little traffic on this road. We could probably hitch a ride if we can't get this thing back on the road."

"Kirk's naked. Who do you think would give a naked guy a ride?"

"Good point," he said, turning to look at me. "I could walk back to the last town. It's only about 5 miles. Or you could hitch a ride to Walla Walla and meet these friends of yours while Kirk and I wait here."

"Or we could all just wait here. When we don't show in Walla Walla, my friends will come looking for me," I replied, hoping I sounded confident. I wasn't sure that's what they'd do, but it seemed likely. "I don't want to split up. I'm the only one that Kirk listens to right now, so I don't think I should leave him."

Jared nodded. "Why don't I go back to the last town then?"

"That was barely a town, Jared. I don't think they even had a gas station. And what are you going to do when you get there? Besides, you don't have shoes. It would be a long and painful walk." I turned away, frustrated. "Let's just wait a few minutes and try the truck again."

"Okay," Jared said softly, coming up behind me. He put his arm around my shoulder, hugging me from the side briefly before letting me go.

Ten minutes later we tried the truck again and managed to drive it three miles at a slow pace before the smoke got so thick we had to stop. We waited twenty minutes and tried again, making it another two miles before we were forced to pull over again. After the third time doing this the truck wouldn't restart again.

"I guess we know why this truck was in the shop," Jared commented as he slid his seat back to get comfortable.

I chuckled and slid my seat back as well. Kirk was still sleeping on the back seat, seeming at peace. "We should have been there by now," I commented.

"Well, yeah," Jared laughed. "We've wasted over an hour messing with this damn truck."

"They could be in Walla Walla by now. Mark said around two

or three they'd get there."

Jared clicked the key over until the clock display lit up. The time was 2:18pm. "It all depends on the traffic," Jared mused. "Let's say they're in Walla Walla already. How long will they drive around looking for a white Blazer before they leave the town and start expanding their search for us?"

"You still think I should hitch a ride with someone?"

"I think it'd be our best bet," Jared replied, glancing at me. "I get why you don't want to go though, and I won't push the issue. I'd go myself, but I don't know what these people look like and it's probably safest if we stick together."

"So we wait."

Chapter 19

By 3:45 we had eaten all the remaining food in the bag and I was anxious. It was early November and the sun would be setting in about an hour. There wasn't a lot of car travel on the road, so every time I saw a vehicle coming towards us I got excited, thinking that maybe it was finally Mark. Then, of course, disappointment would set in when I'd realize it wasn't him.

Every thirty minutes or so Jared would try to start the truck again, but the motor would no longer turn over. It got colder with each passing minute and I was curled up on my seat, shivering. We had been taking trips outside, running and jumping to stay warmed up until the rain had started. It was just sprinkling at first, but now it was a downpour. Dark clouds had crept in, blocking out the remaining sunlight. I didn't know enough about vampires to know if they could come out under cloud cover or not, but the dark sky was making me increasingly nervous.

As the temperature dipped further, Jared and I moved to the back seat and sat on either side of Kirk. Kirk had slept most of the day, but he had woken up as the temperature had dropped. His legs were curled under him and I had pulled the blanket around him the best I could, leaning into him to keep us both warmer.

I was definitely warmer, with my bare feet tucked under me, but Kirk was still shivering beside me. "Kirk, you need to get warmed up." Kirk blinked at me and didn't move. I ran my hands over his arms, trying to warm his skin with friction.

"I knew he was close to the edge before Sarah captured you, but he seems completely gone now," Jared said sadly.

I didn't like Jared getting pessimistic. He was usually the one keeping me in good spirits. "He remembered me before," I retorted.

"He remembered you from the past."

I nodded because it was true. "That's better than calling me Master and waiting to be ordered around."

Jared shrugged, not agreeing or disagreeing with me. "Tell him about the snow skiing trip again. That worked last time."

I sighed. I didn't really want a repeat of what had happened last time, but I tried anyway. I had recounted the whole tale again, stopping at the part where we'd gone back to the lodge. I watched Kirk as I spoke, but I didn't see a flicker of recognition. "We spent the rest of the night warming each other up," I finished. "Kirk, do you remember that?"

Kirk stared at me, but there was no recognition there. I felt tears well in my eyes and I quickly turned away. After a few calming breaths, I turned back to Kirk and grabbed his face, pulling him to me and kissing him. He responded immediately, kissing me back intensely.

I pulled away and looked up at Kirk. "Kirk, who am I?" I asked softly.

He laughed and caressed my face. "You're my fiancée, of course. Izzy, what did you do to your hair?"

I smiled and shook my head. "Oh, I just decided to try something new," I replied.

Kirk nodded and his eyes darted to Jared beside him. "Who's this guy? What's going on, Izzy?" He shivered and scooted close to me, pulling the blanket tighter around him. He took a quick look under the blanket and turned to me, whispering. "Where are my clothes?"

Jared piped in then and I wanted to smack him. "You and Izzy were getting frisky and you threw your clothes out the window. Don't you remember? I think you drank a little too much. Man, that was a *wild* party!"

"I don't feel drunk, just cold," Kirk muttered, before turning to look at Jared again. "You seem vaguely familiar. Do I know you?"

"I'm a friend of Justin's. We met last night, at the party. Ah, well you passed out and then the truck broke down," Jared added. I glanced at him and he grinned at me mischievously. "I can give you my coveralls if you're cold. But then I'd have to use Izzy to get warmed up."

Kirk put his arm protectively around me. "That's my fiancée you're talking about," Kirk replied angrily.

"I'm hurt," Jared replied. "I thought after last night the three of us had really bonded, if you know what I mean. Izzy is absolutely multi-talented."

"That's enough, Jared," I snapped.

"What's he talking about, Izzy?" Kirk asked angrily.

I turned back to Kirk and stroked his face, smiling at him. "Jared's just playing around."

"He'd better keep his hands to himself," Kirk retorted, glaring at Jared and scooting away.

I rolled my eyes at Jared. Kirk had always been a jealous boyfriend and hot-tempered as well, and I really didn't need Jared egging him on. "Kirk, Jared's just joking. He does that a lot."

Jared snorted and shook his head. "Hey, I'm cold! I was just hoping to get warmed up a little." Jared stood up and moved to the other side of me, squeezing in between me and the edge of the seat. "Ahh, warmer already!"

Kirk glared over at Jared and wrapped an arm possessively around my shoulders. He pulled me closer to him and further from Jared. "Jared, stop it!"

Jared leaned over and whispered in my ear. "He's his old self, isn't he? Jealous to the core! At least he's remembering, Izzy. I say we do what we can to keep him from turning back into a pet." He paused, frowning in thought. "Although, I am a little hurt he doesn't remember me."

Why didn't he remember Jared? "Kirk, how long have we been together?" I asked.

He turned and looked at me, frowning. "Is this a trick? You know I'm not good with dates, Izzy."

I shook my head. "No, it's not a trick."

"We've... it's been..." he trailed off and looked away, a frown creasing his forehead.

"Kirk, how long has it been?"

"I...I don't know," he muttered. His arm dropped from around my shoulder as he stared out the window.

Crap. "Kirk?" Kirk turned his face toward me, but his eyes were distant. "Kirk? Rover?"

"Master?"

"Damn it!"

"Try kissing him again," Jared said helpfully from the other side of me. "Or maybe if I kiss you, he'll get jealous and come back."

"Then he'll punch you," I retorted, turning back toward Kirk.

I took Kirk's face in my hands and pulled him in for a kiss. My lips landed lightly on his, but I got no response. I kissed him again, harder this time, but he just sat there staring at me. "Kirk, remember me," I whispered softly as I kissed him again, pulling him toward me.

Kirk responded finally, moving his mouth with mine. His tongue pushed into my mouth in an exploratory kiss. My thoughts drifted away from Kirk, toward Mark. Mark's kiss had been amazing and intense. This kiss felt like I was doing a chore, which I supposed I was. Kirk's hands began moving across my body and I pushed back, holding his hand at bay.

"Car," Jared said suddenly and I looked around Kirk to see a truck pulling over on the other side of the road.

"Kirk, back up," I ordered, pushing at Kirk with my hands.

"No," he said.

I was briefly surprised, staring at him with my mouth hanging open. Kirk ignored me and moved across my body, straddling my legs with his as he began kissing my neck. "Kirk, there's a car here. You need to stop, now."

"Izzy, there's no one here but us," Kirk whispered into my ear. His hands had found the buttons on my jacket and were deftly unbuttoning them.

"Jared?" I pleaded, leaning away from Kirk and pushing at him unsuccessfully.

"There are two trucks here, Izzy, and a couple guys are coming this way," Jared replied. He turned and looked at me, a small smile on his face before he grabbed Kirk and pulled him off me.

Kirk fell onto the floor of the truck and glared angrily at Jared, but the passenger truck door opened at that moment and we all froze. "Izzy?" Mark said and I breathed out a sigh of relief.

"Mark," I said, pushing past Kirk and Jared to climb into the front seat.

Mark grabbed me out of the truck and wrapped his arms around me, holding me tightly several inches above the ground. "Izzy, oh thank God you're all right," Mark murmured in my ear. He held me tight for several moments as the rain poured down on us. I heard him breathe in deeply then his nose began sniffing at me. What did he smell? He set me down on the ground and held me at arm's length to examine me. My coat was unbuttoned, revealing more skin than I would normally show, but thankfully the sash was still held tight. I pulled the pink trench coat tight and redid the buttons.

Mark's eyes met mine and they were golden yellow wolf eyes. He looked over my shoulder and straightened to full height, his arms pulling me tight to him. I turned my head as far as I could to see Jed helping Kirk and Jared out of the truck. Jared moved first, trying to hold Kirk back, but as soon as Kirk jumped out of the truck, he moved straight toward me.

Mark pulled me behind him and glared down at Kirk. Both men were tall to me, but Mark towered over Kirk by several inches. "Get your hands off my fiancée," Kirk said angrily.

"Your what?" Mark asked.

Jared ran over to Kirk and placed himself in between Kirk and Mark. "You must be Mark," Jared said, holding out his hand.

Mark stood still, one hand still held out to keep me back while his other hand was clenched in a fist. The testosterone was so thick I could practically taste it. I gently pushed Mark's hand down and stepped forward. "Kirk, it's okay. Calm down." I stepped toward Kirk and pushed him back, my bare feet slipping in the mud.

Kirk let me push him back until we were next to the Blazer again. His eyes darted around, taking in all the people milling around. Jed was beside the Blazer with his arms crossed, watching everything silently. Hugo towered behind Jed, his eyes focused on the road. The twins were also there, one grinning the other frowning, but both obviously enjoying the show. I ignored them all and grabbed Kirk's face, forcing him to look at me. His eyes were wild, darting everywhere. "Kirk, stay with me. Remember who I am."

Kirk's eyes widened as he looked past me. I glanced over my shoulder to see Mark towering behind me. "Back up, Mark," I said softly. Mark growled, but he took two steps backward.

I looked back at Kirk, but his eyes were downcast. He lowered himself to the ground, bowing at my feet with his arms stretched out. "Damn it!" I yelled, squatting down beside Kirk. "Kirk, who am I?"

"Master," he replied immediately as he rested his face in the mud.

"Fuck!" I screamed, slamming my fist into the side of the truck. "Rover, stand up," I ordered and Kirk immediately stood. Mud covered Kirk's face, hands, chest, and lower legs when he stood, but it slowly washed off with the cold rain.

I turned on Mark, ready to lash out until I saw the confused look on his face. Mark's eyes were on Kirk and they were receding back to their soft brown state. He glanced at me, a frown creasing his forehead. I swallowed my anger and walked back to Mark, resting my head on his chest as tears welled in my eyes. Mark's arms wrapped around me slowly and I grasped his shirt as I tried to hold down the tears. I was tired of feeling useless, and I was definitely tired of crying.

"We should get off of the road," Jed said softly.

I nodded my head and looked over at Jed. "Does anyone have some clothes or something for Kirk?" I asked, glancing around at the werewolves.

"He can wear my sweatshirt," Hugo said, removing his large black sweatshirt in one quick movement. Hugo lumbered over to Kirk and held the sweatshirt out to him, but Kirk stood still, unmoving.

"Kirk, Rover," I ordered, "Put the sweatshirt on." Kirk took the sweatshirt and pulled it on. Hugo was a much bigger man and the sweatshirt went to Kirk's mid thighs.

"What's the deal?" Mark asked, jutting his chin toward Kirk.

"It's a long story and I promise to explain it later. For now, can we get Kirk and Jared somewhere safe?"

"Just Kirk and Jared?" Mark asked, catching my omission immediately.

I sighed. "I need to get my brother. I'm too close to just go home."

"You know where he is?"

"I think so," I said hesitantly.

"You think so?"

"Can you order Kirk into the truck so we can get on the road?" Jared asked, coming up behind me. "Either that or wake him back up like you did last time. Just get him in the truck so we can go. It's getting dark."

I glanced over at Jared, not expecting the look of fear on his face. Jared had been coping so well that I kept forgetting he'd been a prisoner of a sadistic vampire. Perhaps his joking was part of his coping mechanism. The darkening sky was making him nervous. I looked over at Kirk, who stood where I'd left him with Hugo's big sweatshirt on.

"Rover, go with Jared. Do what he says," I added as Jared grabbed Kirk by the arm and drug him behind him across the street with Hugo and the twins.

"The older vamps will be waking up any minute now, if they're not already up," Jed said softly, his eyes glancing my way briefly. "Get in the truck."

Mark pulled me with him to the first of two Suburbans and we climbed in, with Jed following quickly and getting into the driver's seat. Kirk and Jared got into the second truck with Hugo and the twins. Mark and I climbed into the very back seats, past two werewolves I'd never met before and John in the passenger seat. We buckled in and both trucks turned around on the road and headed back toward Walla Walla.

"My brother is the other direction," I said softly to Mark, but I forgot I was in a truck full of werewolves and everyone else could hear me as well, no matter how quietly I spoke.

"It's too close to sunset," Jed replied as he drove us down the road. "We'll head back to Walla Walla, get you and the other humans safe and formulate a plan. I need more information before I go chasing vampires down."

I opened my mouth to argue, but Mark put a finger to my lips and shook his head. No arguing with the Alpha. I sat back in the seat and crossed my arms. My feet were caked with mud and my hair was dripping wet. The truck was toasty warm, but I was still shivering. Mark pulled off his jacket and hung it on the corner of the seat in front of us, letting the rainwater drip off it. He reached over the back seat and rifled around before coming back with a small shop towel, a shirt and a pair of socks.

Mark set the clothes down and took my feet in his hands, wiping the mud off them with the towel until they were mostly clean.

He rubbed my feet with his hands, warming them up before putting the socks on. I smiled at him and curled my feet underneath me to keep them off the wet floor of the Suburban.

"Here," Mark said, grabbing his coat and holding it up to block me from view of the others.

I untied Sarah's trench coat and undid the buttons, but I held it closed and looked at Mark. While he had blocked my view from the rest of the truck, he was still watching me. He grinned and held the coat closer to me, turning his head away. I watched him as I quickly removed the coat. I still had dried blood all over my body, but I didn't have any way to clean up. I grabbed the shirt and hurriedly pulled it over my head. As soon as my head had cleared the shirt my eyes darted back to Mark. He was grinning, but still facing forward. I suspected he had taken a look, but I didn't say anything.

The t-shirt was loose fitting and I was sure it belonged to Mark. It was black with a picture of the Millennium Falcon on the front. I touched Mark's hand and he looked back at me before lowering the jacket. "Thanks," I murmured.

Mark nodded and hung his jacket back up to dry. He took the pink trench coat and sniffed it briefly before tossing it into the back of the truck. "Smells like vampires," he muttered when I frowned at him.

"That's because it belongs to a vampire," I replied.

"So, you want to tell me where you've been and what happened?"

I sighed and sat back, looking toward the front of the truck. I met Jed's eyes in the rearview mirror and John had turned around so he could see me. The two werewolves in the middle seat didn't move. The man on the left had close-cropped brown hair and had a military vibe about him. The man on the right had long black hair pulled back into a low braid and appeared to be of Native American descent. I focused my attention on Mark and tried to ignore the others. It wasn't easy, since I knew they were eagerly listening to my every word.

"The vampire from my dreams, Patricia, showed up at the

house. She said she knew where my brother was."

"So you just went with her?" Mark asked incredulously. "After what we told you about the vampires, you willingly went with one? She says, 'I can take you to your brother' and you just jump at the chance, despite the consequences!"

"She had people attacking you!"

Mark shook his head and looked toward John and Jed in the front, but they said nothing. He took a couple deep breaths before turning back to me, anger still evident on his face. "Those vampires were nothing. John killed one within minutes of their initial attack. They couldn't come in the house without invitation, so you were safe there. All you had to do was stay inside."

I nodded. "I know it was stupid, but between you getting hurt and the possibility of rescuing my brother..." I trailed off, not sure what to say. Mark was going to be mad no matter what. What had I accomplished? A sadistic vampire had beaten me up. I'd been drained of so much blood I'd almost died. I'd watched a man be tortured before my eyes. Oh, and I'd watched my ex-fiancé have sex with my brothers ex-girlfriend-turned-vampire. Despite that, I still had failed to rescue my brother. I wasn't even sure where he was.

Tears welled in my eyes and I silently cursed myself for being so weak. I sniffled and turned away from Mark as I tried to get my tears under control. He put an arm around my shoulder and I immediately pushed it off. I didn't want to cry and if he comforted me I'd be blubbering like a baby. Crying didn't do me any good. I tried taking deep, calming breaths with my eyes closed.

When I finally had my emotions under control, I turned back to Mark. "Sarah, my brother's old girlfriend, is now a vampire and she has Justin somewhere. When I was with Patricia, Sarah kept moving him away so I never saw him. In the town I called you from there's a big warehouse building that Sarah was using. The whole area is abandoned and Jared remembered Justin being there, but he was always housed in a different location. We didn't have time to look around much, but I'm sure she was keeping him close."

"How sure are you that your brother is being kept there?"

"She's keeping him close, and protected. I don't think she'd have him far from her. Now that I think about it, I bet he's in her room."

"Why do you say that?"

I paused, not sure what I should convey to Mark and the truck full of werewolves. It was a gut feeling, but I didn't think they would go for that. What about what Henri had mentioned? How my brother had started this game. What did that mean anyway? I had been silent too long and I immediately looked up at Mark. "Sarah and Patricia both want Justin for something. I'm not sure what, but I think it has to do with his research. Maybe it has to do with the expedition."

"Your brother was only a junior researcher. Why him? What makes him so special?" Mark asked.

I didn't know the answer to that one. I shrugged, "Maybe because the other researchers are either dead or crazy vampires now?"

"What about your old boyfriend and the other guy?" Mark asked and I heard the tightness in his voice.

"You mean Kirk and Jared? Neither of them were researchers."

"That's not what I meant, Izzy. Where do they fit in?"

I sighed. I knew that wasn't what he was asking. Mark wanted details, and I wasn't ready to give them to him. "Kirk and Jared were Sarah's *pets*."

"Pets?" asked John from the front seat.

I looked at John; remembering he was the resident vampire expert. "She kept them as pets and made up dog names for them. She tortured them... until they broke," I stopped, not wanting to continue.

"How did you wind up with Kirk and Jared? Did your vampire friend lead you there?"

"Patricia and I got separated," I said softly.

"Separated? I thought she was leading you to Justin? Is she partners with this Sarah vampire? What happened, Izzy?"

I swallowed hard and looked out the window. We were entering the town of Walla Walla and Jed had slowed the truck down. The sky was dark and the rain had returned in full force, bringing with it a fierce wind. I felt Mark's hand on my shoulder, and I finally turned back. I wasn't sure if I wanted to tell him everything. I'd been avoiding thinking about what had happened, trying to push it to the back of my mind so I could concentrate on Kirk and Jared, and finding my brother.

I had to tell Mark something, so I went with the short version. "I was captured by Sarah and her vampires. That's how I wound up with Kirk and Jared. I don't know what happened to Patricia, except that she got away."

"You were *captured*?" Mark asked, his voice rising in surprise.

I felt his eyes on me, but I turned to look out the window as we pulled into a hotel, ignoring his question. Mark pulled at my shoulder, turning me back toward him. "Izzy," he said softly.

Jed pulled the truck into a parking spot and got out. The second Suburban pulled in beside us and I unbuckled my seatbelt. I couldn't see through the windows to the other truck. "I need to check on Kirk," I said.

I saw the hurt and anger flare on Mark's face briefly, before he schooled his expression. He took a breath and put a restraining hand on my arm. "Wait until Jed gets back," he said simply. "You don't even have shoes on."

"Fine," I said, shaking off his arm as I settled back to wait. I tapped my foot impatiently and kept my eyes glued on the other truck as worry gnawed at me.

Jed came back shortly and we moved the trucks around the hotel, parking in the back. Everyone piled out of the trucks, grabbing what bags they had. I removed my socks before getting out of the truck and stepping onto the wet pavement, but I had left Sarah's coat where Mark had thrown it. I wanted nothing to do with it. We hurried out of the rain and into the building, following Jed's lead down the hallway.

Kirk and Jared had scurried up beside me the moment we'd left the trucks. Kirk had his head down and his good arm clutched around mine. Jared was on the other side of Kirk, speaking softly to him. Mark walked on the other side of me silently, his eyes darting toward Kirk and me.

Jed had rented several rooms along the back of the first floor. He stopped at the first one, handing the key to Hugo. "Hugo, I want you here with Clay," Jed said, and one of the wolves from the other truck went with Hugo. The room across the hall went to the two wolves that'd been in the truck with us, Aaron and Glen.

The third room Jed assigned to John, Kirk and Jared. Kirk whimpered and clung to my arm when I tried to get him to go. I looked at Jed, unsure of his room assignment. Jed must have known what he was thinking, because he said, "John has the most experience helping with... victims. He can handle it. Plus, they'll be safest here."

I nodded and whispered to Kirk. "Kirk, go with John. He will help you. Do you understand?"

Kirk stared at me for several moments, our eyes locked. "Izzy?" he asked softly.

I smiled and nodded my head, relief filling me. "Go with John and Jared," I told him.

"Where are we?" he whispered fearfully, pulling me close.

"We're just staying the night here. You need to go with John now."

"Where are you going?"

I glanced around, noticing that Jed had taken the remaining werewolves down the hallway to their rooms. Mark put a key card in my hand and pointed to the next room. I turned back to Kirk. "See, I'm just in the next room. You'll be fine. John and Jared are friends and they're going to take good care of you."

Kirk frowned, but nodded his head after a couple of deep breaths. He turned and followed Jared into the room. John waited until they were both in the room before he turned to me. "Don't worry, Izzy. I'll take care of them. This isn't my first time dealing with this sort of thing. Is there anything I need to know first?" John asked.

I swallowed and nodded. "They've been tortured quite a bit, and Kirk seems to slip out of reality. If he doesn't respond to his name, try calling him Rover. And Jared was hurt. He hasn't said anything, but he has quite a few burns. We haven't had the chance to treat them, but they're pretty bad."

"I have a first aid kit. I'll tend to them," John replied before he turned and walked into the room behind Jared and Kirk, shutting the door softly behind him.

I moved to the next room and inserted my key card, with Mark following on my heels. "Jed's across the hall and the twins are on the other side of us," Mark said as he threw a duffle bag onto the queen bed. "It'll be safe here."

"Us?" I asked, looking from the duffle bag to Mark.

"You're not staying here alone," he replied gruffly.

Mark seemed angry and I thought I caught a hint of golden yellow around the edge of his eyes. I turned away from him and moved toward the window. We were on the side facing the back parking area and I could see our trucks lit under the lampposts. The twins hurried through the rain to one of the trucks and drove off. Mark moved up beside me and I closed the curtain, turning away. I walked over to the bed, sitting down on the edge.

"The twins are going on a food run," Mark said as he turned back toward me.

I could feel his eyes on me again. He wanted answers and I didn't want to talk about what had happened. I felt so much guilt surrounding the events of the past few days as it was. "Are we really safe here?" I asked.

"That depends on the vampires," he replied as he moved toward me. He pushed the duffel bag out of the way and sat down beside me. "If that Patricia vampire is still alive, she can probably find you again. Can Sarah and whatever other vampires she has with her track you, Jared or Kirk?"

"I don't think so," I replied timidly. "From the sounds of it Sarah wouldn't let any of the vamps exchange blood with Kirk or Jared."

Mark breathed out and he seemed to relax minutely. "And Patricia isn't on the same team as Sarah?"

"No," I shook my head, "definitely not."

"So the only vampire who can find you right now is Patricia?"

And Henri, probably, but I wasn't going to say that out loud. Instead, I nodded my head. "I suppose so," I replied.

"Did she try to strengthen her connection to you at all? Drink your blood?"

"Yes," I replied testily.

"Damn it, Izzy. Did you drink her blood too?"

"Yes, actually, I did," I retorted angrily. "It wasn't by choice, though. I wanted to, or at least I thought I wanted to. She made me... I just did it, okay, Mark. But don't worry, she can't control me anymore."

Mark growled and stood up, pacing in front of me. "Damn vampire games," he muttered. "How do you know she can't control you anymore? From everything we've gathered, every blood exchange deepens the connection. It doesn't remove it."

I shrugged and looked away. Mark would be happy I was free of Patricia, but he wouldn't be happy about the method. "I just sort of broke free," I muttered.

"Izzy, quit evading my questions," Mark growled as he stopped in front of me. "All you've told me is bits and pieces. You just disappeared while we were under attack by vampires, and when I see you again you're half naked with your ex-boyfriend who is totally naked and completely nuts! You smell like blood, sex, your ex, and vampires! Please, just tell me what happened."

"Ahh!" I screamed, standing up and pushing Mark back

several steps. His eyes were wide with surprise. "It's been hell, okay. Don't you get that? Do you really want to hear about every single detail? Is that what you want? What's the point? You can't fix it. I just want to concentrate on finding my brother!"

I started to turn away when Mark's arms wrapped around me, pulling me tightly to him. I fought him at first, but he was too strong. Part of me wanted to just give in while the other more stubborn part of me refused to shed another tear. "What happened to you, Izzy? Just say it. You need to talk about it, whatever it is. Don't hold it in. I... I promise I'll try to be as understanding as possible. Please, trust me."

It was his last few pleading words that got to me. "You think I don't trust you enough to tell you?" I murmured. I laughed suddenly, an almost hysterical laugh.

"Whatever happened that's hurting you so much, you need to face it. Don't worry about what I'll think, or what anyone else will think. We just need to know what happened."

I pushed him back angrily and this time he let me go. "Face it, huh? Fine. Fine." I shook my head and walked back to the bed. I climbed in and pulled the blankets around me, feeling suddenly cold. I was trying to gather my thoughts, still unsure if I should tell him everything or not.

Mark stood at the end of the bed, obviously unsure what to do. He had taken one step toward me when there was a knock at the door. Mark walked to the door and looked through the peephole before opening it. John was at the door and motioned Mark into the hallway. They were gone for several minutes and I took the time to use the bathroom and get cleaned up. I had rifled through Mark's bag and had found a pair of sweatpants that were my size that I took with me into the bathroom, along with some clean underwear and a soft t-shirt. Obviously, a girl had helped Mark pack this bag, and I was thankful for that.

I peeled off Mark's shirt, wincing when the dried blood caking my body stuck to the shirt. I glanced in the mirror before climbing in the shower, but I didn't recognize the blood-covered woman who looked back at me. I took a long shower, relishing in the hot water. Away from everyone and everything, I was able to think and let myself cry in peace. I scrubbed at my skin, trying to wash away the feel of the whip that seemed to linger on my skin. No matter how hard I tried, I kept feeling the sting of the whip. I kept seeing the smile on Sarah's face as she watched my wounds heal so that she could inflict more pain.

When my skin was red from the scorching shower, and the water finally ran clear, I got out and toweled off, avoiding looking in the mirror. I didn't want to see my reflection right now. The knife Patricia had given me was sitting on the counter and I debated what to do with it briefly. I didn't want Mark to see it and ask more questions, so I strapped it to my thigh. The knife felt surprisingly warm next to my skin. Next, I pulled my sweats and shirt on and put the towel on my hair before coming out of the bathroom. Mark was back and had laid food out on the table. I hurried over and sat down, neither of us talking as we ate our burgers and fries.

Mark threw the last of the wrappers away and leaned back in his chair, looking at me as he sipped his soda. "Feel better?" he asked.

I nodded and half smiled at him. "Food and a shower were just what the doctor ordered," I replied.

He smiled back at me and sat forward, taking my hand in his. "I'm sorry I pushed you to talk. If you're not ready, that's okay. Just know that I'm here for you, no matter what. Whatever happened, it's not your fault. I don't blame you for anything."

I took a deep breath and sat back, staring at Mark's sincere face. "Will you help me rescue my brother?"

"Of course," Mark replied, looking hurt that I'd asked that. "I've already spoken to Jed. Jared drew a rough layout of the building you were held in for John and gave him a rundown of what he knew. Hugo will drive you, Jared and Kirk back to Jed's place first thing in the morning. The rest of us will head to Idaho to deal with this vampire issue. We have to be careful, because we're entering another wolf's territory, but Jed is already working something out with the Idaho pack. Nobody likes vampires in their territory. If your brother is there, we'll find him."

"I'm coming," I replied immediately, standing up. Mark opened his mouth and I cut him off. "No, Mark, this is my brother. I'm coming and you can't stop me. You're not going to send me off. You're going during the day, right? When the vampires are asleep?"

Mark nodded his head and opened his mouth again. I was about to shoot him down when he said, "Okay, Izzy, you win. As long as you stay with me at all times, and do as I say. That's not up for discussion. If I say run, you run."

He must have known I wouldn't stay behind, but I was truly surprised he'd given in so quickly. I narrowed my eyes at him. "You knew I would insist on going."

He quirked a smile at me and stood up, chucking me under my chin lightly. "I figured as much," he replied. "I had to take personal responsibility for you if you came, though, or Jed wouldn't have allowed it. So I meant what I said about you doing as I say and staying with me at all times. This is vital. Oh, and I am also being reinstated into the pack."

"Is that what you want?" I asked. He hadn't told me anything about his odd status within the pack, or the reasoning behind it. I wasn't sure what his reinstatement meant, but it seemed important.

He shrugged and plopped down on the bed, pulling a pillow up behind him. I followed him, sliding myself under the blankets on my side of the bed. He flicked on the television and we browsed through the channels, finally settling on a local news channel. We watched TV for a while until Mark finally turned it off and shut the light off, settling in to sleep. Mark was breathing the slow, deep breaths of slumber within minutes, while I lay there with my eyes wide open.

A small stream of light filtered in from the crack in the

curtains, but other than that, the room was dark. Every time I closed my eyes, I saw flashes of Sarah's face and felt the whip sting. I drifted off to sleep only to jerk awake, feeling as though the whip was biting into my skin once more. Mark moved and put an arm across me, pulling me toward him. I stayed where I was as Mark pulled himself closer to me, his arms encircling me from behind.

"It's going to be okay, Izzy. You're safe. Go to sleep," he whispered. His lips brushed across my cheek in a gentle kiss.

I finally let myself relax into his arms, relishing in the comfort. This was safety. I could stay like this without worry, knowing that Mark and the other werewolves would protect me. For tonight, that was what I needed. I eventually closed my eyes and slept, but despite the comforting arms around me, my dreams were still plagued by whips and a vampire in a pink trench coat.

Chapter 20

I awoke with a jerk to the phone ringing, my heart pounding in my chest. I sat straight up as Mark rolled over and picked up the receiver. "Hello," he mumbled. He listened briefly and hung up the phone. "Wake up call." He turned on the bedside lamp and sat up.

I nodded and stretched before crawling out of bed and walking to the window. I peered out the curtains, but it was still dark out. A quick glance at the clock showed it was only 4:30 in the morning. It wouldn't be light for two hours yet and the thought had my heart pounding in my chest.

"Are you okay?" Mark asked suddenly. I heard him walk across the room toward me. "Your heart just started pounding pretty fast."

Damn werewolf hearing. I took a deep breath and nodded my head, pushing the curtain back into place. "Yeah, I'm fine. Why are we up so early?"

He stared at me for a beat before responding. "Jed wants us downstairs in half an hour. If we can get to that warehouse in Idaho early enough, we'll have more time to find Justin. Plus, we have to meet with the Idaho pack at the border."

"But it's still dark out. Won't the vampires be out?"

He shrugged but didn't look concerned. "If they were coming after us they could have just attacked us here at the hotel. This is a public building. They can come and go here the same as anyone else.

Besides, from what Jared said they have a lot of newbie vampires who usually settle down well before the sun comes up."

"You're not worried."

Mark shook his head and smiled. "Do you want to use the bathroom first?"

"Yeah, I'll be quick," I replied.

I got ready quickly, dressing in a pair of jeans and the same shirt. I still had the knife, which I strapped to my thigh again, not because I thought it would do me any good, but more because I had nowhere to put it and I didn't want to lose it. It wouldn't fit under my jeans, so I had to strap it over the top of my clothes. My shirt was long, but only covered the top of the hilt. Mark would probably see it and begin asking questions, but I didn't care at this point.

I let Mark use the bathroom as I quickly pulled on a pair of tennis shoes that had been stuffed into the bag as well. I ran my fingers through my hair, but didn't bother to look in the mirror or do anything more to fix it. I didn't have makeup or hair tools, so there was really no point. Mark showered quickly and dressed in jeans and a t-shirt. He pulled a thick sweatshirt out of the bag and handed it to me while he pulled his jacket back on.

The sweatshirt was navy blue and smelled of Mark. I pulled it on and pushed back the sleeves before following Mark out of the room. Mark hadn't noticed the knife, and with the sweatshirt on the knife was sufficiently hidden from view. The rest of the werewolves were in the lobby when we arrived, already picking through the continental breakfast. Jared spotted me immediately and waved me over to him. Kirk stood beside him, quietly eating a muffin.

"John said you're not coming with us back to Jed's place," Jared said as soon as I was beside him.

I nodded as I grabbed a bagel and began smearing it with cream cheese. "I have to find my brother."

"I drew them a map," Jared replied. "Let them handle this. You may heal fast, but you still get hurt."

"Justin is my brother. He's my responsibility," I retorted.

Jared leaned in close and placed his hand on my arm. "What about Kirk? He didn't do so well without you last night."

I took a bite of my bagel and chewed as I thought, my eyes drifting from Jared to Kirk. When did Kirk become my responsibility? "It'll only be a day, Jared, maybe two," I said finally. "You can take care of Kirk until I get back."

"Kirk doesn't listen to me," he replied, shaking his head. "He did okay with John, but John's going with you guys. The big guy, Hugo, is taking us."

"Jared, please, I have to do this. You understand, right?"

Jared nodded and leaned in close to me. "I get it, Izzy. You think I don't want payback?" I blanched but he continued in a whisper. "Don't try and pretend this is all about rescuing Justin. I was her pet for months! I would love to drive a stake through her heart, but I have a sense of reality, Izzy. Human, remember? Plus, I don't have a death wish. If you go back, she'll be even angrier. She won't just torture you this time. She'll kill you!"

My whole body was shaking by the time he finished. Every werewolf in the room was staring at us, having heard every word despite the fact Jared had whispered it. I felt the tears welling in my eyes, but I shut it down. I looked up at Jared, ready to lash out in anger when I caught the look in his eyes. He was scared. Had Jared had nightmares last night as well? I'd spent one day of torture with Sarah, but he'd suffered for far longer. I felt my anger melt away as I stared into his scared eyes. "I have to do this," I said softly, reaching out a hand to pat his shoulder.

He nodded his head and stuffed his hands into the pockets of the coveralls he still wore. "Okay, I'm going too."

"Jared, no," I replied immediately.

"Why? What makes you so special that you get to go and I have to go run off and hide? I want payback. I want to find Justin. I want the same things, Izzy. I'm going," he said and he turned and walked away before I could say another word.

It felt like the weight of the world was resting on my shoulders in that moment. If I chose to go with Hugo to Jed's house, I'd keep Jared and Kirk safe. If I went with the others to find my brother, I'd risk not just myself and the werewolves, but I'd be risking Jared too. Could I do that to Jared? I didn't know him that well, but we'd bonded during that night of torture. When Sarah burned him, his eyes held mine. And when Sarah's whip had struck me time and time again, I had looked to Jared and found comfort in his eyes.

I ate my bagel in silence, contemplating my decision as the werewolves milled around me. No one spoke to me, but I saw the looks the werewolves gave me, judging me. Kirk stayed close beside me, following me as I wandered around the lobby. I didn't like having someone else's fate tied to mine. It was an unpleasant feeling.

Jed called us together and we moved outside. It was still dark out, but at least it wasn't raining. We moved toward the two Suburbans, and I trailed behind, still struggling to make a decision. The green Suburban would go back to Jed's place and the red Suburban would go to Idaho. Hugo moved to the green one and started it. I looked around at the wolves climbing into the red Suburban, counting their numbers. It would be a very tight fit if Jared and I went too. Jed stood back, watching me and waiting for my decision.

"I'll go with Kirk and Jared back to Oregon," I said before Jared could try climbing in the red truck.

Jared stopped and turned to me, smiling. I didn't return his smile. Inside I was a wreck. I felt like I was letting my brother down, but I couldn't live with myself if my decision got Jared killed. Mark walked up behind me and put an arm around my shoulder in an awkward hug. "I'll go with you," he said softly.

"No," I said, turning toward him. "Mark, I need you to find my brother. If I can't go then at least I'll have you there looking out for him. Please, I'm counting on you."

Mark stared at me silently for a beat before nodding his head. "You'll be safe with Hugo," he said as he pulled me into his arms. "I'll bring Justin back with me. I promise."

My normal response would have been to tell him not to make promises he couldn't keep, but I couldn't do it. I wanted him to keep this promise. "Be safe," I said into his chest. I turned my face up to look at his in the dim light of the hotel parking lot. We locked eyes before he leaned down and kissed me. The kiss was strong, immediate, and full of promises. It was a goodbye kiss, and I felt it settle on my heart like another weight. I didn't want to risk Jared's life, but this felt like I was risking Mark's life.

Mark broke away from the kiss and grinned at me, his eyes lighting up with a yellow ring around the brown. "Don't worry about me, Izzy. I'm a werewolf!" He chuckled and brushed one last kiss across my cheek before turning and climbing into the Suburban.

A small smile tugged at my lips at his words. The werewolves all seemed confident, smiling and joking with one another as they climbed into the Suburban. The twins were placing bets on who would kill the most vampires. I knew they were tough, but I still worried nonetheless. I shook my head and climbed into the green Suburban after Kirk. Jared had taken the passenger seat while Hugo drove.

I watched the red truck drive away with a heavy heart as we pulled out onto the road and wound our way toward Oregon. Kirk sat beside me, dressed in a pair of black sweatpants and the same shirt Hugo had given him the day before. His feet were bare, as were Jared's, but I couldn't do anything to remedy that situation.

The sky was still dark and the clock on the dash said 5:24am as we passed out of the city of Walla Walla. Hugo turned on the radio, flipping through stations before settling on a country station. I was surprised. While Jed seemed the epitome of country-western, Hugo didn't seem the type. The more I thought about it, the more I decided that I couldn't actually fit Hugo into any specific type. A Josh Turner song came on and I smiled as Hugo sang along in a deep bass voice.

I was humming along to the song when the truck suddenly lifted up and rolled end over end, bouncing as it hit the earth. My seatbelt jerked me and I tried bracing myself as we finally rolled to a stop, upside down. I looked quickly to Kirk, who was staring at me with wide eyes; his hands braced against the roof like mine were to help alleviate some of the pressure against the seatbelt. I turned to the front seat and saw Jared slumped down, with blood dripping down his head. My attention turned to Hugo, who had already unbuckled himself and was looking outside.

Hugo sniffed the air and glanced at me with yellow eyes. "Vampires," he whispered.

I felt my heart speed up at his words. I reached up and held onto the seat while I undid my seatbelt. I fell down and righted myself immediately. I helped Kirk do the same before I climbed toward Jared. Hugo unbuckled Jared and lowered him down before kicking out the front windshield. Fur had already started growing on Hugo's large arms, and his hands were lengthening and changing rapidly.

"Call Jed," Hugo murmured as he handed me a phone. I didn't have a chance to reply before Hugo crawled out of the truck on all fours, sniffing the air. He moved around the truck and was quickly out of view. A deathly silence followed his departure.

I scrolled through the phone until I found Jed's cell phone number and quickly dialed it. I examined Jared as I listened to the phone ring. Jared was breathing, but he was unconscious and bleeding from a large gash on his head. The phone continued to ring and finally went to voice mail. I hung up and dialed again. Why wasn't he answering?

I moved close to Kirk, my lips almost brushing his ear so I could whisper to him. "Kirk, I want you to keep calling this number, okay? When someone answers, tell them we were attacked outside of Walla Walla. Can you do that?" I handed the phone to Kirk and he nodded his head, holding the phone to his ear. I watched him as the phone went to voicemail and he hung up and redialed.

I crawled to where the front windshield had been and peered out into the night. I didn't see anything, but I could hear faint scuffling noises to my left. I carefully crawled out of the Suburban and looked around. It was still dark out and only one headlight was still lit, illuminating nothing but grass. I turned and reached back into the Suburban for Jared. I grabbed him by the shoulders and carefully pulled him out of the truck. I waved for Kirk to follow and he crawled out beside me, the phone still pressed to his ear.

We moved around the right side of the Suburban and hunched down, listening. Everything was eerily silent and I had no idea where Hugo was. I took the phone from Kirk and scrolled through the contacts, pulling up John's cell phone and dialing it. It rang several times before going to voicemail as well. I tried the same thing with the twins, Logan and Lucas, but neither answered. The cell phone wasn't doing us any good, so I pocketed it and examined Jared.

The bleeding on Jared's head had slowed considerably, but he was still unconscious. There weren't any other wounds visible, but I needed him to wake up. I shook him slightly and whispered in his ear, trying to wake him without making too much noise. I peeked around the truck, but there was still nothing visible. I hadn't heard any more sounds since we'd crawled out of the Suburban and I was getting nervous. We had rolled quite a ways from the road, but we could probably make it back and flag a car down. I wasn't sure if that was a good idea though. If there were a lot of vampires out, I could end up just putting a random stranger in danger.

I focused on Jared once more, leaning over him and shaking him as vigorously as I dared. His eyes fluttered open and I breathed a sigh of relief. "Izzy," he croaked, and I shushed him, placing a hand over his mouth.

I leaned closer so I could whisper in his ear. "I don't know where Hugo went, but he smelled vampires. Do you think you can get up?"

He nodded and sat up, clutching his head. "They have guns in the truck," he whispered. "I saw them yesterday on the way to the hotel."

"Where?"

"I saw a couple under the back seats."

I nodded and crawled around the truck toward the front window again. I peeked around the edge but still didn't see anything. Fear had my heart beating loudly in my chest. I took a deep breath before quickly climbing into the truck. I stood up the best I could so I could feel under the passenger seat. My hand wrapped around metal and I pulled a semi-automatic pistol out of a holster under the seat. I passed the gun out to Jared and quickly moved to the driver's seat, but I didn't feel anything. I moved to the back seat and immediately felt a longer firearm of some sort strapped under the seat. My hands moved along, unbuckling it until I could pull it free.

I crawled back to the front with a shotgun in hand. Several shells were in a sleeve on the butt of the gun. Jared took the gun from my hands as I crawled out, checking it quickly to see if it was loaded. He nodded and handed the gun back to me as a loud roar sounded somewhere to my left. The hairs on the back of my neck rose as a growl responded to the roar from somewhere much closer.

"Let's get out of here," Jared whispered and I nodded agreement. I was pretty sure the growl had been Hugo, but I didn't want to stick around to find out.

Jared and I crawled along the edge of the Suburban to where Kirk was sitting hunched over and rocking back and forth. "Kirk," I whispered, nudging him lightly. "Kirk, look at me. We have to get out of here."

Kirk looked up at me but I wasn't sure if he saw me. We didn't have time for this right now! I leaned over and kissed him, hoping to remind him of who he was. He returned the kiss and snaked a hand around me. I pulled back and looked at him. His eyes focused on me until a howl broke the silence and he looked around in fear.

"Kirk?"

"What was that?" Kirk asked.

"Let's go," Jared said as he pulled on my arm. "Kirk, are you with us?"

"Jared, what's going on?" Kirk replied. "Where's Justin? Where's the rest of the expedition?"

Jared smiled at me briefly before turning back to Kirk. "We'll explain later. For now, we have to get out of here. Shoot first; ask questions later. Izzy, give him the gun."

I didn't argue as I handed the shotgun over to Kirk. All I knew about shotguns was what I'd seen in movies. Kirk and Jared had both been part of the security detail for Justin's expedition, and they were both well versed in weapons. I just hoped Kirk stayed himself long enough for us to survive. Jared took the lead, with me in the middle and Kirk bringing up the rear as we walked at a crouch to the back of the Suburban. Car headlights were visible on the road, and beyond that was the faint glow of porch lights. If we could get inside a house, we would be safe from vampires.

Jared motioned with his hand and we followed him at a running crouch toward the road. The sky was starting to lighten with a pre-dawn glow, but it was still too dark to make out anything but shapes. A sound behind me made me look over my shoulder and I gasped as a strange vampire came running into view straight towards us. Blood was dripping down the man's chin and he had his fangs bared.

I opened my mouth to scream a warning, but Kirk was in control and sent a shot at the man, hitting him square in the chest and stopping his forward momentum. The vampire's eyes were wide as he stared at the hole in his chest. Kirk pumped the shotgun and fired again, this time knocking him off his feet. We had paused, staring at the vampire's body as he writhed on the ground. His body began smoking as though it was on fire and he let out a blood-curdling scream.

The scream urged us on and we turned as a group and ran full speed away from the shrieking vampire. Jared stopped suddenly in front of me and I skidded into him. Kirk pumped the shotgun behind me and I peered around Jared. A tall man dressed in a flowered shirt and bell-bottom pants blocked our path. His pale skin glowed eerily, and his black eyes gave away the fact he was a vampire.

Jared raised his gun and fired at the vampire, but this vampire was ready for it, and darted to the side faster than we could see before vanishing. We backed away slowly, looking in every direction. Another vampire darted into view, this one dressed in all black, from his greasy hair to his shiny black boots. Kirk shot at him with the shotgun, but he was gone in a blink. The hippie vampire came back as the other disappeared, darting around us at lightning speeds.

We moved backward again as a group, the vampires darting in and out, preventing us from getting away. With each step, we were corralled further from the road and back toward the truck. The vampire in black swept in close and Jared fired again, hitting him in the shoulder. He yelled and lurched at Jared, weaving back and forth as Jared emptied his clip into him. My eyes were on the vamp dressed in black, and I jumped when Kirk fired the shotgun at something behind us.

The vampire in black had a smoking wound in his shoulder and another in his stomach from Jared's shots, but he was still moving. He reached us and grabbed Jared around the throat. I was sandwiched between Kirk and Jared, frozen by fear as I watched the vampire hoist Jared into the air. The vamp tossed Jared through the air effortlessly, where he landed with a sickening crunch. I backed into Kirk, listening to him reload the shotgun behind me.

Kirk pivoted me behind him and shot at the vampire in black. Once again the vampire was too fast, jumping out of the way of the shot. Kirk pumped the shotgun again and fired, and missed again. I grabbed Kirk's arm, pulling him behind me as we ran back toward the Suburban. We had taken three steps when the hippie vampire darted out and grabbed me by the arms. Kirk turned again and aimed at the vamp, stopping as the vampire moved me in front of him.

"Behind you!" I screamed at Kirk.

Kirk turned and fired, hitting the black-dressed vampire square in the chest, but not slowing his momentum. The vampire grabbed the end of the shotgun and yanked it from Kirk's hands, pulling Kirk off-balance. Kirk staggered a couple steps and the vampire grabbed him with two hands, lifting him over his head. Smoke was billowing out of the vampire's chest and his face was contorted in pain and anger. He roared loudly just before he slammed his arms down toward the ground.

There was a loud snap of breaking bones as he bent Kirk in half and dropped him to the ground. I screamed as I stared at Kirk's lifeless body, bent backwards in a position no human could live through. Pieces of broken bone pierced through his skin at unnatural angles. The vampire dropped to the ground behind Kirk, his body smoking and turning to ash as I watched.

The hippie vampire released his hold on me and I crawled toward Kirk, my mind trying to make sense of what I was seeing. Tears poured down my face as I stared at the man I had once loved, who had been broken mind, spirit and now body by vampires. I looked around for Jared, my eyes landing on his body. He wasn't moving and his leg was bent at an odd angle under his body. I stared at his body, watching for a movement or anything to indicate he was still alive, but there was none.

My eyes drifted back to the vampire who had killed Kirk. There was nothing left of him but a human-shaped pile of ash. He appeared to have burned up from the inside. I spotted the shotgun just behind the dead vampire. I glanced up and behind me, where the hippie vampire stood silently, his eyes looking beyond me. I didn't know why I was still alive and I doubted it would last long. I inched closer to the shotgun, cradling Kirk's head in my lap as the vampire's head turned toward me.

I turned my face toward Kirk, while watching the vampire out of the corner of my eyes. When the vampire turned his attention away from me, I slowly reached my hand out until my fingers brushed the butt of the shotgun. I grasped it and scooted it closer as I cried over Kirk's body. My heart ached for Kirk and Jared, but I knew I had to do whatever I could to escape. I felt along the length of the shotgun, feeling the empty spaces where the shells had been. Kirk must have reloaded at some point, and I prayed I still had enough ammo. My left hand was fully around the stock, feeling the hard wood. I would only have a split second to act. I leaned over Kirk, lowering his body to the ground as I reached out and grasped the gun with both hands. In one movement, I swung the gun up and around, pumping the shotgun as I did. I pulled the trigger, bracing myself for the impact. Nothing happened. I fumbled with the gun, trying to slide the pump again as I had seen in the movies, but I was too slow and unfamiliar with the weapon. The hippie vampire grabbed the gun from my hand and glared down at me, as though I was an annoying bug. He hissed through his teeth just before he smashed the butt of the shotgun into the side of my head, knocking me face down in the dirt.

Chapter 21

I was still conscious, but I didn't think the vampire needed to know that. I closed my eyes and pretended I was out, wondering what I was going to do next and marveling at the fact I was still alive. The blessed knife was still strapped to my thigh, but how could I possibly pull it out fast enough to use on a vampire? Kirk and Jared had been good, but they weren't fast enough either. I felt the phone vibrate in my pocket and I risked opening my eyes a slit to look around.

I didn't immediately see or hear the vampire, so I moved my head slightly. I was on my side and I rolled over onto my back, quickly surveying the situation. There was no one around. The sun was almost up now, but there were still dark clouds across the sky, blocking out what little sunlight there was. I had no idea how well vampires fared in daytime.

The phone had stopped vibrating and I pulled it out of my pocket to look at the readout. Someone had called from Jed's house. I redialed and waited a single ring before a familiar woman's voice answered.

"Dr. Humphry?" I asked softly.

"Yes," she said timidly. "Isabella?"

"Yes, it's me."

"Why are you answering Hugo's phone? What's going on?"

"We were attacked by vampires just outside of Walla Walla," I replied as I surveyed my surroundings. The sky was lightening quickly and I could now make out a copse of trees just on the other side of the overturned Suburban. Everything else between the Suburban and the road was open field. There was no sign of Hugo or the remaining vampire.

"Where's Hugo?"

I didn't know what to say. Where *was* Hugo? "I'm not sure," I replied slowly.

"Hang up the phone, Isabella," said a woman's voice from behind me.

I whipped around and looked toward the tree line, where Patricia leaned casually against a tall fir tree. The phone slipped from my hand as I stared past her. Justin stood behind Patricia, next to the hippie vampire. They hadn't been there a moment ago. I stood up immediately, ignoring Mirabelle's frantic voice on the phone.

"Justin?"

"Izzy," he said with a smile on his face. He took a step toward me, but the hippie vampire threw out a hand to stop him.

Justin wore torn, dirty jeans and a denim jacket that had what looked like dried blood on it. His sandy blond hair was a mess and he had a week's worth of facial hair, but he was on his feet and I didn't immediately see any injuries on him. His eyes darted around the field, settling on Jared's still form. I was thankful the Suburban was between us and blocked his view, so he couldn't see Kirk on the ground at my feet.

"Isabella, come here dear," Patricia said sweetly.

I stood still, weighing my options. The sun was rising quickly now, although obscured by the thick clouds. I knew Patricia would be awake for a while yet, but I wasn't sure how long I actually had. Patricia looked relaxed, but the hippie vampire appeared nervous, his eyes darting toward the sun rising in the sky.

I had stood still for too long. "Isabella, I said come here," Patricia repeated. "I order you."

She still thought I was under her influence, which might be the only reason I was still alive. I walked slowly toward her, trying to think fast. I had seen no sign of Hugo, Kirk and Jared were dead, and Jed wasn't answering his phone. I was on my own here. I moved slowly around the Suburban, taking my time. With each step I took, the sun climbed higher in the sky. I was racing the clock. I stopped just short of the tree line, out of arm's reach of Patricia, not that that would do me any good.

"Look at this! Brother and sister reunited!" Patricia crowed, smiling at me. She turned around to look at Justin, the fake smile slipping from her face. "Now, Justin, where is the serum?"

Justin pursed his lips and looked at me. Now that I was closer, I could see the wear on his face. He had dark circles under his eyes and looked like he hadn't slept in days. His cheekbones were disturbingly visible, and he appeared almost gaunt. He took another step toward me, but the hippie vampire pushed him back again. He swallowed visibly and locked eyes with me. I knew he was trying to convey something, but I wasn't sure what it was. "If you want my cooperation, you'll let my sister go unharmed," Justin said as he turned his eyes to Patricia.

"You're not in a position to negotiate, Justin dear," Patricia said as she flung a hand out and grabbed me by the arm.

Patricia pulled me in front of her before I had a chance to react, one hand clutching my arm tightly while her free hand stroked my neck. I tried to push away from her, but she tightened her grip on my arm until I cried out in pain. I felt pain in my neck, and it took me a moment to realize she had bitten me. Where her previous bites had been pleasant, this one was nothing but pain. I cried out as she tore at my neck with her fangs. She pulled back and released me while the blood continued to flow at a rapid pace down my neck. I placed a hand to my neck, trying to staunch the blood but it just kept pouring out between my fingers. She had torn the artery, and I would be dead within minutes.

"She won't heal this fast enough," Patricia said calmly to Justin, as though she were talking about the weather. "She only has a few minutes before she loses consciousness. Then, she will die from blood loss. Is that what you want? Perhaps she still has enough vampire blood in her to become a vampire herself. That could be interesting."

"No!" Justin yelled.

I fell to my knees as everything grew dark around me. I was losing blood too fast. Patricia was right; I was going to die. I could hear Justin and Patricia arguing, but I couldn't make out their words any longer. The world was going fuzzy as though I was entering a long, dark tunnel. I'd noticed while Sarah had been torturing me that I wasn't healing as quickly. Each time I was injured I healed slower and slower. The vampire blood was leaving my system. Maybe that was a good thing. At least if I died I didn't have to worry about coming back as a bloodthirsty demon. I'd just die.

I closed my eyes and rested my head on the soft grass, ready to surrender. I could still hear Justin and Patricia, but their words were slow and muffled. Then another voice intruded, and I opened my eyes to see Henri Donovan leaning over me. "I told you to kill Patricia if you had the chance," he said to me. He seemed rather disappointed in me, as though he had been counting on me and I had let him down.

"I didn't have a chance," I replied. "And now I'm too weak. I'm out of time."

"You're dying," he said simply and I nodded weakly. "Are you ready to give up so quickly?"

I didn't reply. He leaned over me and held out his wrist to me. Blood dripped from it and I shook my head. "You're not really here. That won't help."

"I told you before I am the Master of Dreams. What happens in my realm affects the real world. Drink quickly. You will have strength and power, but it will only last for a short time. Use it. Kill her!"

He pressed his arm to my mouth and I drank the blood he offered. Would I turn into a vampire now if I had dream vampire blood in me? This was probably all in my head anyway. I was on my way toward death, so why wouldn't I dream of the sexy vampire? But why would I dream of him giving me blood? That seemed rather odd. My thoughts flittered around in a jumble. If this truly were real, then why would he help me? What was I to him? Was I just a means to an end? A thousand thoughts skittered across my mind in those few brief seconds as I drank his blood.

Suddenly the world came back into focus. Henri was gone and I was still lying on the ground, staring up at Justin and Patricia. Justin was screaming at Patricia, begging her to help me. He offered to do anything, and I think that's what Patricia was waiting for. Patricia smiled and knelt down over me, rolling me onto my back to look up at her. I didn't feel like I was dying any more, but I didn't feel quite normal either.

Time was moving slowly for me, or perhaps I was just in shock from blood loss. Patricia put her wrist to her mouth and bit down. Justin fell to his knees beside me, tears in his eyes as he stroked my hair. I looked up at Justin, but my mind was on the warmth spreading across my thigh. I moved my right hand across my leg, wondering what was causing the warm sensation. The knife! I had been carrying this knife around with me like a security blanket, but had never really thought about it.

Patricia leaned over me and held her bleeding arm over my face. I blinked as I saw a flash of movement behind Justin. The hippie vampire was leaving and I realized why. A small ray of sunlight was peeking through the clouds, illuminating the edge of Justin's face. I smiled up at him before turning my attention back to Patricia. She had moved closer, moving her wrist against my mouth until I could feel the wetness dripping on my lips.

I kept my mouth closed, not wanting her blood inside me

again. This angered her and she moved closer, pushing her wrist against my mouth forcefully. I pursed my lips tighter together and refused to drink, turning my head to the side. I tossed my head dramatically, hoping to distract Patricia as I pulled the knife free of its sheath. I knew I would have one chance only. Patricia reached across me with her other hand, forcing my mouth open.

I struggled against her as I moved the knife in close to my chest. Patricia had just managed to pop my jaw open as I used all my strength to thrust upward with the knife, aiming for her heart. Patricia screamed and sat back, but I held on tight, using my whole body to push her backward onto the ground. The area of skin around the knife quickly turned black and then gray, like an old burnt piece of wood. Patricia's movements slowed, and eventually stopped, her mouth still open in a silent scream as the blackness covered her entire body, spreading from the knife wound. I yanked the knife free and Patricia's body turned to dust, leaving just an ash-shaped figure on the ground amidst a pile of clothes.

Justin's arms were suddenly around my shoulders, hugging me from behind. I patted him awkwardly with my left hand until he let go. My hand holding the knife was shaking as I stared at what was left of Patricia's body. I spit out the blood that had dripped into my mouth and timidly felt at my neck. The wound had closed up already, leaving just sticky, drying blood.

I felt strange and lightheaded, but not as though I was going to pass out. Something was different, although I couldn't pinpoint what. The knife in my hand was no longer warm, and just felt like a normal knife, except it was completely clean of blood or ash. I stared at it briefly before putting it back in its sheath and standing up. Rain was starting to fall and the clouds had obscured the small amount of light from the rising sun. The hippie vampire wasn't in sight, but I didn't want to take any chances that he might come back under the cloud cover.

Justin clung to me as I stood, hugging me from behind once

more. I turned in his arms, pulling myself close to him in a tight embrace. I held him for a few seconds only before pulling back. "We're still not safe," I said finally.

He nodded, looking toward the sunrise and the obscuring clouds. "Most of them should be asleep by now."

"Except the older ones, like Patricia," I added with a glance back at Patricia's clothes. "How many vampires did she have with her? Did you see?"

Justin stared at Patricia's remains before turning back to me. "She had four vampires with her here, and she sent five others to attack some other truck."

I closed my eyes, soaking up this information. That explained why Jed and the others weren't answering their phones. Vampires had attacked them as well. I counted the vampires I'd seen, and came up one short. "Did you happen to see a werewolf?"

Justin's eyes widened and he nodded his head, pointing back toward the forest. "I didn't know they existed until he came barreling through the woods, covered in fur. All four vamps all ganged up on him and I have no idea what happened. I could hear them fighting for a long time, but they got further and further away." He stopped talking and suddenly turned around, his eyes going to Jared's body. "Jared!"

"Justin, no," I said, but Justin ran toward Jared anyway. I followed him with a heavy heart, remembering the sickening crunch I had heard when the vampire had thrown him.

Justin crawled on the ground beside Jared and placed his head on his chest. "He's alive!" Justin shouted back to me.

My heart sped up as I ran toward Jared. His leg was obviously broken and he was covered in blood, but he was breathing. Justin was examining him quickly, assessing him to see if he had more complicated injuries. The leg would obviously need to be realigned and braced, but it could wait until we were safe.

"Is he going to be okay?" I asked as I squatted down beside my brother.

"I think so. I don't see any obvious injuries except a head wound and his broken leg, but I'm not a doctor."

I nodded and reached my hand out, placing it on Jared's chest so I could feel his chest move with his breaths. I sighed in relief at the steady breaths and the heartbeat I could feel pulsing under my hand. He was still unconscious, but I felt a tiny glimmer of hope that he would survive.

"What about Kirk?" Justin asked suddenly and I blanched. I shook my head, my eyes going toward Kirk's mangled body. Justin followed my eyes and stood up, running toward Kirk's body. I didn't want to leave Jared, and I really didn't want to see Kirk's body again. Tears were swimming in my eyes as I watched my brother kneel next to his friend, my ex.

I looked over Jared quickly to make sure he seemed stable before I followed my brother over to where I'd left Kirk. I avoided looking at his crumpled body, instead keeping my eyes on Justin. The last time I'd seen Justin cry was at our dad's funeral, and it had torn me apart then. I didn't know if I could bear watching him cry again. I squatted down next to my brother and put a hand on his shoulder. "We need to get Jared and get out of here before someone shows up," I said softly. Justin sat with his eyes transfixed on Kirk. He nodded once and stood up stiffly before walking back to Jared. The cell phone still lying on the ground caught my eye. I scooped it up and hurriedly followed my brother back to Jared, casting one last glance back at Kirk. I wish I hadn't. The sight of his mangled body would haunt me for the rest of my life.

I walked up behind my brother, my eyes scanning our surroundings constantly. More and more cars were visible on the highway, and sooner or later someone was going to report our wrecked truck. When that happened they'd come across the bodies. Then the police would arrive and we'd have to explain what happened to Kirk and the piles of clothes and ash made by the vampires. What about Hugo? Was there also a dead werewolf to add to the mix?

Together Justin and I were able to drag Jared back to the edge of the woods. Justin wanted to flag down help and get Jared to a hospital. I just wanted to get away from the scene of this mayhem. The edge of the woods offered a little shelter, and we could follow it for quite a ways back toward Walla Walla. We wouldn't venture in deeper though, in case the vampires were lurking nearby.

As soon as we were out of sight of the wreck, we lowered Jared down and I pulled out the cell phone. I debated who I should call, but decided I'd better try Jed again first. The phone had ten missed calls on it; eight from Jed's house and two from Jed's cell phone. That was a good sign, I thought. I dialed the cell phone and waited, but no one answered. I tried a second time, but had the same result. I sighed in frustration before I tried Jed's house.

Mirabelle answered on the first ring. "Isabella?"

"Dr. Humphry," I began, but she cut me off.

"Jed and the others are on their way to your location. They're in wolf form, so they won't be answering the phone."

"So they're all okay?" I asked.

She paused before answering. "They're all alive. What about you? You stopped talking earlier."

"A lot happened. I don't really have time to get into it now," I said. I didn't want her to start asking questions about her husband that I just couldn't answer. "How soon will they be here?"

"I'm not sure. Jed said that if I spoke to you again to tell you to get somewhere safe. They'll find you. Wolves have excellent senses."

"Okay, thanks Dr. Humphry."

"Wait, Isabella, what about my husband? Where's Hugo?"

I had been dreading her asking that question, although I couldn't really blame her. I took a deep breath and answered her. "I don't know where he is. I'm sorry I don't know any more."

"It's okay," she replied softly. "Jed will find him. My Hugo is tough; I'm sure he's just fine. Call me if you need anything." I hung up the phone and pocketed it, marveling at Mirabelle's optimism.

Justin had been making a makeshift litter for us to drag Jared on. It wasn't much, just a couple long branches braced against his body and tied with strips of cloth torn from his coveralls. Justin and I each took a side and drug Jared along as carefully as we could. I kept my eyes open as we traipsed through the edge of the woods, looking for any sign of Hugo or the vampires.

The rain started pouring and I was thankful for the shelter of the trees keeping us mostly dry. Unfortunately, rain meant clouds and clouds meant no sunlight. We stopped periodically to check on Jared, but there was no change in his condition. We didn't talk much, both of us lost in our own thoughts. We'd been walking for about a half an hour when we heard the first howl. Justin stopped and looked at me with worry on his face. Another howl sounded, closer this time. I stopped and lowered Jared carefully to the ground before I sat down, feeling the strength ebb from my body. The adrenaline that had been spurring my body into action was gone, leaving me suddenly exhausted. I smiled up at Justin as a third howl sounded. Help was on its way.

The first wolf we saw came running straight toward us. He was a large gray wolf with black-tipped ears, and he skidded to a halt right in front of us. He stopped and tipped up his large muzzle, sniffing the air around us. Justin was still standing, backed up into a tree and visibly scared. I was sitting on the ground next to Jared and I think I had no fear left in me. Maybe I had no emotions left at all.

A second wolf arrived just after the first. The second wolf was just as big as the first one, but with thick brown fur. The wolf moved cautiously toward me, sniffing the air. His large head turned from side to side as he took in the scene with his wolf eyes. I stayed completely still as the wolf stepped up next to me and nuzzled my neck. "Mark," I said softly. The wolf rubbed his head against my neck before moving several feet away and dropping to the ground.

I watched in fascination as the wolf morphed and changed.

The thick fur across the wolf began to ripple, thinning out to reveal human skin beneath. The wolf's muzzle shrunk and squashed, and the wolf made grunting noises as the joints flexed backwards. Within moments, there was no longer a wolf there, but a strange hybrid of wolf and man. The transformation progressed further and human hands and feet emerged, as the wolf seemed to dissolve into the human body, leaving a very tired Mark lying on the grass in place of the wolf.

Another wolf arrived and ran past us, further into the woods. The first wolf, who I suspected was Jed, stayed where he was watching everything. Mark crawled toward me slowly, his naked body covered in sweat. He scooted next to me and laid his head on my lap, exhausted. Mark looked up at Justin, who still stood backed up against a tree, his eyes wide with fear.

"Compared to the vampires, we're tame," Mark said to Justin.

I chuckled, but Justin just nodded his head and stayed as he was. I wanted to give Mark a few minutes to recuperate, but I was antsy to leave the area. "We need to get out of here," I whispered to Mark.

Mark sat up slowly and looked at the wolf. He was silent for several minutes, and I wondered if he was communicating with him somehow. "We didn't smell any vampires nearby," Mark said. He paused, his eyes jumping toward Justin and Jared and back to me again. "Do you know where Kirk and Hugo are? I don't smell them either."

I shook my head and looked down at my hands. "Kirk's dead," I said softly, my voice breaking. I cleared my throat and continued. "I don't know what happened to Hugo."

Mark placed his arms around me and held me tightly. I didn't cry though. I think I was too numb to feel anything. Maybe I'd cry later, when I really thought about what had happened. For now, I just wanted to be anywhere else but where I was. Mark pulled back finally and stared at me, his yellow and brown eyes searching my face. "We'll leave soon. Lucas and Logan are bringing vehicles. You can relax, Izzy. You're safe now. Everything is going to be okay."

Chapter 22

I slept through most of the drive back to Jed's house, curled up between my brother and Mark. As soon as we arrived at Jed's house, I took a shower then immediately went to my room and fell asleep. Mark woke me up periodically with updates, but I mostly just slept. I woke up again to the smell of food. The clock said it was 6:15 and I was so confused I didn't know if it was morning or night. My stomach rumbled, urging me to get moving. It was probably time to face the world again.

I didn't bother turning on the lights as I rifled through the dresser. I pulled on the first clothes that came to my hand and ran downstairs to the small living room, which had been turned into a makeshift hospital room for Jared and Hugo. Hugo's throat had been torn open by one of the vampires and they had left him for dead. Thankfully, he was a werewolf and not that easy to kill. I walked over to his temporary hospital bed and looked at him. He was asleep and had IV's hooked up to him, but he looked better than he had when they had dragged him out of the woods, covered in blood and a sickly green color.

I patted his shoulder as I passed by and moved to Jared's side. He was also hooked up to IV's and still unconscious. A splint was on his leg along with a contraption to keep his head stable. Lucas had driven a truck with Hugo and Jared in it to Dr. Humphry's clinic as soon as we had gotten into town. They had moved them to the house sometime during the night.

Dr. Humphry walked in from the hallway and smiled tentatively at me. "Good to see you're up, Isabella. I wanted to examine you earlier, but Mark insisted on letting you sleep. If you'll sit down, I'd like to check you over."

I complied and sat down in a chair beside Jared. Dr. Humphry examined me as I spoke. "Is Jared okay?"

She didn't answer right away as she examined my eyes and head, assessing me. I felt completely fine, just drained. She finished her exam and looked at me directly, her arms crossed over her breasts. "Jared should be in a hospital," she said softly as she flicked a glance at Jared before turning back to me. "We did scans at my clinic. He has a fractured femur, multiple broken ribs that look old and partially healed already, and he has significant spinal damage along with a lot of bleeding on the brain, not to mention all the burns across his body. He's been through a lot. I don't know if he's going to wake up, Izzy. I'm so sorry."

"What? What do you mean? There has to be something that you can do. Let's take him to the hospital then and get him treated!" I stood up, instantly agitated. After everything that had happened, I had thought if we got Jared back here, he'd be okay. He had become my responsibility, him and Kirk. I had failed Kirk, and now he was dead. I couldn't lose Jared too. "Please, there must be something you can do."

"I'm sorry, Izzy," Dr. Humphry replied, patting my hand. "There's nothing more I can do here."

"There may be one option," Jed said, walking into the room. He sauntered across the room, dressed in his usual cowboy boots and flannel shirt. He stopped beside Jared's bed, but his eyes were on me. "Normally I'd ask Jared before making this kind of decision, but he isn't capable of answering. Are you willing to take responsibility for him?"

I had no idea what Jed was talking about, but I had already taken responsibility for Jared. We had been through so much together in a short amount of time. I moved closer to Jared's bed and stared down at his face. My heart ached for him and I felt tears threaten at the thought of losing him. He had become family to me, as much as my brother was. I looked back at Jed and nodded my head. "He already is my responsibility," I replied.

Jed smiled minutely and said, "I thought you might say that. He's going to die if we do nothing. We could take him to a hospital and they *might* be able to do surgery and save his life, but he would never be the same. Best-case scenario is he'd be paralyzed, and never walk again. He could also have permanent brain damage. No matter what the hospital did, he would never be the same. Is that the kind of life he'd want? I've spoken to your brother and he seems to think Jared would rather die than live paralyzed. Do you agree with that assessment?"

I shrugged. "I don't really know Jared that well, but Justin did. I'd trust his judgment on that."

"What does your gut tell you?"

"He's a fighter," I responded immediately. "He's tough and he could live like that, but I think it might crush his spirit. He's been through so much already, and despite everything, he has persevered. Even when things were at their worst, he was cracking jokes. He's tough, but I don't know if he could take much more. There's only so much a person can handle."

"He was tortured." It was a statement, not a question.

"Yes," I responded, stroking Jared's hair.

"I could turn him," Jed said softly, and I looked up immediately. "If I bite him, he could become a werewolf and heal from this."

"Then why haven't you done it? Jared would be fine as a werewolf!"

Jed looked at me directly, his eyes turning golden between

one blink and the next. "Not everyone survives the bite. You must understand this before making a decision for someone else. There are no guarantees. With as many injuries as he already has, he could very well die from the bite. The first bite can bring on the transformation immediately, or it could take a few days. Everyone is different. Some people are bitten and never become werewolves. Some people die as soon as they are bitten. It's a roll of the dice, Izzy."

I tried to think about what he was saying rationally, but there was nothing rational in my decision. My heart had already chosen a course of action. "Do it," I said assuredly. "Please, Jed, do it right away."

Dr. Humphry was shaking her head, but she didn't say anything as she began prepping Jared. Jed took a deep breath and looked at me. "You're sure?" I nodded my head in response. "We'll take him to the barn for the transformation. It's safest for everyone that way. You should stay here. I'll find you when we know something."

I pursed my lips, ready to argue, but Jed looked at me once more with his piercing golden eyes and I simply nodded my head. I leaned over Jared, still stroking his hair as Dr. Humphry moved around me to secure him to the bed. Jed's words had me worried, but I knew I had no other choice. Dr. Humphry tapped me on the arm, indicating they were ready to wheel Jared to the barn. I nodded and leaned close to Jared so I could whisper in his ear, even if he couldn't hear me.

"Jared, please fight," I whispered softly. I kissed Jared on the forehead before standing back to let Jed and Dr. Humphry wheel his hospital bed out of the room. I stood there silently for a few moments before making the decision to go in search of the food I smelled.

I stopped at Hugo's bed, noting he was awake and looking right at me. I smiled timidly at him and he grinned back at me as he sat up. "Glad you're okay," he said simply.

"You too, Hugo," I replied as I walked out of the room.

"You made the right decision," he said as I reached the hall leading to the other living room. I turned and looked back at Hugo. He was pulling his IV's out, but he stopped to look directly at me. "Jared will make a fine wolf."

I smiled and turned away, hoping he was right. Mark was sitting in the living room when I walked in, waiting for me. He stood as soon as I entered and strode toward me, pulling me toward him in a fierce hug. I stood still and let him hug me, but I didn't return the embrace. He held me for several moments before finally releasing me, his expression worried.

"Are you all right?" Mark asked.

I didn't know how to answer that. No, I wasn't all right. I was desperately trying not to think of everything that had happened, and I was worried about Jared. My stomach growled loudly and I grinned sheepishly at Mark. "Hungry," I said simply.

He grinned back at me and flung an arm casually across my shoulders. "Well, let's get some food," he said simply. I let him lead me into the dining room, where several werewolves were already eating. Mark pulled out an extra chair for me beside Justin and we sat down to eat.

The lone wolf, Leon, was sitting at the table chatting amicably with Logan. As we ate, Mark filled me in on what had happened after I left the house with Patricia. Patricia's vampires had attacked the barn, releasing the caged werewolves. Leon had stepped in and killed one of the vampires, protecting the young Michael in the process and securing his place in the pack.

We finished our meal and all moved into the large living room to wait for Jed. More wolves showed up and the house was soon filled with people. I sat in one of the smaller couches, smashed between Justin and Mark. Justin hadn't spoken about what had happened to him over the last several months yet. He sat uneasily beside me, wringing his hands nervously. He still didn't seem comfortable with the werewolves. I patted his leg reassuringly as Jed entered the room and silence descended.

Jed looked directly at me; his eyes still golden wolf eyes. "The transformation has already started. John is going to keep an eye on Jared, but if he can survive the night he'll be okay." I nodded and Jed continued on, addressing the group. "I have received word from the Idaho pack. They went to the vampire den, but it had already been burnt to the ground by the time they got there. We don't know what happened to the vampires there." Jed's eyes moved around the room to Justin and settled there, waiting.

Justin shifted nervously in his seat and bit at his lower lip before finally raising his eyes to meet Jed's. I reached out and grabbed Justin's hand, squeezing it reassuringly. He turned to me when he spoke. "They destroyed my research," he began quietly. "That's why the building was burnt down. It's the only explanation."

"What research Justin?"

He looked down at his hands, intertwined with mine. He sat there silently for several minutes, collecting his thoughts. He kept his head down as he spoke, his sweaty hands clutching mine as though I was his lifeline. "I had heard rumors about a village in the Carpathian Mountains where no one ever got sick. They didn't get the cold, the flu, or anything. No one had died there for over 40 years! I thought there must be something in the water, or their food, or something that was keeping them healthy. I thought this discovery could make my career! Sarah and I could finish our PhDs and we could be married.

"It took a while, but I was finally able to assemble a team. We headed straight to the village, but the villagers were close-mouthed. No matter what we tried, we couldn't get any cooperation from the village. We were ready to leave, when a man named Petrivian approached us and said he could help. He was a bit of a scientist himself, and with his help, we developed the vaccine. I didn't know what he truly was. I didn't ask questions. I followed blindly; too ambitious to stop and question what I was doing, or whether it was ethical."

Justin stopped and cleared his throat, his head still down. His hands were shaking holding mine and he risked a glance up at me, his face pale and drawn. "We kept making batches of the serum, but it didn't work on any animals we tested. Petrivian insisted it would only work on humans, so Sarah volunteered. I tried to stop her, but she insisted. She said she was doing it for us, and for the world. She was so ambitious. I should have fought harder against her taking the serum, but I was selfish. Petrivian gave her the serum and it changed her," he said, pausing again. "At first, I thought we had just made the best discovery ever. Her hair was more lustrous, her skin was flawless, and she couldn't get injured or sick. It was a miracle cure, just like we hoped. We sent a report back to the States about our unofficial trial, and were immediately ordered to come home with all our research. We hadn't mentioned Petrivian in our reports. He insisted on accompanying us, and that's when everything went wrong."

Justin paused, taking a deep breath. He looked around the room, before settling once more on me. "Sarah wasn't the only one in our expedition who had taken the vaccine. By the time we got on the plane to leave, most of the expedition had taken the serum and were now under Petrivian's control. I didn't understand what was happening at the time. I had grown suspicious of Petrivian, but I thought it was just insecurity. He had taken a liking to Sarah and I was jealous of their relationship. She was so enamored with the charming Petrivian, but she wasn't the only one. She spent more and more time with him, secreted away at all hours of the night. I didn't realize..." he stopped, swallowing hard.

"He turned her into a vampire?" I asked softly and he nodded his head.

"He wanted her to be like him, to do his bidding. She agreed to it! He had shown her his power and she agreed to be like him. She didn't even tell me." His voice broke as he choked back tears. "She slaughtered most of our team while we were stuck on that damn plane. By the time we landed, the plane was red with blood and only

Jin, Kirk, Jared and I were still human. Everyone else was either a vampire, or dead.

"That was when I realized what was happening. Petrivian had already bought out NuvaDrug and the other pharmaceutical companies. He managed to get his vaccine pushed onto the market. Every person infected with Petrivian's blood was now under his control, and he was mass marketing it. Kirk, Jared and I managed to escape for a short time with Sarah. We had her contained, but she escaped and came back even more ruthless than before." He stopped talking as a single tear trailed down his face. He quickly wiped it away and stared back down at his hands.

The room was silent as we took in his words. Everything he said added up with what we had suspected about the vaccine. There were still gaping holes in his story though, and I found I had a million questions racing through my mind. I opened my mouth to ask him, but Jed beat me to it.

"Why were they still after you? They could have easily killed you, but they kept you alive and vampires keep coming after you, and your sister. Why?" Jed asked.

Justin took in a deep breath and looked up, facing Jed. "They want my research. They want the project I've been working on," Justin replied, pausing. He glanced at me and pulled his hands out of mine, guilt etched on his face. "I've been working on making the vaccine airborne... and permanent."

BLOODY BEGINNINGS

About the Author

Laura Hysell is a freelance writer who lives in the countryside of the Willamette Valley in Oregon with her husband and two daughters. She has been writing since childhood and has received Honorable Mention in two short story contests. Her hobbies include bow shooting, photography and playing piano. *Bloody Beginnings* is her first novel.

www.laurahysell.com
facebook.com/laurahysellauthor
twitter.com/laurahysell

Printed in Great Britain
by Amazon

29723849R00142